The Hunted

Paul Cuddihy is a writer and journalist whose first novel, *Saints and Sinners*, a historical adventure set in Victorian Glasgow, was published in 2010. He is the editor of the *Celtic View*, the official magazine of Celtic Football Club, and in 2009 he wrote the best-selling biography *Tommy Burns: A Supporter Who Got Lucky*. He was also the co-author of *Century Bhoys: A History of Celtic's Greatest Goalscorers* (2010) and *The Best of the Celtic View* (2007), while he also edited a number of books for the club including *The Road To Seville* and *The Official Tribute To Henrik Larsson*. In 2004 he was one of the prize-winners of the inaugural Scotsman Orange Short Story Competition. Paul Cuddihy was born in 1966 and lives in Bishopbriggs, Glasgow with his wife and three children.

D1323813

Capercaillie Books

The Hunted

Paul Cuddihy

Capercaillie Books

First published by Capercaillie Books Limited in 2011.

Registered office 1 Rutland Court, Edinburgh

© Paul Cuddihy. The moral rights of the author have been asserted.

Printed and bound by CPI Group (UK) Ltd, Croydon, CR0 4YY

Set in Galliard by 3btype.com, Edinburgh

A catalogue record of this book is available from the British Library.

ISBN   978-1-906220-42-6

In memory of Helen Quail
'Een Skeen Boxaleen Jeryx'

Acknowledgements

So many thank-yous, so little space, but here goes . . . This book, like everything else in my life, is for Karen, Louise, Rebecca and Andrew. There would be no point without them.

I would like to thank Kay Strang and Capercaillie Books for having faith in this novel, and for allowing me to continue to live the dream.

Thanks, as always, to my mum and dad, and to John Quail, especially for the t-shirt!

To Stephen Maule, for more years of friendship and support than either of us care to remember.

To Nichola Fullerton, who remains an inspiration to me. I'm glad you were the first to read this book too.

To Lynne Hamilton, who has been a wonderful help and encouragement, and to Tony Hamilton, for many great car journeys and fried breakfasts – the important stuff!

To Chris Dolan and Professor Willy Maley for their advice and friendship, and thanks also to Allan Dougall, Craig Dunbar, Hugh Macdonald and James MacMillan.

And to John McLaughlin . . . thank you for the music and the songs I'm singing!

I continue to thank God for the life I have and count my blessings for everyone in it.

Bloody Rain

Tom Costello felt like he'd been plunged into a bath of ice-cold water and held there until he was so wet and numb that if someone punched him he wouldn't feel a thing. It had been raining for hours, even before they'd arrived and taken up their positions amongst the dripping conifers overlooking the single-track road as it forced its way up the steep hillside. The tall grass would also have to play its part in providing them with necessary cover and it had long since ceased to be uncomfortable lying on its saturated surface.

There were eight of them, split into two groups of four, who had planted themselves on either side of the road. It was the perfect spot for an ambush. A blind man in a snowstorm could have seen that, and Tom could hardly believe anyone would be so careless as to navigate this narrow stretch of track. That was the Brits for you, he thought – arrogant to the point of stupidity. He would make sure they'd soon come to regret their decision, even if a tiny doubt continued to gnaw at the back of his mind that this might all be a pointless waste of time. What if the intelligence was false? They'd eventually have to trudge home frustrated, their rifles still full of bullets and their bodies already in the grip of colds that would probably floor them for a few days at least.

Tom sat up and stared through the sheets of rain that poured relentlessly across the dismal landscape. There was no sign of life in any direction and he cursed the spy who'd tipped them off. He was probably sitting in front of a peat fire at this very moment, thankful that all he'd been asked to do was provide information. If it was wrong, Tom knew he'd have to fight the temptation to shoot the messenger. It would be a waste of a bullet, he thought, but a couple of well-aimed punches would still make him feel better.

There was a cough, quick and urgent, and he glanced round, hoping it was a signal that something had been spotted. It was only Danny Doyle clearing his throat before pushing a cigarette between his lips and cupping his hand round it to offer shelter from the rain as he tried to light it.

'Get that out of your mouth,' Tom hissed.

Danny looked up.

'They'll see the smoke, you feckin' eejit.'

Danny shook his head and snatched at the cigarette, crushing it angrily in his palm and throwing it away.

'No-one's coming, Tom,' he said.

'They'll be here. Bide your time.'

'We've been here for hours and there's been nothing. I'm so bloody cold I feel like pissing myself just to get some feeling back in my legs.'

Tom said nothing. He knew Danny was right but he didn't want to be the one who suggested they abandon their saturated vigil. In any case, it wasn't his call to make. Seamus Kelly was in charge and they would only be able to go home on his order. After all, he was the one who would have to answer to their superiors, so Tom could understand the reluctance to acknowledge what increasingly seemed like a fruitless expedition.

Danny was glaring straight ahead, sulking like a child and Tom wasn't sure whether to laugh or slap the boy. Danny was only eighteen but he'd already proved himself on numerous ambushes before this one. No-one ever mentioned his age when it came to operations, though it never stopped the rest of the men teasing and tormenting him when the subject of women was mentioned and in particular the boy's lack of experience in that department.

Tom would laugh along with everyone else as Danny's embarrassment and rage built to a crescendo, though he never said anything himself. Danny was his cousin, after all, and there had to be some family loyalty. He felt protective of the younger man and he was glad they were part of the same flying column. He'd promised his Aunt Theresa that he would look after her son and that's what he always tried to do, though he had to leave Danny to deal with the verbal abuse he received by virtue of being the youngest member of the group.

He began imagining the bowl of steaming hot potato soup that would be waiting at Theresa's when they finally got away from here. He always called in on his way home, making sure that his cousin was safely delivered back to his parents, though the prospect of getting fed would be enough to lure anyone into their cottage at any time of day or night. Theresa's soup was legendary – better even than his own mammy's though he never told her that – and it would certainly be welcome on a day like today. He hoped Seamus would make a decision soon, licking his lips in anticipation of the soup that he swore he could almost taste already.

Murphy stood up and stretched, groaning as he held his rifle above his head.

'It's always feckin' raining here,' he said.

'Stop your whining,' said Seamus.

'I'm only saying.'

'We all know it's raining. You don't need to state the bloody obvious.'

Murphy held out his rifle and waved it in front of him.

'We're fighting for this, you know,' he said.

'What?'

'To live in a country where the heavens drown us every day.'

'Well, at least we'll be wet and free,' said Seamus.

'I'd love to live somewhere warm.'

'If you don't shut up, I'll send you to hell right now and you can warm your bony Armagh arse on the devil's pitchfork to your heart's content.'

Murphy shook his head but turned away and began staring towards the road, not wanting to run the risk of the threat becoming a reality, but he continued muttering under his breath. Seamus always wore an air of quiet authority which it was never wise to question. The men respected him – he was a veteran of nineteen-sixteen, after all, and had fought alongside James Connolly in Dublin – but they had seen enough of him in action to fear him as well.

Seamus was fed up. They all were and Tom knew the four men on the other side of the road were feeling exactly the same. It must have been at least two hours since they'd arrived and not a single vehicle had passed. They might have expected at least one tractor or truck from one of the nearby farms but there had been nothing. Even a passing cyclist might have caught their attention and given them something to talk about but instead they were stuck with their own company and the incessant rain which had long ago soaked through the many layers of clothing they'd all put on. Every topic of conversation had been exhausted and now they were wet and tired and on the verge of mutiny.

Tom glanced at Seamus, and shook his head.

'Right lads,' Seamus said.

'Something's coming.'

'What?'

'Down there. Look.' Danny pointed towards the bottom of the hill where they could see a truck beginning its slow ascent.

'Heads down, lads. Now!'

They all dropped to the ground, not caring that the grass was wet and soggy. Hoods were pulled up, rifles pointed at the road and a silent determination quickly took over. Tom could feel his heart racing, the anticipation provoking a heightened sense of excitement, and he knew the rest of the men would be experiencing the same thing. He would have been worried if he didn't feel this way. That would mean complacency on his part and it was not a welcome companion. Complacency could lead to death – his own – and he wasn't ready for that just yet.

It would take less than five minutes for the truck to reach them and with each passing second his focus became narrower and sharper. It was a familiar sensation and it brought him a sense of comfort. He allowed a tiny smile to creep out from the edges of his mouth, though he could barely feel it, so numb was his face. This was what he was trained for. This was why he had volunteered. This was what he enjoyed most, even if he sometimes felt guilty at having such feelings.

Seamus had no need to issue any final instructions. They all knew what they had to do. They'd gone over it so many times before and had carried out enough ambushes in the past to know their respective roles.

Tom would fire the first shot. He was their top marksman, the finest shot in Donegal; some said he was the best the IRA had in the whole of Ireland but he would always dismiss such praise even if, secretly, he hoped it was true. His first bullet would be for the commander of the army patrol.

'Shoot the head and the body loses all direction,' is what he'd always been told and it was true. Panic would spread through the rest of the soldiers when their commanding officer was taken out and before they had time to re-organise, most of them would also be dead. That's why there was no room for error. The first shot had to be perfect.

Tom lay absolutely still, the safety catch on his rifle cocked, his eye, steady and unblinking, trained through the sight on the road ahead. His finger gently caressed the trigger and he licked his lips again. It wouldn't be long now till he was wolfing down that potato soup.

It began as a distant growl, like a roll of thunder from many miles away, but slowly the rumbling of the truck grew louder, the engine seeming to groan and grumble as it pulled the weight of the vehicle and the group of soldiers sitting in the back up the steep road. Tom pictured the soldiers hunched together, as wet and miserable as he and the rest of his comrades were, probably cursing their own bad luck at having to patrol this deserted stretch of Donegal on what felt like the wettest day of the year. None of them would be thinking that they were about to die, and even those who had contemplated such things in the past couldn't have pictured the last few minutes of their lives being spent in the back of a rain-soaked truck.

Tom glanced to his left where Danny lay, pressed to the ground. His cousin winked at him and Tom winked back. It was a ritual they had before the shooting began which made them both feel better because they realised they were not alone. Danny pulled out the silver chain he wore from under his jacket and kissed the medal of Our Lady. It was his lucky charm, he always insisted. Religion was not for Tom. He couldn't understand why anyone would pin their hopes and dreams on a bunch of superstitious nonsense that never put any food on the table and always let you down, and which made people accept their suffering in this life with the false promise of a better time after they died. He'd learned all that on his mother's knee and he'd never forgotten her words.

Danny hid the medal back under his clothes and grinned at his cousin. Tom shook his head dismissively and touched the trigger again as the rumbling truck drew ever closer.

Another minute passed and then it re-appeared round the bend in the road, inching its way forward as the track flattened out. The driver gripped the steering wheel and stared intently through the windscreen that was cleaned intermittently by a temperamental wiper. Another soldier sat beside him, arms folded, with his boots up on the dashboard.

The back of the truck was uncovered. Five soldiers sat

against one side, facing five of their colleagues while one man stood in the middle of them, hands on hips and staring ahead. He was the officer. Tom grinned and shook his head. It was as if they'd drawn a target on this man just to help him. He'd heard that British officers weren't the brightest but this really took stupidity to a new level. If he'd been in charge, he would have been beside the driver and dressed as a regular soldier so as not to draw attention to himself. Instead, this officer posed proudly in front of his men, his uniform distinct and dashing, his hat almost shouting out 'Look at me, I'm in charge. Shoot me first!'

Tom closed his left eye and stared through the sight with his right, focusing the target on the officer's forehead. He'd see if he could shoot the man without knocking his hat off. He squeezed the trigger, feeling a jolt to his shoulder as the rifle recoiled while from the other end the bullet exploded out of the barrel, though it had almost reached its target before the noise reached the ears of the soldiers. In the same instant the tiny piece of metal crashed through the skull of the officer, lifting him off his feet and sending him crashing backwards where he toppled over the end of the truck and landed with a dull thud on the wet road.

For a few moments the soldiers were stunned, gripped by an inertia brought on by the sight of their commander vanishing, remnants of his brain splattered on several of their faces, and it was in those seconds that the rest of Tom's comrades began firing. Bullets rained down on the truck which came to a sudden halt when the driver slumped over the steering wheel, having been shot through the throat. It was Tom's second shot.

Short explosions filled the Donegal countryside, soon followed by the panicked shouts of desperate soldiers mixed in with the screams of the dying. Several of the soldiers had managed to clamber over the side of the truck but while they sheltered at one side of the vehicle, trying to fire off some sort of response at their attackers in front of them, they were picked off from behind, unaware that they were surrounded.

Tom kept his sight trained on the front of the truck, watching as the passenger opened the driver's door and kicked his dead colleague out on to the road. He tried starting up the engine and after two failed attempts managed to spark it into life. It was at this point that Tom pressed his trigger again and a burst of lumpy red liquid smeared the inside of the windscreen.

The shooting continued for five minutes, most of it coming from the hillside, before Seamus shouted a ceasefire command. Immediately the guns drew silent, though some echoes of their activity resonated through the rain. Weak clouds of gun-smoke hung briefly in the air before finally being extinguished by the endless downpour and Tom caught a hint of the odour of burning cordite. No-one moved and rifles remained trained on the truck, waiting for any sudden movement that would indicate any unfinished business.

After a few minutes Seamus got to his feet, a signal for the rest of the men to follow suit.

'Careful, lads,' he shouted automatically as he led the way down the hill. Tom looked at Danny as he pushed himself on to his knees, feeling himself relax. It was another job safely and successfully executed. He knew they didn't have too long to complete their work, which involved stripping the soldiers of any weapons they had, before army reinforcements might arrive, and they all quickly followed Seamus down the hill and on to the road, rifles still poised, but they were now gripped with a sense of elation and one or two whoops of delight filled the air.

This had been the perfect ambush, thought Tom as he began lifting weapons from the dead soldiers and stacking them at the side of the road. He nodded to Seamus as he passed him, a silent gesture of congratulation that the other man acknowledged. It wasn't always as easy as this. They both knew that and had seen enough comrades fall by their side not to get too carried away by one successful operation. Still, it was one they would enjoy when they finally all returned home.

Tom wasn't sure where he would be staying tonight. He was moving between safe houses, never feeling comfortable if he remained more than a couple of days in the one place. There were soldiers everywhere, and spies too, and he'd been warned on more than one occasion that he was considered a prize well worth capturing. Seamus knew where he was to go but Tom would wait until he'd dropped Danny off before finding out. The fewer people who knew the location the better and that included his cousin.

He didn't pay attention to the men he was relieving of their weapons. It was best not to look into their dead eyes lest he was haunted by them in his dreams, nor would he glance at their blood-soaked bodies which would only remind him of their youthfulness, which he had brought abruptly to an end. To him they were simply uniforms – enemy uniforms – and that was the only way to deal with it.

A sudden gunshot startled him and he spun round. There was a split second of silence before Murphy and Cahal Kennedy, one of the men from the other side of the hill, began firing their rifles at the back of the truck and he raced towards them as a low moan broke clear of the gunfire which had now ceased again. Danny was lying in the middle of the road, his knees pulled up towards his body and his hands clutching his stomach.

Tom glanced towards Murphy and Cahal. Their rifles were pointed at a soldier whose body, riddled with bullet wounds, was slumped against the tyre, and Tom immediately knew what had happened. Dropping his own weapon he stumbled forward and sunk down beside Danny whose groans were getting louder and more incessant. His cousin's hands were bright red like he'd dipped them in a pot of paint.

'Danny! Danny! It's okay. I'm here.'

'I'm shot, Tom. Oh God, I'm shot!'

'I know, Danny, but you're going to be okay,' he said automatically.

The teenager let out a sharp cry as a sudden pain surged through his body. Tom tried to pull Danny's hands away from his stomach to examine the full extent of his injury but the younger man showed a surprising surge of strength to resist his efforts and he knew anyway that there was nothing he could do.

Tom looked round as the other men inched forward. Seamus barged his way past them and knelt down beside Tom. There was a detached calm about his demeanour as he gripped Danny's shoulder, his touch seeming to soothe the boy's frantic squirming but it was only for a few moments.

'Help me, Tom,' he pleaded.

'I'm here, Danny,' he said, taking his cousin's bloody hand and managing to wrench it away from his stomach. He squeezed it tightly, muttering 'It'll be okay,' over and over again. He looked at Seamus, whose eyes confirmed what he already knew, and he glanced away, leaning into Danny's face and gently kissing his cousin's forehead. The gesture took him by surprise and he could feel his face burning brightly. He wondered what the rest of the men would think about it and hoped they'd forget what they'd seen.

Danny was gasping for breath now and every time he tried to speak, blood poured out the side of his mouth.

'I'm scared, Tom,' he mumbled. 'I don't want to die.'

'Danny, Danny,' he said, blinking furiously to force back the tears that were threatening to soak his cheeks. He didn't know what else to say. There was nothing he could say. Danny managed to muster one final burst of energy and let out a cry that could only have lasted for a few seconds but which seemed to hang in the saturated Donegal air for as long as they all remained there. Then his body went limp. Tom felt his cousin's hand effortlessly slip out of his own palm and he let it fall to the wet ground.

He remained on his knees staring at the dead body, studying a face he knew and loved. He wanted to commit it to memory because he would never see it again, never see it relax into a warm, innocent smile, or clench up with youthful anger. Danny's eyes had closed over but Tom would remember them as green and inquisitive. He felt a hand on his shoulder.

'We have to go,' Seamus said and Tom nodded. He was grateful for the strong grip Seamus took of his arm as he helped him back to his feet, and he needed the support as he swayed unsteadily. The rest of the men were gathering up the weapons, all of them keen to keep busy and avoid any eye contact with Tom. He was vaguely aware of the activity going on around him though he could only look down at his cousin.

Once they'd gathered everything up, Seamus ordered two of the men to lift Danny and they gripped the arms and legs of the dead teenager. Seamus began walking back up the hill but Tom stopped him.

'I'll lead the way,' he said, moving ahead and striding up the wet grass, the rest of the group following behind. Even if he closed his eyes he would have been able to find his way to Danny's house but as they got nearer he felt himself slowing down. He could hear the forced breathing of the men carrying the body – Seamus had made sure they had all taken turns – but he never glanced round once.

Tom's heart sank as he caught sight of the cottage. He knew the big pot of soup would be warming on the stove in the kitchen at this very moment and he wondered what he was going to say to his Aunt Theresa.

Glance Back, Look Forward

The rain had eased as clouds of smoke drifted out across the grass towards the garden and it looked at first glance as if the oak tree was smouldering at the base of the trunk. Behind the smoke, however, Tom sat in silence, a lit cigarette constantly at his lips. He desperately wanted to be alone though he knew he had to remain nearby just in case he was needed. The rest of the men had stayed for as long as was polite though they were all anxious to return to their own homes. Even if they couldn't articulate it, they would all be relieved to be with their families again, thankful still to be alive when one of their own had fallen. Seamus had left too, though he promised to return later. He knew where the safe house was and it would do for tonight, though Tom realised that, tomorrow, he would have to go home and break the sad news to his mother.

The local priest had arrived just as the men were paying their final respects to Danny. 'Nothing personal, Father,' Seamus said as they trudged out the cottage. Tom would have liked to stay with Danny, even if he didn't know what to say to Theresa or his Uncle Pat, but he knew he wouldn't be able to tolerate in silence the religious incantations unless he bit his tongue off. It wasn't that he hated the priest, or any priest for that matter. There were plenty who provided sanctuary when it was needed most, or offered a hiding place for weapons, and he'd been grateful for that on more than one occasion. It was the religion he despised as opposed to the men who preached it.

Father O'Brien didn't seem at all perturbed that the busy room he'd entered was suddenly cold and empty. He made the sign of the cross on Danny's forehead and then knelt down at the side of the bed, blessed himself and began praying out loud. He was joined by Theresa and Pat who knelt at the opposite side of the bed, while Tom stood at the door for a few seconds before quietly wandering over to the tree facing the house. He sat down on the ground. It was damp though nowhere near as wet as it had been up on those lonely hills. The ancient tree provided a degree of shelter from the last of the rain, though Tom was soaked beyond caring.

His rifle remained propped against the trunk as he sat and smoked, desperate to keep his lungs fully filled with tobacco. He kept going over every moment of what had happened during the ambush, trying to figure out what they could have done differently – what he could have done – to save Danny. Someone should have double-checked to make sure all the soldiers were dead before they'd emerged from the hillside. It didn't matter now, anyway. Even if he did stumble upon something, it wasn't going to bring Danny back to life. His cousin was lying in the cottage just now – soon he'd be under six feet of earth – and there was nothing Tom or anyone else could do to change that fact.

He'd seen plenty of dead bodies before, some of whom had fallen by his side, men whose names he knew, whose families he'd had to tell. Some of them had died instantly, barely able to take a final breath before it was snatched out of them. They were the lucky ones. Others took longer to die, their agony almost enough to tempt Tom to end their suffering with a bullet of his own. Others still he had been responsible for despatching, like those lifeless souls lying on the cold and wet Donegal hills at this very moment. If he didn't kill them, they would kill him. He understood and accepted that and he knew the men who trained their sights on him and his comrades did too.

This time it was different, however. Danny was family and Tom knew he'd miss him long after the weeds had taken up pernicious residence on his grave.

Tom watched as his Uncle Pat slowly trudged the few yards across the grass from the cottage to the tree. A tall, broad man, it seemed as if he was visibly shrinking with every step, each one more laboured than the last. Tom began to push himself up on to his feet but Pat shook his head.

'Sit down, son. Don't be daft,' he said as he lowered himself awkwardly to the ground beside his nephew and leant against the tree.

Tom held out his tin and Pat removed a thin cigarette with a grateful grunt, accepting a light and adding his own contribution to the balls of smoke that rolled towards the cottage before reluctantly evaporating in the rain.

'Pat,' Tom began.

'It's alright, son. You don't need to say anything.'

It was a comfortable, almost welcoming silence which nestled between the two men, only broken by the sporadic sobs emerging from the cottage. Tom snatched occasional glances at his uncle, who wore a bemused frown. Pat was a farmer. That's what he knew and understood, along with the pleasures to be had from a few pints of the black stuff after a long day in the fields. He was floundering now, drowning in a storm of emotions that had suddenly engulfed him. His wife was crying over the body of their dead son and his only answer was to sit out in the rain, smoking.

'He was a good boy,' Pat muttered.

'He'll be a great loss to the movement. Ireland has –'

Pat snorted.

'What?'

'You don't need to give me all that patriotic gibberish. Remember, it's your Uncle Pat you're talking to now.'

'I'm sorry.'

'It's fine, son.'

'I should have been there for him.'

'Don't be daft.'

'I was meant to look out for him, Pat, look after him, and I didn't, and now he's dead.'

'Now don't be blaming yourself. It's not your fault.'

Tom sighed and flicked away the tiny stump of his cigarette, still conscious of the heavy burden of guilt that was crushing his shoulders despite Pat's words. He didn't have the luxury of the confessional box to unburden himself, though that was by choice and he wasn't about to change now, even if someone was to tell him it would help. It was just something else to bottle up and bury in a hidden compartment of his mind, never to be dug up again.

'How's your mammy?' Pat asked.

'She's okay. You know. . .'

'Go and see her.'

'I'll go tomorrow.'

'Make sure you do. It'll do her good.'

'This'll break her heart.'

Pat nodded, coughing up a mouthful of phlegm which he spat on the ground before drawing on his cigarette again.

A figure appeared at the side of the cottage, nodding towards Tom when he looked over. It was Seamus. Tom stood up, automatically brushing his trousers with his hands before picking up the rifle. Pat remained sitting, legs outstretched and crossed. He looked as though he was enjoying a warm Donegal evening rather than sitting in the rain mourning the loss of his youngest child and his only son. Tom threw the cigarette tin gently towards him where it landed on his stomach.

'That'll keep you company for a while,' he said.

Pat nodded, and began rummaging in his pocket.

'Here,' he said. 'This is for you.'

He held out a silver chain, on the end of which was a medal of Our Lady. Tom took a step back, shaking his head.

'Don't be an eejit,' Pat said. 'Danny would have wanted you to have it.'

'I don't know, Pat. It's just . . . I don't believe . . .'

'It's nothing to do with that. You can think of Danny when you look at it and forget about all the other nonsense if you want. Here, take it.'

Slowly, Tom held out his hand and his uncle dropped the chain into his palm. He studied it, immediately picturing Danny kissing it for good luck before every operation. He could feel his eyes filling up and he knew it was time to leave before he embarrassed himself or Pat.

'Look after yourself,' he said with a nod.

'You too, son.'

'And can you tell Theresa . . . '

'Don't worry, son. She'll understand.'

Tom turned and began trudging towards Seamus who stood, hands in pockets, at the side of the cottage.

'And don't forget to go and see your mammy,' Pat shouted after him. Tom nodded again, though he didn't look round.

They were ten minutes down the road before Seamus spoke.

'The Big Fella wants to see you,' he said without glancing round or breaking a stride.

'When?'

'Now.'

'The Big Fella's here? Where?'

'Where we're going. That's where.'

Tom shook his head as Seamus grinned. He knew he wouldn't get any more information out of the other man, even if he was a trusted comrade, and he thought it better to walk in silence rather than waste his breath with questions that wouldn't get answered.

They called him the Big Fella but never to his face. Not that he would have minded. Tom knew he'd relish the nickname, but the men referred to him as the Chief while those who knew him best called him Mick.

Michael Collins was their leader. He might not have the title as head of the IRA but he had the stature, reputation and respect of every volunteer from Dublin to Belfast, and from Cork to Donegal. The Brits wanted him more than any other man in Ireland but he was smarter than them. Now he was in Donegal and Tom could feel his stomach churning, even though he was going to meet an old comrade.

As they continued walking, Seamus occasionally breaking the silence with a poorly-whistled version of *The Wearing of the Green*, Tom realised where they were going. It was a familiar trail that would lead all the way to the Paterson house. He'd stayed there before and it was no surprise that this was where they were to meet the Big Fella. It was one of their safest houses, after all.

The Patersons were a well-respected family in the county, good, God-fearing Protestants who would never arouse any suspicions, certainly none that would mark them down as sympathetic to the cause. Robert Paterson let them into the house after Seamus had knocked just once on the front door, immediately nodding towards the stairs. The two men tipped their caps as they made their way upstairs.

Seamus knocked on one of the bedroom doors and was shouted inside. He gestured for Tom to wait. Tom could hear the murmur of voices before Seamus re-appeared, holding the door open.

Tom stepped into the room and Seamus closed the door, disappearing down the stairs, no doubt to take advantage of Alice Paterson's home cooking, which could satisfy even the hungriest stomach.

Michael Collins was standing, hands on hips, and staring out through the rain-washed window at the fields which stretched as far as the eye could see. Isolated farm-houses were dotted on the landscape, with thin trails of smoke crawling out from chimneys alerting observers to their presence. At night the flickering candles holding lonely vigils at the windows offered the only signs of life amidst the rugged landscape while the cries of restless animals would struggle to be heard above the manic howling of the wind as it soared and swooped across the land.

There were many nights when Tom had been out there, snatching precious moments of sleep in hidden culverts or trudging wearily over muddy fields towards one of those candles where he would be greeted with some warm food and a place to rest his eyes for a few hours. It was never a peaceful sleep, or a deep one. There were people scouring the countryside hunting for him and his comrades and he was always on edge, waiting for a door to come crashing down at any moment and a dozen rifles to be aimed at his head.

Collins slowly turned round, his face immediately breaking into a broad smile.

'Tom, it's good to see you,' he said, striding across the room. He held out his arms and the two men gripped each other in an affectionate bear hug. After a few moments Tom tried to break away but he couldn't get free of Collins' grip. He squirmed and struggled but instead of releasing himself, suddenly got caught up in a head-lock. He threw his arm round Collins' waist and began squeezing it.

'Tickling's a dirty trick,' Collins laughed. 'That's almost torture you're using there, Tom. Remember, we're not Brits.'

The two men, grasping and grappling with each other, stumbled back towards the window, crashing into the table and chair which sat beside it before bouncing back into the middle of the room. Tom could feel himself toppling over and he knew Collins' grip wouldn't hold him up. As he hit the ground, bringing the other man tumbling down with him, he suddenly felt himself released and he rolled across the floor, narrowly avoiding a boot in his face. Collins was on his knees, recovering his breath and still grinning like a maniac.

'Give us a hand now,' he said as Tom slowly got to his feet.

'Not a chance,' Tom said. 'I know your game.'

'I'm calling a truce,' Collins said and Tom reluctantly held out his hand which the other man gripped, dragging himself to his feet.

'It's good to see you, Tom,' he said again.

'You too, Mick.'

'Are you well?'

Tom nodded, picking up the chair and dropping on to it. Collins was more restless, sitting on the edge of the bed for a few seconds before springing to his feet again and pacing up and down the room.

'That was good work today,' Collins said. 'The Brits are going to hit us hard now, that's for sure.'

Tom grunted in agreement.

'It's a bad business too. I'm sorry for your loss.'

'Thanks.'

Collins sat down on the bed again, pushing himself back until he could lean against the wall. Rummaging in his pockets, he produced a packet of cigarettes and threw them to Tom, quickly followed by a box of matches. Tom gratefully lit a cigarette, filling the room with smoke before lobbing the cigarettes back on the bed. Collins lit up too and both of them sat smoking in silence.

There wasn't much between them in age – Collins was the older by a couple of years – and they enjoyed a similar stature, both of them big, broad men with rugged looks that always caught the eye of the opposite sex. The biggest contrast was in their personalities. Collins was gregarious and outgoing, exuding an infectious enthusiasm wherever he went. That, along with the aura of his position and the legend of his activities, ensured an almost reverential hush would fall over any room he entered until he filled it with his own laughter. Women were drawn to him and he enjoyed the attention, easy in their company and revelling in their flustered admiration. Women were drawn to Tom as well, though as moths to a flame. He was quiet, almost sullen at times, but there was a scent of danger that set many hearts racing. They found out too late that his heart was ice-cold when it came to such matters.

They had met in Wales, thrown together in a prison camp after the failure of the rising in nineteen sixteen. When they'd returned to Ireland, Collins headed immediately for Dublin while Tom was Donegal-bound, ready to take up the fight once again, but more comfortable in his own county and among his own people. That had only been three years ago but sometimes, to Tom, it felt like a lifetime after what had happened in the intervening period.

'I've got a job for you,' Collins said, taking a final draw on his cigarette before flicking it on to the floor where it smouldered until he stood on it.

'Sure. What is it?'

'I need you to go to Glasgow. . .'

'Glasgow?'

'Is that a problem?'

Tom shook his head.

'I want you to go there and take someone out.'

'Who?'

'It's Maxwell.'

Tom whistled.

'I know. It's the big one. That's why I need our best man.'

It was an important job and Tom should have been flattered that he was the one being asked – or told – to carry it out – but one factor made him pause; he was going to Glasgow. His mammy wouldn't be pleased about him going over to 'that God-forsaken city,' as she always described it. He didn't know if he would tell her, especially when he still had to break the news to her about Danny. It was probably better she didn't find out because he knew she would try and talk him out of it.

'So what of it then?' Collins asked.

'I'm your man,' Tom said, standing up. Collins did too.

'Seamus has all the details. I've got to be off now. No rest for the wicked,' he laughed.

'That's what they say.'

'Look after yourself now,' he said, holding out his hand. As Tom took his firm grasp, he felt something being pushed into his palm. Collins gripped his hand and held his gaze. 'Later,' he said as Tom tried to see what it was. With a final nod, Collins turned and strode out the room, slamming the door behind him.

Tom walked over to the window and stood with his forehead pressed against the cold glass, waiting until he saw The Big Fella appear from the house and get into a car which had drawn up at the front door. He glanced up at the house, and Tom was sure he winked before disappearing inside the vehicle which immediately drove off. He remained staring out the window, even after Seamus had walked into the room, though the piece of paper Collins had left him was now safely buried in his trouser pocket.

Mammy's Boy

Tom hadn't seen his mother for almost three weeks. It wasn't a long time but he was still shocked when he set eyes on her. She'd appeared to have shed most of her skin and was now wearing only the flimsiest layer of flesh that barely covered bones which were desperately trying to break free. Her eyes had sunk deep into their sockets like they were deliberately trying to avoid the light and it was as if she was peering through a tunnel to see him. He stood in the middle of the room, towering over the bed where she lay, while her sister – his Aunt Annie – sat on a chair beside her, a bundle of knitting on her lap and a basin at her feet.

'Look what the cat's dragged in, Kate,' she said as his mother used up every ounce of energy to turn her head a few inches to look at him.

'Who is it?' she croaked.

'It's me, mammy. Tom.'

He wanted to say that her eyes suddenly sparkled or that her face shone with a smile as bright and dazzling as the sun on a summer's day but all she could muster was the slightest movement at the edges of her mouth. He could see that even this effort seemed to stretch her skin taut and he almost wanted to tell her to stop.

'So it is now,' Annie said, standing up. 'It's been that long I hardly recognised him.' She shuffled over and hugged him briefly, the knitting needles pressing against his stomach, before ushering him towards to the stove.

'And I suppose he'll be wanting fed as well? He's some boy to be one boy, Kate. Is that not what I've always said?'

Kate's head bobbed slightly in agreement as Tom looked for Annie to put words to the picture he saw in the bed. Three weeks ago his mother was still on her feet, and though he saw then that even the effort of putting one foot in front of the other visibly drained her, Tom looked at the inevitable being months away at least, if not a year or two. Now it seemed like they were counting down the days – hours maybe – and he didn't know what to do or say.

He did know that he wouldn't tell her about Danny. He wasn't sure she'd even take the information in, and as for Glasgow . . . he didn't think he would have mentioned that even if she'd come running across the field to greet his return.

'It's good that you're home,' Annie said. 'God's made sure you're here for your mammy in her hour of need . . . and you can wipe that frown off your face right now, Tom Costello. I know the nonsense that my sister's put in your mind about religion and that's all it is – nonsense.'

Tom shrugged. He would never argue with his aunt at the best of times, and since this was the worst of times, he knew better than to open his mouth. Instead he took up vigil at his mother's bedside, though she'd already fallen asleep again by the time he did so. He sat and stared at her, unsure whether he wanted her to wake up or if he preferred that she continue sleeping. He placed her hand on his palm, lowering it until it rested on top of his own flesh, his touch as delicate as if he was handling a freshly laid egg.

Annie busied herself at the stove, eventually calling him

again when she'd made a fresh pot of tea, and he moved over to the table, feeling more comfortable with the distance between him and his mother, like he was trying to keep her dying body at arm's length so that it might be easier for him to try and make sense of it.

'She'll be delighted you're back,' Annie said, taking a sip from her own mug. 'That's all she talks about – 'Tom this, Tom that.' It'll do her good to see you.'

Tom glanced over at his mother and then back at Annie.

'I didn't say it was going to make her better. Jesus, Mary and Joseph,' she said, blessing herself. 'Will you look at her now? She's a poor soul.'

'I know,' Tom said. 'I didn't expect it. . . '

'Maybe it's a blessing? She could suffer for months on end and that would be a lot worse. At least she's got her boy back.'

'I'm leaving tomorrow.'

'Oh, Tom, you can't. Look at your mammy, for goodness sake. She needs you.'

'I've no choice,' he sighed. 'I've got to go.'

'Where?'

Tom shook his head. They drank their tea in silence now, Annie's occasional snorts indicating she wasn't happy but he knew he couldn't tell her anything.

'It's an awful business, all this fighting,' she eventually said.

'It is that.'

'Well, just you be careful now.'

He watched her sleeping, sometimes straining his eyes to make sure that her chest continued to rise and fall, though the occasional rattle that escaped from deep in her throat as if her whole body was being shaken was strangely comforting. It was the sound of silence that he feared most. It was dim in the corner of the room where she lay, the candle sitting in front of him not able to cast light on her despite its best efforts. He sheltered behind the flame as it swayed and swooned in the draft which had raced in under the front door and swirled mischievously round the cottage, and he continued to sip at a mug of tea that had long ago gone cold but was still preferable to making a fresh pot.

The peat fire remained a smouldering presence, emitting a few waves of heat which he would occasionally encourage with the bellows that lay on the hearth and he briefly thought of moving the bed nearer to the fire, though he wasn't sure whether she would be able to cope with even the tiniest hint of smoke in her lungs.

Two pillows at her back gave her body the necessary elevation while providing a degree of comfort. If she lay flat out she was likely to choke, possibly to death, Annie had warned him, though she patted his arm to reassure him when she saw the lines of panic break out across his face. His aunt had left after finishing her own tea.

'Spend some time with your mammy,' she'd told him, hugging him warmly and giving him a quick kiss on the cheek. 'I'll be back in a wee while,' she said as she closed the door behind her and he hoped she wouldn't be too long.

Sometimes when he looked at the frail figure in the bed, he had to remind himself that this was actually his mother. If he closed his eyes, images of how she used to look – the way he remembered her, and always wanted to – danced before him; she was laughing, singing, offering him words of comfort if he was upset, or words of encouragement if he'd done anything worthwhile. Always, she was the centre of attention in any room. He found it a comforting vision and he was reluctant to open his eyes to reality.

He could have sat wishing things were different but he knew it was a pointless exercise. It still didn't stop him from keeping his eyes closed more often than not, and in every image he recalled, it was her eyes which sparkled brighter than anything else he could see.

He missed those warm brown eyes which always seemed to shine brightest for him. When he was younger, Tom believed that he was able to make them light up whenever he entered the room.

'Here's my best boy,' his mammy would say, her arms open and welcoming as he raced towards her, allowing himself to be engulfed in her embrace.

It was just the two of them for almost as long as he could remember. There were vague memories of his granny which would occasionally re-surface. She was old and slow, with a spine that had bent over and made it look like she was permanently on the verge of toppling over. She died when he was young – four or five – and after that it was just him and his mammy.

Not that they were alone. The house always seemed to be filled with aunties and uncles and cousins, so it never really felt to Tom like he was an only child anyway. He knew he was different since he only had his mother but she had enough love to compensate.

'What happened to my daddy?' he would occasionally ask but she never really told him, save for muttering bitterly about Glasgow, and he knew that no matter how many times he pressed her, she was never going to tell him.

He did know the story, though, hearing her tell Annie when she thought he was sleeping. It was the only time he ever heard her talking about him – Mick Costello – and he committed every word to memory. He was confident he could repeat it word for word if anyone pressed him.

Mick Costello was the father he never knew. Mick hadn't known about his son either. He'd been murdered by someone his mother had once been involved with. She hadn't the chance to tell him she was pregnant before he bled to death on a Glasgow street. That's why she hated the city so much. 'Glasgow' was a dirty word in the house and always had been, for as long as Tom could remember. Now he was heading there for the first time and he was glad his mother would never find out about that.

Kate stirred in her bed and opened her eyes.

'Mick?' she mumbled.

'It's Tom, mammy. I'm right here.'

He took her hand and gently stroked the back of it. She started coughing, a low rumble that sounded to Tom like the groans of a hungry dog, but when it gripped her, he tipped her body forward slightly with one hand while he grabbed the bucket with his other. He held it under her chin and she spat thick mouthfuls of blood into it, though some of it dribbled on to her chin. He wiped it off with his jacket sleeve.

The sight of blood was not an unfamiliar one to him, but this was different. This was his mother and she was dying. Slowly. He suddenly wished he could have said a prayer for her. It was a fleeting thought, as brief and barely notice-able as a sudden gust of wind on a bright summer's day, but it took him by surprise nevertheless. There were prayers he could have summoned from the depths of his childhood. Religion might have been an unwelcome guest in the house but he still had to experience it every day at school.

Yet he wasn't sure a prayer was what his mother would have wanted, and the thought of it made him feel uneasy. He suspected his Auntie Annie sat at his mother's bedside muttering a whole litany of prayers to every saint in heaven, which would make up for his own shortcomings.

His mother mumbled something and he moved closer to her.

'What did you say, mammy?'

'I want my box.'

He nodded and dropped to his knees to peer under the bed. Lying in the far corner was a box and Tom could just about reach it at full stretch, his fingertips touching it, and it took a few minutes before he managed to manoeuvre it into his grasp. Sitting up, he placed it on the bed.

The box had been in the house forever. He suspected it was at least as old as him, and it brought more memories of childhood flooding back. It had been the forbidden fruit. He wasn't allowed to touch it. Ever. Under pain of death or other punishments that he imagined in his youthful naiveté were even worse, his mother had warned him never to open the box. He wasn't used to seeing her so serious about anything and it took a great deal of effort to suppress his natural curiosity. He did try to open it once but he got caught. His mother skelped his backside for that and he never tried again.

He stared at it now, a battered navy object, until his mother's tired sigh told him to open it. With trembling fingers he slowly removed the lid and placed the box on her stomach. Her skeletal hand began rummaging in it and she removed what looked like an old shirt which she discarded on the bed. She continued searching until she found what she was looking for. A silver chain and medal dangled on her fingers.

'For you,' she whispered.

Tom looked at her and she nodded, pushing her hand towards him. He let the chain drop on to his palm and he stared at it, not recognising which saint it was. Another bloody holy medal, he wanted to say, but he held his tongue. He studied the medal more closely. It was silver, though it was also covered with dark stains. His mother whispered something and he moved closer to her.

'What did you say?' he asked.

'It was your daddy's.'

He closed his hand tightly over the medal and laid his head on the bed beside his mother. She managed to muster enough strength to lift her arm and she let her hand rest on his head, gently caressing his hair with her bony fingers. He could feel himself drifting off to sleep and he smiled, remembering all those times from his childhood when he'd snuggled into her lap at night. It always felt like the safest place in the world to him. Those warm brown eyes were the last thing he saw before he shut his own and they were always there to greet him when he woke up. He couldn't believe that wouldn't always continue to be the case.

Paying the Price

There was a detour to be made before he headed to Glasgow. That's what the Big Fella's note had ordered. There had been a surname scrawled on it, along with the name of the house – Caislean Mhaigh Eo. He'd quickly memorised both pieces of information and then burnt the piece of paper.

Now he sat in the tree and watched the house – Mayo Castle. He had been there one hour at least, perhaps even longer, and nothing much had happened in all that time. As far as he could figure out, there were just two men who strolled round the grounds in opposite directions, stopping for a cigarette whenever their paths crossed. They didn't exchange too many words during their break but they'd always bid each other farewell when they resumed their patrol, even though they'd meet again at the same point within the next ten minutes. Both of them had rifles slung casually over their shoulders and Tom knew it would take a few vital – or fatal – seconds for them to be in a position to fire their weapons. By then it would be too late for either of them.

He could have shot them both from his vantage point – a tall oak tree, thick with branches and greenery which provided the perfect camouflage for his observations – but he required the element of surprise so he wouldn't be able to use his own rifle. Instead, he would have to be quiet, though hopefully just as deadly.

It was a beautiful house which stood alone and proud in the Mayo countryside, visible to the naked eye from miles away, and an obvious sign of wealth that could only be imagined and envied. The man had done well, thought Tom, though he quickly reminded himself how that wealth had been accumulated just in case any sense of admiration began to creep into his mind and cloud his judgement.

He counted the windows on the back of the house. There were four on the ground floor, two either side of the imposing, wooden door. If this was the servants' entrance, Tom could only imagine how impressive the front door was. The house was on two levels and a further six windows ran along the first floor. He had never been in a house this size before and he couldn't even begin to guess how many rooms there were, even though he realised there were more than the ten to correspond with the number of windows he could see. The house had a light sandstone exterior that looked as smooth as marble from where Tom sat, though he knew it would be rough to touch when he got up close.

It was peaceful in the tree, silent save for the occasional bird calling out for companionship or the rustle of leaves from busy animals on the move or the restless wind which glided through the branches. It smelt of the countryside whenever Tom breathed in and he closed his eyes, remembering the fields from his childhood that seemed to stretch out into infinity, each one a different shade of green.

Certainly, it seemed to him that there were more than forty varieties. That was his own secret playground – the whole of Donegal – or so it felt to his young and inquisitive mind, though it was only later that he realised his mother always knew where he was, even as it seemed to him that he discreetly slipped away from her sights to explore on his own or with any one of his cousins who were like brothers and sisters to him.

Tom snapped his eyes open, aware that he was drifting off into a dangerous daydream – dangerous because he could topple to the ground in a moment if he wasn't careful, and then he'd be worse than useless; if the fall didn't kill him he'd be bound to break a limb or two.

He was beginning to stiffen up, having remained in the same position for so long. He knew better than to move, aware that even the slightest adjustment might catch the eye or disturb something else in the tree which would have the same effect of alerting the guards or at least arousing their interest. He was glad of the clouds which provided a natural barrier to the sun whose rays would have sought him out even amidst the foliage he hid within; a tiny sparkle as sunlight hit metal might prove fatal, even though he had examined himself several times, concealing anything which might cause that to happen. His rifle was hidden under a pile of leaves at the foot of the tree, though he had a pistol tucked into his belt buckle. It was concealed by his jacket though it could be called into action at a moment's notice.

After watching the guards repeat their circuit of the house, stopping again for a cigarette, he used the window of opportunity that presented itself when they slipped round either corner of the house to scamper down the tree with the agility of a creature which had lived its whole life in these environs.

The rifle remained in its hiding place, only to be redeemed when he'd completed the job in hand. He patted his waist where the pistol was, just for reassurance, and then produced a knife from his inside jacket pocket. It was like those fishermen used to gut their catch, its edge serrated and sharp. He quickly sprinted across the grounds, some twenty yards or so, before reaching the right-hand corner. He glanced down to the other end of the house and saw the guard disappearing round the far corner, no doubt heading towards the front door of the house.

Tom moved in the same direction, glancing around him for any other sign of life, though all was still and silent. He had a fleeting thought that the men were guarding an empty house and that his target was elsewhere, but he quickly dismissed it. What would be the point of the two men patrolling the house if there wasn't something – someone – worth protecting?

The house was wider at the front than at the back. Tom imagined it would look like a fat 'T' shape if he could have climbed to the top of a tree which overlooked it, and it was this extension which provided him with the necessary cover.

He stood, knife poised in his hand, and heard the lazy footsteps getting louder and louder, as the guard completed another tired lap of the house. A throat was cleared and the contents spat on the ground. The crunch of leather boots on the gravel growing ever louder. The grip on his knife tightening. The footsteps louder . . . louder . . .

The guard didn't even see Tom. He emerged round the

corner with his head bowed, watching his boots like he was tracking every footstep, perhaps counting each one in his boredom, working out how many it would take to complete a circuit, though each lap would vary and he'd inevitably lose count or forget the number when he stopped for a smoke.

Tom took one step forward, grabbed the man's shoulders and spun him round before drawing the blade heavily across the exposed throat. Blood burst out of the wound and the guard's hands automatically began trying to clutch at the flesh in the futile hope of binding it together again. It was an instinctive gesture of survival that was doomed to fail. Tom lowered the man to the ground as gently and quietly as he could, kneeling on his back to squeeze the last few frantic breaths out of him. He wiped the knife on the man's jacket and snatched the cap, pushing it down on his own head.

He stood up and jabbed the body with his boot. The man was dead. He took up the rifle, slinging it over his left shoulder and walked briskly towards the back of the house. He knew the other guard would already be there and realised any delay could be suspicious.

The guard stood leaning against the wall, blowing clouds of smoke out into the air. He heard the footsteps approaching but didn't glance round at first. They were quicker than usual, however, and it was their urgent approach which alerted him. He turned round, straight into the butt of a rifle which smashed into his face. The force of the blow knocked the man to the ground. He was choking already – Tom guessed he'd swallowed his cigarette – before a knee pressed down on his chest almost crushing his rib cage, and then a sharp edge sliced force-fully across his stubbly throat.

Tom tried to spring back before the blood began to spurt out but a few thin lines of spray caught the bottom of his trousers. He cursed his luck even though he knew that fresh clothes would be waiting for him before he set sail for Glasgow. The second guard took longer to die, writhing on the ground in silent agony, Tom's blade having severed the man's vocal cord.

Tom lit a cigarette as his eyes darted frantically in their sockets, watching for any sign that he'd been detected, waiting until the sound of the body rolling in the gravel ceased before glancing back down at the ground. He finished the cigarette and then peered through one of the ground floor windows. The room was empty except for a wooden table and four chairs. A lonely cup and saucer sat on the table, with a silver teaspoon leaning lazily in the cup. He elbowed one of the glass panes, cracking it with his first blow and then shattering the glass with his second. He carefully pushed his hand through the ragged hole and unclipped the window catch. Then he gently slid it open and climbed into the house.

He stood perfectly still for a minute or so, waiting to see whether the sound of breaking glass would bring anyone scurrying through to investigate. He heard nothing and eventually crept over to the door, edging it open and peering out into the corridor. It was empty. He didn't know exactly where he was going but instinctively he knew it would be upstairs.

He still clutched the knife though he hoped he wouldn't have to use it again on some innocent member of the house staff who just happened to stumble upon his unexpected intrusion. The element of surprise was vital, however, and if it meant sacrificing a cook or cleaner, then it would have to be done.

By now he was at the front of the house and he stood at the foot of the staircase which had one central stairway that branched right and left about halfway up. He could hear voices now, the sound of a child laughing, an occasional low murmur of an adult voice, the slow and laborious clinking on piano keys by a careful but inexperienced student. All of the noise seemed to be in one of the upstairs rooms to the right so Tom opted to go to the left, figuring that the man of the house would want to keep a distance from the rest of the noisy family life so that he could concentrate on his business matters, whatever they might be.

Creeping slowly along the top corridor, the sound of the piano drifting ever louder from the other side of the building, Tom stopped at every door and pressed his ear close to the wooden frame, staying in that position until he was convinced it was empty. At the fourth door, a deep cough was enough to tell him this was the room.

Taking out his pistol, he breathed in deeply. As his free hand hovered at the door handle, Tom instinctively glanced round as if he was expecting Danny to be there, winking at him, but there was no-one, and there never would be.

'Sit down, shut up and don't move,' he barked to the man in the far corner of the room as he burst in, pointing the pistol at him, 'or I'll shoot you and every other person in the house.'

The man was sitting behind an imposing desk near the

window. He held up his hands and Tom could see they were trembling. This would be easy, he realised.

'What do you want?' the man mumbled nervously.

'I told you to shut up,' Tom snapping, bringing down the pistol handle on the side of the man's head, knocking him on to the floor. He groaned as he slowly pushed himself back to his knees and then, with the aid of his desk, he clambered back on the chair. A trail of blood began to run down his cheek and he wiped it with his sleeve.

'It's time to pay for your past, Mister Walsh,' Tom said, cocking the pistol.

'Who are you?' Walsh whispered.

'You must have known we'd find you eventually?'

'I don't know what you're talking about.'

'Well, it's not my job to explain.'

'I've got money if that's what you want. Take it, and anything else you want.'

'On your knees,' Tom said, shaking his head.

'Please, I'm begging you. Don't do this.'

Tom made to hit Walsh again with his pistol and the man cowered back before stumbling off the chair. He fell to his knees and clasped his hands together as if in prayer.

'If you believe in God now would be a good time to pray to him,' said Tom.

Walsh was shaking, crying too, a soft sob that was broken up with just one word repeated over and over again.

'Please. . . Please. . . Please. . . Please. . .'

Tom stood directly behind Walsh now. He didn't want any more blood on himself. He cocked the pistol just as the door opened and a girl came running into the room. She was only about eight or nine-years-old. Her eyes, hypnotically blue, darted between Walsh and Tom before they settled on the kneeling man.

'What are you doing, daddy?'

Walsh didn't reply at first and Tom nudged him discreetly in the back with his pistol.

'Nothing, darling,' he said. 'Daddy's just playing a game.'

The girl looked at Tom now and he found it difficult to hold her gaze. Her face was impassive, neither a frown nor a smile broke across it, but Tom felt uneasy, sensing that she'd guessed what was happening. He nudged the kneeling man again.

'It's okay, darling. Daddy's fine. You go back and practice piano for me. Play a song for Daddy.'

Walsh's voice quivered and he began coughing, trying to force back the tears which were desperate to burst out.

Tom often wondered what people thought about when they knew they were going to die. More often than not, his victims were unaware of their fate until a bullet slammed into their body, and then it was too late, but occasionally they had time to contemplate. It might only be for a minute or two, but it was enough to think of something, or someone. He was curious as to what that might be.

What was going through Walsh's mind at this very moment? Was his life flashing before his eyes? Did he remember sitting on his mammy's knee while she gently sang him to sleep? Or was he thinking about his first kiss? His first love? His wife? Maybe a lost love, or lips that he always wished he could have caressed with his own but never did?

Or was he thinking about his daughter, whom he loved more than life itself? Was he looking at her standing before him right now and realising that he would never see her grow up to become a woman? He'd never watch with pained paternal reservations as she fell in love herself. He would never see her married, and the grandchildren that she would bear were just a flimsy figment of his imagination. Tom nudged Walsh again, sparking another coughing fit.

'On you go, darling. Daddy and his friend are just playing a game.'

The girl still hesitated, watching Tom while glancing occasionally towards her father, who said, 'Go.' She turned and ran back out of the room as Walsh whispered 'Sarah,' and Tom realised he didn't have long before the girl returned with her mother. He walked over to another chair and snatched up the cushion.

'Please don't do this,' sobbed Walsh. 'I've got a wife and children . . . My daughter . . . I love my family.'

'You have to pay for your past,' Tom said with a sigh.

'I don't understand.'

'You have to answer for Dan Foley.'

There were a few seconds of puzzlement on Walsh's face before he remembered. His trembling shoulders seemed to sag and the colour began to vanish from his face like he was accepting his fate. He shrugged and shook his head. He knew now that there was no point in any further pleading.

'I was only doing my job,' he mumbled.

'And I'm only doing mine,' said Tom, stepping forward and pushing Walsh to the ground with his boot. He placed one knee firmly on Walsh's back and placed the cushion on the back of his head.

He stared at the body which was beginning to tremble increasingly violently. This was the man who had caught

Dan Foley and brought him back to Ireland to be hanged. Tom had heard the story – the legend – countless times in smoke-filled rooms, and it felt strange to him that he should now be standing over the man who was responsible for the death of a fellow Republican. Foley had been caught in Glasgow planning to smuggle guns home for the Irish Republican Brotherhood and the Big Fella wanted revenge for that.

It might have happened back in eighteen ninety-two, but the Brotherhood, which Collins now led, had a long memory, and the past had finally caught up with Walsh. Perhaps he thought he'd evaded them for ever? After all, most people now spoke only about the IRA and its fight to free Ireland, but the Brotherhood remained, as secretive and sinister as it had always been, lurking in the background and operating at the Big Fella's behest in the shadows of the struggle.

It was Walsh's name that was on the piece of paper that had been left in Tom's hand; it was his death warrant and now it was time to carry out his order.

'Please,' Walsh sobbed. 'My family. . .' Walsh thrashed about on the ground, though he was restricted in his movements by Tom's weight on his back.

'Erin Go Bragh!' Tom said quietly as he pressed the trigger, firing the bullet through the cushion and into Walsh's skull. Suddenly the air was filled with feathers, many of them blood-splattered, while the echo of the gunshot, dulled slightly by the cushion, reverberated around the room.

Tom heard the screams when he was back at the tree, having retrieved his rifle which he was wiping clean. He pictured the woman sinking to her knees beside the body of her dead husband, not caring that she was kneeling in a pool of his rapidly congealing blood. She would shake his body, screaming his name over and over again, oblivious to the gaping hole in the back of his skull. All the while, a little girl and her brother stood silently at the doorway, witnesses to a scene they could barely understand, but which would change their lives forever. The girl, a couple of years older, instinctively held the boy's hand, a silent gesture of comfort that he'd never forget.

Tom slipped quietly away through some heavy bushes and out of sight and earshot of the house.

Choppy Waters

He stood at the doorway, hands in his pockets, and waited. The kitchen conversation drifted on aimlessly and oblivious to his lurking presence, though neither man sitting at the table said anything of note. They continued talking behind clouds that fluctuated in density, depending on how heavily both of them were smoking. A shaft of sunlight struggled to push its way through the smoke-filled room leaving a ghostly blue streak in its wake.

Eventually, Tom grew impatient and cleared his throat. The two men looked round in unison, and the heavier of the two nearly fell off his stool while his companion choked on the mouthful of tea he'd just swallowed, some of the brown liquid dribbling out of his mouth and down through his beard, which was already a strange collage of black, grey and ginger hairs.

'Sorry, Father,' said the heavy man, standing up unsteadily. 'We didn't realise. . .'

Tom nodded and walked towards them as the bearded man scrambled to his feet as well. It took all his will-power not to start laughing, but since they obviously thought he was a priest – and why wouldn't they – he didn't want to spoil the illusion.

The suit had been laid out neatly on the bed and Tom had stared at it for a few minutes, not really sure what to think. He knew Seamus would laugh if he could see him now – he was probably in on the joke anyway and the thought of it was keeping him warm at this very moment while he trudged across some remote Donegal field.

He knew Danny would have laughed. He wished his cousin was here with him now to share the joke or to be the butt of his momentary and misplaced anger. His fingers moved instinctively towards the medals round his neck though he stopped himself from actually touching them. He'd been doing that a lot recently, either for luck or when he remembered Danny. When he thought of his mammy, lying in her bed and counting down the days under the compassionate vigil of her sister, it was his father's medal he held.

She had kept it all these years, hidden in the box that held all the tangible memories of her time in Glasgow. He wished he'd been able to speak to her about it. He wanted to know what had happened to her there, but more than that, he wanted to know about his father. What did he look like? The sound of his voice? His personality? Tom wanted to ask his mammy if she saw Mick Costello when she looked at her son and, if so, was that memory one of pain or pleasure?

He'd tried bringing it up before but she'd always evaded his nervous enquiries. Now it was too late to get any answers. She could be dead already for all he knew. She didn't have long – he knew that without being a doctor – and the guilt at leaving her still weighed heavily on his shoulders.

He didn't have a choice. That's what he told himself whenever the temptation to head back to Donegal started to prey on his mind. When he'd volunteered, there had been no get-out clauses. It was all or nothing and now was not the time for faint hearts. Michael Collins had chosen him to do this job because he was the best and he knew that, if anyone could carry it off, then Tom could. He wouldn't let the Big Fella down, Tom resolved.

He shook his head again as he looked at the clothes. Someone was definitely having a laugh at his expense. He didn't mind the black suit or the matching shirt. It was the white dog collar he was expected to fasten round his neck that he objected to. He knew it was just a disguise, and one that made sense but still, Tom Costello as a priest? What would his mammy say?

Once he'd changed his clothes, Tom looked himself up and down. They'd even given him a new pair of shoes which shone impressively out from the hem of his trousers. He wished there was a mirror in the room so he could give himself a better inspection. He was curious to see what he looked like. Did he make a convincing priest? He would soon find out, he thought, as he left the room and made his way through to the kitchen.

They had arrived after he did, taking over from a comrade

who had brought him to the house. He'd heard them clattering noisily at the sink as he changed clothes. They remained standing now, both of them throwing nervous glances in the other's direction, but neither seemed willing to break the awkward silence that now hovered in the room.

'Shouldn't we get going?' Tom asked, and both men shrugged. 'What time's the boat?'

'I don't know, Father,' the heavy man said. 'We were just told to wait here until someone came to get you.'

He looked round at the bearded man, who nodded vigorously in agreement.

'Well, a cup of tea would help pass the time,' Tom said, sitting down. The bearded man shuffled over to the sink and began filling up a pot with cold water while his companion took a seat at the table alongside Tom. He produced a small tin from his inside jacket pocket and prised open the lid, holding it out to Tom, who took a cigarette. The man did the same before striking a light and holding the match close to Tom's face until puffs of smoke began escaping from his mouth.

As they sat in smoky silence the bearded man began humming a tune which Tom instantly recognised. It was *The Ballad of Dan Foley*. Tom smiled at the irony of hearing it now, though in the same instant an image of Walsh's dead body flashed before his eyes. Thankfully, it vanished just as quickly.

He'd learned the song on his mammy's knee. She had a beautiful voice that would sing him to sleep every night with a whole host of songs. 'Dan Foley' was one of his favourites though he now found it strange to think she might actually have known Foley, or been in Glasgow at the same time.

Tom began singing. ''Twas in Glasgow town for to take on the crown, Dan Foley he did go. . . But the traitors they sang, and brave Dan did hang, and all Ireland she did mourn. . .'

He was suddenly aware that the humming accompaniment had stopped and two pairs of curious eyes were staring at him.

'A fine song,' he said with a nervous laugh. 'We learned

that in seminary. Old Monsignor Donnachy, God rest his soul. That was his favourite . . . He buried Dan, you know.'

'He did not, Father, did he?'

Tom nodded and both men blessed themselves. He knew they'd be desperate to tell anyone who'd listen about the tenuous link to a republican hero that they'd stumbled upon. They weren't to know that Tom was lying, and he had no doubt that what little he had said would later be embellished with the encouragement of a few pints. He thought of saying more, just for his own amusement, but he decided against it. He didn't want to run the risk of tripping himself up.

A mug of tea was placed in front of him, though just as he picked it up, there was a knock on the door, one solid thud that seemed to reverberate around the room. The bearded man shuffled over to the door and opened it. Michael Collins walked in, followed by two other men. Tom recognised one of them, the smaller of the pair, as Joe Dolan, one of the Big Fella's most trusted lieutenants, but the other man was a stranger to him. He closed the door and stood in front of it, arms folded, no doubt so that his fingers could caress the pistol Tom was sure would be in his jacket pocket.

'Father Costello, how are you doing?' Michael Collins said, holding out his hand which Tom grasped.

'I'm grand, Mr Collins. Just grand.'

'Call me Mick,' he said, patting Tom on the back. 'And I hope these two have been looking after you?'

'They've been fine,' Tom said, raising his mug of tea.

'Well, I don't know if you'll have time to finish that, Father. You've got a boat to catch.'

Tom put the mug down on the table as Collins handed him a heavy black coat.

'For the journey over. It'll keep you warm,' he said as Tom slipped the coat on. 'A perfect fit,' Collins said with a laugh. 'And tell me, how's the view from Mayo Castle?'

'Just as you'd expect,' said Tom. 'All quiet.'

Collins nodded and held out his hand again, giving Tom's hand a quick squeeze before releasing it.

'I just wanted to wish you good luck on your journey and I hope everything goes well when you're there.'

'I'm sure it will,' Tom said.

'Denis will take you to the dock,' Collins said, nodding towards the man at the door whose face remained impassive even under the sudden scrutiny from everyone else in the room. 'I'm going to stay here and have a cup of tea with these two fine gentlemen.'

The bearded man immediately hurried over to the sink again and Collins grinned.

'I'll be seeing you then, Mick,' Tom said as he walked to the door, which had now been opened.

'I'm sure you will, Father,' Collins said. 'Look after yourself now,' he said as he dropped on to the chair Tom had been sitting on.

'God be with you, my son,' Tom said with a grin before the door closed behind him and he was following Denis out to the car which was parked in front of the building.

Once he was safely aboard the boat, Tom glanced back towards the dock but Denis had already melted into the heavy crowd which was milling about. He had been a man of few words on the short journey from the house, though he did provide Tom with the details of who would meet him in Liverpool and how he would then get to Glasgow.

The quickest route would have been to sail from Belfast to Glasgow but that was also the most dangerous. Belfast wasn't a friendly place at the best of times, but with the war against the Brits now on, it had become even less hospitable, and Tom knew that the dog collar might well prove to be a hindrance rather than a help. There was also the risk of him getting caught – people were hunting for him – so it was best to avoid a city where republicans were not welcomed with opened arms but with loaded ones.

He wanted to find a quiet corner of the boat where he could sit and smoke and sleep and think about what he was going to do while trying to forget what he'd already done.

By now he was used to the nods and bows, the raising of caps or gentle curtsies which seemed to greet him wherever he went. At first he was puzzled, taken aback by the sudden deference towards him until he realised why. Then it had amused him, but that too soon passed. Now he accepted it with a casual nod or smile, which always seemed to satisfy whoever had offered the greeting.

The boat was busy, mainly filled with travellers escaping to England in search of work. Some, he could tell, were simply going where they hoped the money was, but there were others who pined for a better life rather than a few pennies in their pocket. They clung to bags and cases like life-belts as if they were survivors of a sunken vessel and were barely able to keep themselves afloat in restless waters. He could tell that they were holding all their worldly possessions, their entire lives crammed into tiny pieces of luggage.

As he ventured further along the deck, he was brushed aside by a couple who stormed passed him. A man as tall as himself was leading a wispy, black-haired girl and showing scant regard for anything in his path.

Tom watched as the man gripped the girl's arm, her face flinching as he kept dragging her towards the far corner of the deck. At first she reluctantly moved with him though after a few steps she began to resist, making it more difficult for the man to continue. He stopped, spun round, and with his free hand, punched the girl in the face. Her legs buckled but he wouldn't let her fall, instead using her temporary immobility to drag her more quickly towards the shadows. Tom walked briskly after them.

'Excuse me,' he said loudly when he'd nearly caught up with the couple. The man stopped and both of them looked round. The girl was blinking furiously and blood poured out of her nose. 'Is everything okay?'

'Everything's fine, Father,' the man muttered.

'Your friend here doesn't look so fine.'

The man glanced at the girl and then back at Tom.

'I said, everything's fine, Father.'

'This might help,' Tom said, stepping forward and holding out a white handkerchief towards the girl. Her nervous fingers began to reach out for it before the man knocked her hand away.

'Maybe you didn't hear me, Father?' he said.

'I heard you fine,' Tom said, still holding out the handkerchief.

'Well, you'll hear my advice to turn and walk away then?'

Tom didn't move.

'I don't want any trouble,' the man said, pulling a knife out of his jacket pocket and pointing it at Tom. 'So mind your own business, priest.' He spat out the last word and a few stray drops of spittle landed on Tom's coat.

Tom held his hands up, the white handkerchief dangling in his fingers like a flimsy flag of surrender. 'I get the message,' he said, taking a step back as the man nodded and slipped the knife into his jacket. In that same instant, Tom sprang forward, one hand gripping the man's throat while the other snatched the knife out of his pocket. He pressed the tip of the blade against the man's flesh, and every increase in pressure that he applied produced more terror in the man's eyes.

'Did no-one tell you that you should never ever pull a knife on a priest?'

The man shook his head slightly, still terrified of being cut by his own weapon.

'What do you think they teach us at seminary?'

Tom pushed him back, flicking his wrist at the same time so that the knife pierced the skin of the man's throat. A tiny trickle of blood appeared, though it looked no more than a shaving cut. The man clutched his flesh in a panic but relaxed slightly when he realised he wasn't going to die. He still stared nervously at Tom, though his eyes followed the knife as it disappeared inside Tom's coat pocket.

Tom held out the handkerchief again and the girl took it, holding it to her nose to stem the blood which immediately darkened the white material. She wore a startled look like she'd stumbled into a strange dream.

'Sit down over there and don't move,' he said to the

man, gesturing towards the corner where he'd been heading. 'You can sit with me,' he said to the girl, who shuffled over and cowered behind him. The man sat down and leant against the side of the boat. He took his hands away from his throat and examined them. There was barely any trace of blood.

'If I see you stand up before we arrive in Liverpool, you'll be getting your knife back, if you know what I mean,' Tom said.

The man frowned but said nothing. He pulled his knees up to his chest and wrapped his arms round them. Tom and the girl sat down at the other side of the deck where he could still see the man.

'What's your name?' he asked.

'Kathleen.'

Tom smiled. 'That's a beautiful name,' he said.

Kathleen blushed and held out the handkerchief.

'You can keep it,' he said.

'Thanks.'

Tom fished out his cigarette tin, opening it and holding it out to Kathleen. Her fingers hovered over the tin, nervously debating whether to take a cigarette but worrying that, if she touched the thin white sticks sleeping in the tin, the lid would instantly snap shut. Her eyes darted anxiously between cigarettes and the man slumped sullenly in the corner. After a few seconds, Tom took one out of the tin, lit it and handed it to her.

'It's okay,' he said and she took it with a grateful smile, instantly placing it between her lips and drawing heavily on it, releasing the smoke into the air with a long and satisfied sigh. Tom watched her. She was staring ahead as if in a trance and he wondered what she was thinking. A stray strand of black hair dangled across her cheek. She pushed it away absent-mindedly but it quickly fell back out of place. Tom lit his own cigarette, the grating of match on box dragging Kathleen out of her secret daydreams. She smiled weakly at Tom.

'He's not always like that, you know.'

'Who?'

'Matty.'

'Who's Matty?'

'Him,' she said, nodding towards the man still sitting at the opposite end of the deck. 'My husband.'

'He's your husband?' Tom asked, shaking his head with a sigh.

It was going to be a long journey over, he realised, glancing at Kathleen. Her snow white skin looked as smooth as marble. He wanted to touch it but the gesture would most likely shock her. It would certainly scandalise any other witnesses, though he was also curious to discover what it felt like before her husband intervened again because Tom knew that, at some point, husband and wife would be reunited on dry land and he wouldn't be there to protect her from blade or fist then.

He couldn't concern himself with that, however. He had a job to do in Glasgow and nothing, or no-one, was going to get in the way of that. He took one last, lingering look at the marble of Kathleen's face, suspecting it would soon enough be ruined for ever, and the thought made him feel sad.

Obeying Orders

Harrison sat down on the single wooden chair holding a lonely vigil in the corridor. The soldier who'd accompanied him from the reception disappeared into the room beside the chair, closing the door quietly behind him. He noticed the brass numbers on the wooden door – '27' – though it gave no clue as to who or what was inside. In truth, he didn't know either and couldn't even begin to guess. The telegram had been short and to the point.

'REPORT TO MINISTRY OF DEFENCE, LONDON. STOP. TUESDAY, JANUARY 26TH, 1919. STOP. 09.30 HOURS. STOP.'

There had been no name to ask for, though when he produced the telegram at the reception, the soldier knew immediately where to take him. He'd been asked to sign the visitors' book and he scrawled his signature beside his name which had already been written on the page in capital letters. He was obviously expected.

He stared down at his shoes, almost convinced that he could see his face in their shiny toe-caps. He'd been up since five – a force of habit learned in the trenches that had never left him – and he'd spent the best part of an hour polishing his shoes, enjoying the rigorous monotony of the task. He'd always prided himself on his appearance. Even in the bleakest of conditions during the war, he'd always made an effort and did what he could to make himself presentable. His boots were always the cleanest, no matter the weather. Days of rain could have filled the trenches with muddy water, but there was still a shine to his footwear.

'You can always judge a man's character by his shoes,' his mother would say, throwing a disdainful glance towards his father, who simply folded out his newspaper and hid behind the headlines. He knew his father's shoes, bruised and battered and bearing holes that got bigger with every step taken, were lying by the front door; he never asked his mother what they said about his father, but as he got older he realised she wasn't being complimentary about her husband.

He knew whoever was in Room 27 would be impressed by his footwear, along with the rest of his uniform. There had been no indication as to what he was expected to wear. He didn't know who he was going to see or what the purpose of the meeting was, but he thought it best to wear his parade uniform which, washed and starched, looked impressively formal.

A door slammed at the far end of the corridor and he flinched, closing his eyes tight and clutching the sides of the chair as if he were about to fall off. It was only for a few seconds but he was glad no-one had seen him. He glanced down towards the source of the noise but the corridor remained empty. Whoever slammed the door had disappeared. As he released his grip on the chair, he realised this had been happening more often. Every noise brought a reaction, sometimes mild, sometimes more extreme. There was no way to predict what he would do. He felt a single bead of sweat run down his spine and he pressed his back against the chair in the hope his shirt would mop it up. He remembered the explosions that seemed to go on forever.

BANG!

BANG!!

BANG!!!

BANG!!!!

Each one would get louder until he was sure the next shell was going to land on top of him. He'd been showered with earth more times than he cared to remember. His uniform had worn the blood of colleagues who'd been blown apart beside him. The trousers that he still kept in a suitcase under his bed bore the imprint of Arthur, who had lain lifeless in his lap while a gaping hole in his best friend's side spewed the contents of his body into the trench at Harrison's feet. He'd pushed the intestines away with his boots, throwing up over his friend's head in the same instant but not concerned that he had, realising Arthur was well beyond caring. He'd had to scrub his boots for hours that night.

He feared it was only a matter of time before he was the one bleeding over another soldier. Sometimes he had wished it would happen sooner rather than later, the prolonged agony of living with the awful anticipation at times almost unbearable. Then, like a miracle, he'd escaped the trenches. He believed it was a miracle. Certainly, he thanked God every day for it, and he continued to do so even now.

The door of Room 27 opened and the soldier re-appeared. Closing the door behind him, he didn't look at Harrison but instead marched back down the corridor towards the reception. He watched the soldier getting smaller and smaller until he disappeared round a corner.

His mouth was dry, while his throat was beginning to sting. He wanted a cold glass of water and a cigarette. He glanced up and down the corridor, briefly tempted to get a cigarette from the packet in his jacket pocket, if only for a few quick draws, but he knew it would be a foolish move. He was liable to light up just as the door opened again and then he'd be in trouble. He had plenty of self-discipline to resist any such urges. He would be out soon enough anyway, when his cigarette smoke would be able to mingle freely with the oppressive smog which always seemed to hang in the London air.

He heard footsteps approaching and looked back down the corridor. It was the same soldier as before. As he got nearer, Harrison could see that he was carrying a brown folder under his arm. The soldier opened the door of Room 27, standing aside in a gesture of invitation. Harrison stood up immediately and stepped past the soldier and into the room.

The door closed behind him and the soldier brushed past him, walking briskly to the large oak desk which sat impassively in front of the window, but which dominated the whole room with its silent presence. Dropping the folder on the desk, the soldier saluted before turning and walking back past Harrison, staring intently at something behind him and refusing to make eye contact. When the door closed again, he was left alone in the room except for the figure who stood looking out the window, arms clasped behind his back.

He knew it was someone important. He could tell by the uniform, which looked brand new and without a single crease, and from the gold braiding that adorned the shoulders, though he couldn't tell what rank the officer was. He'd have to wait until the other man turned round. Harrison wondered what he was staring at. All he could imagine was visible from the window was the sight of countless people filling up the London streets far below as they hurried to and fro, like a billion worker ants, all contributing to the smooth running of the ant hill that was the capital, even if their role was only a minor one.

The London sky was all that he could see – grey and oppressive as always. He'd stopped just inside the room and stood to attention. He would wait for an invitation before he ventured further forward and there was no way he'd ever be presumptuous enough to plant himself on the seat in front of the desk.

He didn't want to cough or make a sound – he felt like he was barely breathing – though he knew the officer was aware of his presence. It was like he was back at school again, summoned to the headmaster's study to be punished for crimes that were often vague or never even specified. 'You know why you're here, boy, so don't act all innocent with me,' the headmaster would say, pre-empting any pleas for clemency, before producing a cane from inside the black cloak he always wore and waiting for the out-stretched hand so that he could dispatch summary justice.

He knew he hadn't done anything wrong now – at least, he didn't think he had – so there wasn't any need to worry, though a wave of unease still washed over him.

The officer sighed wearily and turned round. It was a general, but not just any general. Standing in front of him was General Sir John Maxwell, the former Military Governor of Ireland. Harrison's body automatically jolted into a rigid salute which he held until Maxwell returned it in a more languid style.

'Please sit,' Maxwell ordered, nodding to the chair as he sat down on the leather chair behind the desk. It looked like a throne, Harrison thought, imagining Maxwell producing a crown from his desk and placing it on his own head. Instead, the general brought out a pair of gold-rimmed spectacles which he put on, though he still held them in place with his hand as he scanned the loose-leafed pages contained within the folder the soldier had left on the desk. Occasionally, he would nod or grunt – Harrison took that as a sign of approval – and once he looked up, staring at him from behind his glasses for a few seconds before resuming his examination of the folder.

It was the only time that Harrison felt self-conscious and he automatically reached towards his face. He had a purple birth-mark that he wore like a patch across his left eye. It had long since ceased to bother him, except when he became aware of the curious stares of strangers who couldn't help looking even though they probably guessed it made him feel uncomfortable. Maxwell hadn't taken such sensitivities into consideration.

He stared at the bowed head before him. Thin strands of black hair stretched across the skull, barely covering it, but what little hair was still there had been smoothed down with corn oil, which made his head glisten. Harrison wondered how the general managed to avoid his hat sliding off. It sat on the edge of the desk, the insignia adorning it another sign of rank and importance. Harrison's own, inferior cap remained sandwiched under his arm.

He knew who Maxwell was. Most soldiers did. Certainly

anyone who had been posted to Ireland in the past three years would have heard the name of General Sir John Maxwell mentioned. His reputation, particularly in that country, went before him, and Harrison certainly knew all about him.

Maxwell had been the man in charge of Ireland before Harrison had found himself sent there. In truth, other soldiers complained about the posting but he couldn't believe his luck. It felt like someone had lifted him from the trenches of France where he'd resigned himself to dying, and deposited him as far away from the guns that were out to kill him as it was possible to get. It was still dangerous, and he'd seen soldiers falling at his feet even in Ireland, but it was heaven compared to the hell he'd been mired in before.

That had been nearly two years ago, in November nineteen-seventeen. By then, Maxwell had made his reputation, cracking down hard on the rebels who'd dared to rise up against the might of Britain the year before. Many of the leaders were tried and executed, with Maxwell the judge, jury and executioner, though he wasn't actually part of any firing squad. Still, that didn't mean he didn't have blood on his hands. That's what the Irish thought and it was the trouble his 'justice' created which Harrison and others had been sent to combat. By then, Maxwell had left, though what he'd done hadn't been forgotten, and shouts of 'Maxwell's Murderers!' were often fired at him and his comrades as they marched through the streets of Dublin, though the verbal marksmen or women always managed to remain hidden.

Maxwell put down the spectacles and sat back, stroking

his thin moustache thoughtfully. His eyes narrowed as if he was peering into a misty night and Harrison wasn't sure whether to look away or stare back. He coughed nervously, which seemed to rouse the general.

'Very impressive,' he said, tapping the sheets of paper on the desk which he'd been reading. He picked one up.

'Corporal James Stanley Harrison. Born in Coventry, September fourth, eighteen ninety-two. Enlisted with the Royal Warwickshire Regiment in nineteen fourteen. Saw action at Passchendale and the Somme . . . Distinguished Conduct Medal for bravery at the second Battle of Ypres.'

Maxwell nodded. 'Very impressive indeed, Corporal Harrison.'

'Thank you, sir.'

'I read the account of what happened at Ypres and I am honoured to be in the presence of a man who possesses such courage and character.'

'Sir.'

'You've been in Ireland these past two years?'

'Yes, sir.'

'That country . . . ' Maxwell sighed, shaking his head, 'that country is like a boil on the arse of the Empire which should be lanced for good. Let me tell you, Harrison, that I have fought the Boers. I have fought the Huns. I have even fought those blasted Turks, but nothing gives me greater satisfaction than the spilt blood of an Irishman.'

'Yes, sir.'

'What have you made of Ireland?' Maxwell asked.

Ireland was wet. That's what Harrison thought. It always seemed to be raining and his uniform never managed to dry out before he was back on patrol again, but he never complained because it was better than having to stand knee-deep in brown, rat-infested water while bullets flew past him and shells exploded overhead. He shuddered at the memory.

Ireland was hostile. He could feel it in the air. The animosity was almost tangible in every town or village they walked through. Doors remained locked, shutters closed over windows and streets became deserted. They still had to remain alert, however, knowing that also lurking in those houses were loaded guns and home-made bombs.

He preferred to be out in the country, sitting in a ditch, the local shrubbery offering natural camouflage, waiting for a target to appear. He would happily sit there for hours without getting bored. When the time came, he was able to train his sights, pull the trigger and hit the target with lethal precision. Whether he was killing a German or an Irishman made no difference to him. He was only obeying orders.

'They want me dead, Harrison.'

'Sir?'

'The Irish. They've been waiting for a chance of revenge and now they want to take it.'

Harrison nodded.

'I am going to Glasgow next week and we have intelligence that the IRA are going to try and kill me . . . Now, I can see what you're thinking – that I shouldn't go, but that would just be surrendering to them and I will not do that. I have a job to do for King and country and these damn rebels won't stop me.'

Maxwell stood up and walked back over to the window, peering out again at the London streets below.

'I have important work in Glasgow that must be done,'

he said without looking round. 'There is unrest in the city. Communist unrest, and we must be ready to crush it.'

'Yes, sir.'

'So where do you come in, Harrison? I know that's what you want to ask me.'

Maxwell strode to the desk and lifted out a photograph from under the pile of paper.

'This is the man who is going to try and kill me.'

Harrison took the photograph and studied it. The face that stared up at him was stern, almost sullen. He was probably about the same age as Harrison, who also recognised the cold eyes which had seen and done so many terrible things that any trace of humanity had long since disappeared. It was like looking in a mirror. Harrison stared hard at the image, committing the face to memory; the untidy dark hair, slightly crooked nose and those eyes. He would have no problem remembering them.

'His name is Tom Costello. He's the IRA's top marksman and they've sent him to Glasgow. Your job is to kill him before he kills me.'

Harrison looked up, startled. He knew he was a good shot himself, one of the best in the British Army. That's what they'd said when they'd given him his medal for bravery and that's what they'd repeated when they brought him to Ireland to 'shoot a few paddies' as his commanding officer had put it. This was different, however. It wasn't simply a case of hiding somewhere and training his rifle sights on the target before pressing the trigger. He would have to hunt for this man, which wouldn't be easy in itself, and in the middle of a busy city too, where his target was bound to have more friends than he did.

'How do you know he's going to kill you?'

'He's not, Harrison, because you're going to kill him first. And I can't tell you how we know but trust me, our intelligence is as reliable as it is possible to be. So what do you say? Will you go to Glasgow and kill Tom Costello?'

'Yes, sir.'

Harrison stood up, still holding the photograph in his hand. He had no choice but to agree to the mission. It was an order and he would have to obey it. He glanced down at the face in the picture, which sullenly stared back up at him. Next time he saw Tom Costello he intended to kill him.

Dear Green Place

The handshake was firm but fleeting and the hand disappeared back into a trouser pocket as quickly as it had appeared to greet him. Tom stared at the man facing him who studied him through thin wiry glasses that looked as though they'd snap in a gust of wind. Tom guessed he was probably only nineteen or twenty and he found it hard to believe that someone so young was running the whole organisation in Glasgow. Still, he'd only been twenty-three at the time of the Rising, and he'd long since fired his first shot in anger at the Brits before then.

'Connor Daly,' the younger man said.

'Tom Costello.'

Connor turned and walked over to the kitchen table, noisily dragging a seat out and dropping on to it. He nodded towards the seat facing him and Tom slowly trudged across the room, biting the inside of his cheek until he could taste blood. He didn't look at the other men in the room – two of whom stood in front of the fireplace while the one who'd met him at Central Station, Declan, leant lazily against the front door, his arms folded. Connor's actions had been for their benefit. He was showing his men who was the boss, and it wasn't the big shot that Michael Collins had sent from Ireland.

Tom sat down and took out his cigarette tin, lighting one in silence without offering them round to anyone else. The smoke seemed to hang in the air like an awkward silence and he noticed Connor blinking furiously behind his glasses as it stung his eyes. He obviously didn't smoke, Tom thought as he blew another nicotine cloud in the direction of the younger man.

Tom knew that Connor was trying to impress his men, so he decided to let it go, just this once. He only hoped Connor was clever enough to realise that. Tom sensed that the men looked up to their leader, and he knew it would be an unfair fight if he tried to start one now.

It was the way Declan had spoken about Connor on the way to the house. They'd taken their seats on the top deck of the tram, waiting a further five minutes until the last of the passengers had shuffled on before it finally moved off, pulled slowly but steadily by a horse that was taking its instructions from the driver at the front of the cabin downstairs. Declan's Belfast brogue offered a running commentary on their journey.

'And this is Argyle Street,' he said as the tram glided round the corner. Tom stared down at the street, noticing people hurrying along the street in both directions, an occasional body darting out ahead of their tram or appearing from the front of it, usually followed by a volley of abuse from the driver. Argyle Street teemed with trams and carts and people – lots of people – though it appeared to Tom that everyone had something to hide. The men concealed faces behind caps that were pulled tightly over foreheads, while women walked briskly, heads wrapped in shawls bowed low as if in deference to some hidden superior. He spotted a car too; he heard it first, actually, its horn sounding loudly ahead of them, its angry riposte a novel sound amidst the hustle and bustle of the city street, and a few heads looked round towards the source of the strange noise.

'We'll be turning just at the corner there,' Declan said, pointing ahead and blessing himself. 'The Tolbooth,' he muttered by way of explanation when he saw Tom's puzzled frown. 'They used to hang Catholics there . . . John Ogilvie for one, God rest his soul.'

Tom didn't know the name and wondered if he'd been an Irish rebel from years gone by. He decided against asking Declan, however.

'This is the Albert Bridge,' the Belfast man announced as a swift breeze from the river buffeted the tram as it edged its way up a slight incline and then on to the bridge proper. Tom could see all the way up the busy waterway, crammed with ships and boats and barges, and he wondered how they all managed to avoid each other.

'And that one's called the Victoria,' Declan said, pointing to a bridge about one hundred yards down river. 'Victoria and Albert,' he said with a shrug and Tom nodded to let him know he understood.

As the tram pulled into Crown Street – 'Nearly our stop now,' Declan announced – he began talking about Connor. He called him 'The Boss', which made Tom smile. As far as Tom was concerned, there was only one boss and he was the man who'd given him this mission. Everyone else was equal, doing their bit for Ireland regardless of rank or task. It was clear, however, that the Glasgow Brigade had a respectful deference for their commander that left Tom feeling slightly uneasy.

Connor ran his hand through his hair, short and brown, and tugged nervously on his fringe before sitting back and folding his arms. Tom continued smoking, enjoying the sensation as each gulp of nicotine galloped down his throat towards his lungs and enjoying the discomfort of the man facing him even more.

'How was the boat over?' Connor eventually asked.

'Fine,' Tom shrugged.

'So how long are you here for?'

'As long as it takes.'

Tom knew Connor wouldn't have been told what the mission was. The less people knew about it, the better. That was Collins' policy and it wouldn't have changed for this. Connor's instructions would have been to provide whatever assistance was required, without question. All Tom wanted for now was somewhere to stay and weapons. He still didn't feel comfortable dressed as a priest, but knew it provided cover while he found his bearings in the city, and Maxwell wasn't due for another few days – so a change of clothing would have to wait.

There was a bowl of warm water on the small table in the bedroom and he'd gratefully splashed it on his face a few times, feeling instantly refreshed. He hesitated at the door, patting his jacket pocket for reassurance that the new orders Michael Collins had left him were still there. He'd already memorised them and he knew he should have destroyed the written evidence but he would wait for an opportunity to burn it later, when he was alone.

Returning to the kitchen, he noticed that all four chairs round the table were occupied, with the three men listening dutifully as Connor conducted an impromptu history lesson, condensing into a matter of minutes hundreds of years of British oppression of Ireland. Tom wasn't sure how much the men were absorbing. He would have simply told them the Brits were bad and they had to fight them until they were driven out of Ireland. At least they would have understood that. Instead, they stared at Connor, trying to appear interested but looking baffled instead. He stood at the sink, vaguely listening until they became aware of his presence.

His arrival seemed to call an end to Connor's lecture, much to the relief of his audience who, individually, nodded gratefully if discreetly in his direction. The Big Fella didn't usually like intellectuals – 'They always think with their head and not their hearts,' he'd say – and Connor also seemed very young. He must be really good to have won the approval of Michael Collins, thought Tom. So long as he was as good as his word and provided help when required, then Tom would approve too.

'I've organised a wee party for tonight, just to welcome you to the city,' said Connor.

'Parties are not really my thing,' Tom said, sitting down at the table.

'It's just a few of the boys. We don't want you thinking we're not a hospitable lot over here.'

'It's not that. It's just. . .'

He didn't want to appear ungrateful or inhospitable himself, and he finished speaking with a sigh, shrugging his shoulders as if resigned to the party. He'd stay for a while, no more than an hour or two, before he'd make his excuses and leave, blaming the journey over for his weariness. Connor smiled, though it gave him the look of a constipated man rather than a happy one.

'A few drinks and a few songs and you'll feel right at home,' he said.

Nodding towards each man at the table, Connor introduced them. Tom already knew Declan. The Belfast man tipped his cap and continued playing with a match between his teeth. Beside him was Sean. He was tall and handsome, as a folk song might describe him, with blue eyes as clear as the ocean. He held out his hand which Tom shook. It was warm and sweaty. The last of the three men was Kilkenny. Tom didn't need to ask where he was from. He grinned when Connor introduced him, proudly displaying a mouth that had more gaps than teeth to boast of. He wiped his hand on his sleeve before offering it to Tom who took it with a smile.

Declan was nominated to make tea for everyone, which he agreed to without any protest. Tom held out his cigarette tin, knowing the gesture would be seen as a friendly one, and everyone except Connor took one. He liked these moments of smoky silence, when comrades could sit contentedly enjoying the company of others who knew what they were thinking without having any great desire to talk about it. They were few and far between, particularly now the war was at its fiercest, so every opportunity was seized on hungrily, and even though he didn't know any of these men, he accepted them as comrades, all with a common bond and fighting for the same cause. The unifying power of nicotine, he thought, holding his own cigarette up and admiring its slender body which was slowly disappearing.

'When do you want to get started?'

'Tomorrow,' said Tom. He could tell that Connor was desperate to find out what was going on and he smiled inwardly.

'Just let me know what you want and what you're planning to do.'

'I've a few things I need,' said Tom, 'but I can't tell you what's happening.'

'This is my city,' Connor said, 'and I like to know what's going on.'

Tom nodded.

'So I'd much rather you run things past me. Just to keep everyone happy.'

Tom sensed that everyone else was watching him. He knew these men didn't really care what he was up to. They'd do as they were told without asking any questions . . . though they answered to Connor.

'It's best you don't know,' Tom said. 'It's safer that way. But I'm grateful for the offer of help.'

'Maybe you don't understand,' said Connor, 'but I'm in charge here, and in this city I want to know exactly what's going on.'

'And maybe you don't understand,' Tom said. 'The

Chief has asked me to do something here and he's told me not to tell a soul. So I can't tell you, even if I wanted to.'

He had a strong urge to hit Connor and watch as blood poured out of his nose and on to the table, but it was an urge he knew he had to suppress. He could feel Connor's eyes on him but he didn't look at the younger man, preferring to focus on the front door. Declan, who'd taken up position there after making the tea, looked as if he was sleeping, though he quickly jumped to attention when there was a knock from outside, three in quick succession. The noise seemed to shatter the tension that had suddenly built up in the room and Tom relaxed as well. Quickly composing himself, Declan slowly opened the door and a red-haired girl barged past him.

'Sorry I'm late,' she said, stopping in the middle of the room.

'Tom, this is Bernie. . . Bernie – Tom,' said Connor, standing up and making the introductions. Tom nodded and so did the girl. She folded her arms nervously, aware that she was the centre of attention. Tom couldn't take his eyes off her.

'Someone give him a pencil and some paper and he can draw a picture,' she said and Tom could feel his face burning, but even though he looked away, he found his eyes couldn't resist returning to her. She sat down on the chair Sean had vacated, giving Tom a quick smile which sent his heart into a spin. That was the last thing he needed in this city.

Welcoming Committee

The low rumble woke Tom. It sounded like thunder. In truth, he thought at first it was his stomach, still churning from all the drink he'd consumed the night before. It had been a while since he'd taken so much. He couldn't actually remember the last time a drop had passed his lips. He was wary of it, having seen what it did to too many men. Quiet souls became boisterous, the excitable became emotional and the loud wanted to fight. It dulled the senses, even the morning after the night before, and he wanted to be alert at all times should he be called upon, or just so that he was prepared if the Brits suddenly turned up.

What had been different about last night? He knew the answer, even if he was reluctant to admit it even to himself. It was her. Bernie. She had handed him the first drink and he couldn't say no. It wasn't her hair, flaming and angry like an early-morning sun. Nor was it her eyes, green and lively and captivating though they were. It wasn't even her skin, fresh and freckled and tempting; he had to fight the urge to reach out and caress her cheeks. It was when their hands touched for the briefest of moments. He felt a surge through his body like he'd been hit by lightning. It left him feeling disorientated, as if he'd already drunk ten pints instead of having just accepted the first of the night.

'I thought you might be thirsty,' she'd said as he took the glass with an awkward smile.

Her voice was pure Galway. He'd recognised it straight away when she'd first spoken. He didn't tell her even though he knew, or hoped that she'd be impressed. Most people were. It was a gift he had. 'Just like your daddy,' his mother once said before clamming up when he tried to press her for more information. Just one sentence and he'd pinpoint the county. He was always right too; the ones who weren't impressed thought it was some sort of trickery but they were always careful not to call him a fraud. That could have unpleasant consequences.

He hadn't spoken much more to her. She seemed to float around the periphery of every conversation he had or every song that he joined in with, though she always seemed to appear just at the very moment he'd drained the last drop of liquid from his glass, taking it from him and returning moments later with it miraculously filled again. Each time he couldn't say no.

He'd watched her – he knew she was aware of his eyes following her but he didn't care, certainly not after a few drinks. There was even a hint of jealously when he saw her with Connor. He'd kissed her brazenly on the lips in front of everyone, though it seemed to Tom that he was the only one who found it strange. No-one else seemed to notice. He knew it was Connor's way of letting everyone – Tom – know who Bernie was with. He got the message, loud and clear.

Tom opened his eyes. He knew it wasn't his stomach and it wasn't thunder either. He was out of bed and on his feet just as the creak of the handbrake echoed along the street below; the harsh crunch of boots landing on the cobbled surface told him that this wasn't a social call. His own feet were already in his boots as the sound of loud voices came bounding up the stairs announcing the presence of soldiers. He raced through the house, shouting warnings as he went and kicking any sleeping bodies that lay in his path.

'Where's your gun?' he snapped at one of the men who stirred on the floor and groaned. 'Hurry up!'

The man pointed towards the table in the corner of the room where a pistol lay beside a small lamp. Snatching it up, Tom quickly checked the carriage – it was fully loaded – and made his way towards the front door. The voices and the footsteps were getting louder as the soldiers made their way up the stairs, stopping at each floor to break open doors and conduct searches of the houses, no doubt paying scant regard to any protestations of innocence which were most likely answered with a rifle butt in the face.

He ran back to the other room and peered out from behind the net curtain which had offered a flimsy shade from the intrusive and persistent dawn sunlight. There were two army trucks parked across the middle of the road. Five soldiers stood behind them, using the vehicles as a protective barrier, their rifles trained indiscriminately on the building. Crouching down, he pulled at the window, needing to put the pistol down at his feet in order to prise it open.

He could hear noises filling up the house. Everyone was awake now and slowly beginning to realise what was happening. He smiled as he heard the groaning man shout, 'Where's my feckin' gun?' though he hoped that the rest of them had located their weapons. They'd need them soon enough.

He picked up the pistol and then lay down on the floorboards, slowly pointing the gun through the gap in the window.

'What are you doing?'

He looked round. It was Bernie.

'Get down on the floor.'

'Why?'

'Just trust me. Lie down now against that mattress and don't move.'

She hesitated but slowly dropped on to the floor as he glared at her. As soon as her head rested against the wooden surface, he looked back and took aim.

One of the soldiers seemed to be pointing his rifle towards Tom's window, though he didn't notice the pistol appearing. He had a brown moustache and he ran his tongue along it, perhaps wanting to rescue any remnants of the breakfast he would have enjoyed before setting out on his mission. Tom shot him through the head.

The roar of the gun blasted up and down the street, ricocheting off tenement walls and ensuring no-one was going to remain sleeping in Rose Street now, though it also managed to silence the commotion from inside the building as if the soldiers had been frozen in mid-search while their brains tried to process the noise and what it meant. Tom fired off a second shot, hitting another of the soldiers behind the truck whose cheeks were smeared with his comrade's blood. The bullet blew a hole in the man's face which would leave him unrecognisable and unidentifiable to grieving relatives, but it was the last free shot Tom would enjoy. He slid back across the floor as a barrage of bullets blasted the building.

The soldiers didn't know where the fatal shots had come from, so their furious response hit every window they could see. Glass shattered, opening up gaps to the outside world through which the terrified screams from each house escaped. There were screams too, coming from the next room and Tom crawled across the floor until he reached the doorway.

'Someone stand at the top of the stairs and shoot anything that moves,' he said.

No-one moved.

'You!' he shouted at a small chubby unshaven man who sat cowering on a chair and shaking his head. 'Get out there or I'll shoot you myself.'

He pointed the pistol at the man who slowly dropped off the chair and shuffled over to the front door which he opened nervously, pointing his gun into the corridor before venturing out himself.

'Remember, shoot anything that moves,' shouted Tom. 'Anything!'

He crawled back to the window as bullets continued to smash into the thin walls, spraying plaster all over the room so that it felt like it was snowing indoors. He moved close to Bernie who'd pressed herself tight against the side of the mattress and he, in turn, pressed himself against her. The sudden contact startled her and she craned her neck to see who it was.

'What do you think you're doing?'

'Keeping you alive, that's what.'

'Aye, and getting a cheap thrill while you're at it.'

Her red hair was tickling his nose and he resisted the urge to breathe in deeply and commit her odour to memory. He knew she'd not be happy if she heard him. Still, the warmth of her body was seeping into his and for the most fleeting of moments he allowed himself to forget that he was under attack and imagined instead that he was lying beside a beautiful woman, ready to see her naked for the first time. She thrust her elbow into his stomach and he took the hint to move back a few inches so that they were no longer touching. Strawberry shortbread, he thought, as he took a deep breath, smiling for an instant before a bullet whistled by his head and smashed into the wall.

He could hear gunfire out on the stairs now, and hoped that the chubby man would be able to keep the soldiers at bay for a few minutes at least. Once he'd fired his first shot, however, they would realise where the initial bullets had come from and then they'd really be in trouble.

There was another scream from the next room and Tom knew that a bullet had hit flesh rather than plaster. It was a cry laced with terror and torment that came from a fear which gripped the mind. The man thought he was going to die.

He crawled back towards the window, ignoring Bernie's urgent warning that he stay back. He knew it was dangerous – it was stupid – but he wanted to kill at least one more soldier before it was all over. He didn't think that would be too long because he couldn't see any way of escaping. There was a fierce battle going on at the stairs. The chubby man had evidently taken his advice but he didn't imagine he or any of his comrades would be able to delay the soldiers for much longer.

There were still three soldiers outside training their guns on the building. Tom could see them through the curtain, narrowing his eyes and peering at them as if he was staring through a wall of fog. He pushed the pistol out through the window and took aim, though he knew, even before he pressed the trigger, that the shot wouldn't be as accurate as his two previous attempts because he had to keep his head hidden in case it became an easy target.

He was already shuffling back across the floor when the bullets came crashing in through the window in response to his own shot, and he realised he hadn't managed to hit anyone.

'There's no way out,' he shouted to Bernie when he reached her again. He thought of his mission and what Michael Collins would say when he heard about his failure. He thought of his mammy, lying in bed coughing up blood while her sister mumbled her way through successive decades of the Rosary, probably knowing in her heart that it wasn't going to make any difference. There would be no miracle in Donegal and it didn't look likely that there would be one in Glasgow either.

'Where's Connor?' he asked.

'I don't know. He was gone when I woke up.'

'Just as well. At least they'll not get him, even if the rest of us have no chance.'

He wondered briefly if he should have told Connor about the mission. Then, he might have been able to complete it and Tom could have consoled himself with the knowledge that his own death hadn't been in vain. Bernie gestured with a nod for him to follow her as she began crawling across the floor.

He saw the dead body as he reached the doorway. It was Sean. He shook his head, reaching for his medals and then stopping himself, realising there was no point. Sean's blood was spreading out across the floor and they had to lift themselves up to avoid crawling through it.

'Where are we going?' he asked as they reached the door.

'You need to get out of here,' Bernie said. 'Connor said we had to look after you because you had something important to do, so that's what I'm doing.'

She stretched an arm up and grabbed the handle, turning it quickly and opening the door. Immediately the chubby man tumbled into the room. His body had been slumped against the wooden barrier. He had three gaping holes in his chest, all of which were weeping blood, while a trail of crimson liquid ran out the side of his mouth and down his chin. His place at the top of the stairs had been taken by Kilkenny who didn't glance round as Bernie and Tom, crouching low, crept towards the door across the landing.

Bernie tried the handle but it was locked. She knocked on the door, loud and furious, but the noise was drowned out by the gunfire. She glanced round at Tom, who didn't need to be told what to do. He stood up and ran straight at the door, hitting it with his left shoulder and falling into the room as the lock burst and the door flew open. Bernie rushed in after him, closing the door behind her.

'Is anyone there?' she shouted anxiously but there was no reply. The flat was empty. As Tom got to his feet, she grabbed his arm and dragged him towards the set-in bed which was concealed behind a makeshift barrier of towels hanging drunkenly down from the ceiling

'Quick, sit here,' she said pulling him on to the bed.

'What?' Tom said, watching open-mouthed as she pulled off her jumper and began unbuttoning her blouse.

'Hurry up!' she shouted.

'But –'

'They'll be here soon.'

'But I hardly know you.'

'You're kidding, aren't you?' she said, as she stopped undressing.

'I'm meant to be a priest,' he said, pointing at the dog collar.

'You'll soon be a dead priest if you don't do something.'

Shaking her head, Bernie slid into the bed under the cover, pulling it up to her chin. He stood staring at her as the crashing boots approaching angrily up the stairs grew louder and closer, broken only by an occasional burst of gunfire.

'Are you just going to stand there?' she snapped.

'You want me to get in there with you?' he asked.

'No, you daft eejit! You're a priest. Of course I don't want you to get into bed with me.'

'Well, what then?'

'Hear my confession, pretend you're giving me communion. Give me the last rites. Just do something that looks bloody holy!'

Shaking his head he moved over to the side of the bed, kneeling down and joining his hands together as if in prayer. Suddenly the front door crashed open and Tom blessed himself, swiftly followed by Bernie as three soldiers appeared in the room.

'Don't move!' one of them shouted.

'Don't shoot,' Tom said quickly, raising his hands in the air. Three rifles were pointed at them and Tom could feel his heart racing. One wrong move, or even one sweaty trigger finger and they were dead.

'You! Get over here!' An English accent barked the order at Tom. He couldn't guess where the soldier was from. His gift didn't extend beyond his own island. He began to get up slowly off his knees.

'Keep your hands up,' the soldier shouted, pointing the rifle at Tom who nodded, hoping it would offer reassurance. He could tell the boy was nervous – he looked no more than eighteen or nineteen, not much older than Danny had been, he thought.

Two of the rifles were now trained on him while the other one continued to keep Bernie in its sights. She remained hidden under the cover and Tom was glad of that. He knew what the Brits were capable of and three soldiers full of aggression after a gun battle and with adrenalin still flowing through their bodies could react in unpredictable ways to the sight of a female.

'Against the wall. Now!'

The soldier prodded Tom with his rifle, directing him towards the wall facing the bed. His arms still raised, he placed his hands on the plaster and pressed his forehead gently against the cold surface. One of them began firing questions like a verbal machine-gun and Tom felt pressured into answering them in the same rapid manner.

'Name?'

'Father Daniel Foley.'

'Where are you from?'

'Ireland.'

'Where abouts?'

'Belfast.'

'Is this your house?'

'No.

'Where do you live?'

'I'm a priest at St Mary's.'

'When were you last in Ireland?'

'Three years ago.'

'Who's that?'

'Who?'

'The girl?'

Tom hesitated, and was prodded with the rifle again.

'Who is she?' the soldier shouted.

Tom looked round and nodded at the soldier to come closer. He did so warily, while his colleague seemed to stiffen and point his rifle at Tom with a greater sense of purpose.

'She's one of my parishioners,' Tom said in a low voice when the soldier was close enough to hear. 'I was just hearing her confession . . . she doesn't have long left, I'm afraid,' he said, shaking his head and slowly making the sign of the cross.

The soldier stared back towards Bernie and then at Tom again, who leant in closer.

'Consumption,' he whispered.

The soldier almost recoiled from Tom, then immediately realised that it was taking him a step nearer Bernie.

'But she looks . . . so healthy.'

'I know. It's very sad,' Tom said.

The soldier glanced over his shoulder, shaking his head.

'You just never know,' he muttered.

'There's no hope for her,' said Tom. 'That's why she wanted me to hear her confession.'

The soldier nodded.

'I'm taking her to the doctor after this, though I don't know why. Her lungs are ruined, but if you breathe in the air near her. . .'

The soldier nodded again, a nervous look washing across his face.

'Right lads, he's fine. Let's go,' he said quickly to his colleagues. The other two soldiers watched the first one walk out of the house, still shaking his head before they followed him. Tom waited until the door closed before he turned round. He leant back against the wall and sighed.

'What did you say?' Bernie asked as she dropped the cover and stepped out of bed.

'Nothing. It doesn't matter.'

She frowned at him but didn't press for an answer and he watched her as she tidied up the bed cover. His eyes drank in every inch of her body – the curve of her hips, the long slender neck, and her breasts, small but still defined beneath her blouse.

'Stare any harder and I'll have to charge you,' she said as she folded her arms. He shrugged apologetically as she shook her head with a smile.

'Where will we go?' he asked.

'We've got another house in the Gorbals that'll be fine for now.'

'The Gorbals?'

'It's not far from here. We'll be among friends.'

They waited another ten minutes, sitting silently side by side on the bed and listening to the boots that stamped up and down the stairs. Tom presumed they'd be carrying out the bodies of Bernie's comrades, men he'd barely known long enough to remember their names.

Eventually, they crept to the front door and opened it slowly. Tom peered out. The landing was empty. He stepped out, noticing the pools of blood on the floor which he stepped over. Bernie was right behind him and did the same thing. They reached the first floor where a rifle and a tense voice stopped them in their tracks.

'It's alright, Terry,' a voice shouted from behind the soldier. 'They're fine. You can let them go.'

It was one of the three soldiers who'd burst into the flat and he nodded grimly, staring at Bernie as Tom took her arm and guided her down the stairs.

'What did you tell him?' she whispered.

'You don't want to know,' he said.

They reached the ground floor and sunshine at the far end seemed to lure them like light at the end of a tunnel. They both had to resist the urge to sprint towards its tempting glare. As they reached the mouth of the close, a man bounded up the stairs. His eyes were fixed on his feet and he didn't see what was in front of him. His shoulder barged into Tom's

'Sorry, padre' he muttered, stopping and looking up. He stared at Tom for a few moments and Tom noticed the red blotch on the man's face that crept out from the corner of his left eye. Bernie tugged at his sleeve and he began walking away.

'No problem,' he said to the man who continued staring at him. Out on the street Tom picked up their pace, eager now to get away as quickly as possible. They were nearly at the corner when he heard the shout.

'You two! Stop!'

They kept walking.

'Now! Stop or I'll shoot!'

Tom grabbed Bernie's hand and began running. He wasn't sure why but he sensed that he had to get away now. It was the man in the close who had shouted. He knew that even without looking round. It was the way he'd kept staring, as if he recognised him even though Tom knew their paths had never crossed before. His instinct had served him well in the past and he was sure it would again.

He heard the crack, like a branch snapping underfoot, as he reached the corner and he knew what it was. He pulled Bernie forward and pushed her towards the corner. She stumbled with a cry of protest but still managed to steer herself round into the next street. He was almost beside her when he felt a blow on his shoulder like he'd been punched and he fell down, dragging Bernie with him.

'Get up, Tom,' she cried as she pulled herself to her knees.

His shoulder felt like it had been scorched with a hot poker and when he leant on his right arm, a pain shot through his body as if he'd been skewered with a bayonet and he couldn't suppress a scream which filled the air. Bernie was over him now, gripping his left arm and offering herself as a human crutch so that he could get to his feet. He staggered back but she still managed to hold him up.

'Can you move?'

'I don't know,' he mumbled.

'We need to get out of here.'

They began heading down the street, though Tom was moving slowly, the pain in his shoulder getting worse with every step. He could hear footsteps racing towards them, getting louder and louder, and he knew they weren't going to get away. He was holding them back. He stopped running and Bernie looked round.

'You go on,' he said. 'I'll keep them at bay for as long as I can.'

'No,' she said. 'I'm not leaving you.'

He took the pistol out of his jacket pocket and cocked it.

'Bernie! Over here. Quick.'

They both looked round to see Connor waving frantically from the front of a cart which had halted across the road.

'Hurry up!' he shouted and they both staggered into the street. He helped Bernie push Tom on to the back before she clambered up beside him and then the cart sped off with Tom's legs dangling out the side. A bullet screamed towards them and slammed into the side of the cart but Connor kept driving, the horse's hooves clattering noisily on the cobbled streets as it galloped away. Tom lay back with a groan as a sudden pain gripped his whole body. He closed his eyes, relaxing slightly as Bernie placed her palm soothingly on his forehead. It felt as cool as the underside of a pillow and he even managed a weak smile before passing out.

Battle Scars

She took the towel and tugged at it roughly until she heard the tiniest of rips, which was her cue to pull it with as much force as she could muster, slicing through the material until she held two separate pieces of cloth in either hand. One of them she draped across the back of the chair while she dipped the other in the basin, immersing it in the murky liquid. It had been clear when she'd filled it, but once the anti-septic liquid had been added, the hot water became cloudy though, hopefully, more useful. She pushed the towel around the basin until she was sure it had absorbed enough water, before taking it out and squeezing it to get rid of the excess. Then she turned to face her patient.

He was lying face down on the bed, naked from the waist up, and the wound was clearly visible on his right shoulder. It was red and raw as if the skin had just been expertly sliced off with a knife. He had been very lucky. That's what the doctor told him. The bullet had gone through the flesh without shattering any bones. It was a clean wound, and one that would mend easier. The doctor had left instructions with Bernie on how to clean it though she could probably have figured that out herself. He'd also left some tablets to dull the pain, though they still lay unused on the table underneath the window.

Tom had floated in and out of consciousness in the cart

all the way to the house, barely registering the fact that he was hastily carried up two flights of stairs. When Connor and the doctor had removed his jacket and shirt, however, he'd woken with a jolt and sat up as if someone had fired an electric shock through his body and he let out a deep and mournful cry that made the two men temporarily stop what they were doing. Just as suddenly he lay back on the bed and remained silent as they continued their delicate but necessary task, even though Bernie could tell from the way the skin tightened on his face that he was in pain.

Neither Connor nor the doctor had noticed the piece of paper which floated silently to the floor as they'd moved him on to his front and Bernie quickly bent down, unnoticed, and snatched it up, slipping it into her pocket. Now she patted it again for reassurance even though she knew it was still there.

She hesitated at the side of the bed. A solitary drop of water fell from the wet towel and landed on Tom's back. He tensed slightly and Bernie studied the taut and defined muscles before they seemed to vanish into his body again. Unravelling the towel she leant over and gently placed it on his back, covering the wound. He flinched and groaned, a low, lingering murmur like the sound of a tram approaching from a nearby street, though it didn't get any louder but instead melted away into silence. She left the towel on his back. The doctor had told her to keep it on for about five minutes so that the warm, cleansing liquid could seep slowly into the wound and begin the healing process.

Bernie walked over to the window and looked out into the street below. Two boys were kicking a lump of coal along the road, both of them chasing the rapidly-disintegrating black rock, but still jostling with each other to get the next kick, laughing and shouting as they did so. They were no more than five or six-years-old. One of the boys, who had blond hair with black streaks through it as if it had been washed with the coal, took a final kick and the makeshift football rolled towards the kerb, breaking up into a thousand tiny fragments the instant it hit the concrete. The boy stopped, stunned at the abrupt end to the game while his companion, whose hair was as bright as Bernie's, so much so that she might have been mistaken for his mother if she'd gone out into the street at that particular moment, stood beside him.

The blond boy continued staring at the coal, picking his nose casually as he did so. Occasionally his attention would be diverted when he examined what was on the tip of his finger, and Bernie turned away with a rueful smile when the finger disappeared into the boy's hungry mouth.

It was time to take the towel off Tom's wound and she did so with the same delicacy with which she'd laid it on his back. This time there were no groans. She put the wet towel back in the basin and then took the dry one from the chair and gently dabbed at his wound until she thought she'd wiped away any traces of dampness. The doctor told her it was a process she'd have to repeat three times over the next two hours and she glanced at the clock hanging on the wall just to give her an idea of when she'd have to apply the wet towel again.

She studied Tom's wound, staring intently at it and frowning. Her eyes remained focused on his back for a minute or so until her face brightened as it suddenly dawned on her what she was looking at. Tom's wound looked to her like a map of Ireland.

Bernie gently closed the bedroom door and walked slowly across to the table where Connor sat nursing a mug of tea.

'There's still some left,' he said, scraping his chair on the wooden floor as he stood up, Bernie dropping on to the other chair in the same instant. She smiled gratefully and watched as he busied himself at the sink, retrieving a mug and giving it a cursory rinse under the tap before filling it with tea that she saw was thick and brown as it dribbled into the mug.

Tom was sleeping. He'd been a restless patient throughout the time she was cleaning his wound, though after she'd dried it a final time his body seemed to relax, as if he realised that all her work was done. She still had to wrap his shoulder – the doctor had left some bandages – but for now she preferred to let him sleep. She'd draped the cover across his back, covering him up to his neck, and watched him for a few minutes as he slipped into a more contented sleep before leaving the room.

Connor placed the mug in front of her and sat down, instantly draining the last remnants of tea from his own mug. She took a sip – it was lukewarm – but she wasn't complaining.

'We lost four men today,' Connor said, shaking his head. 'Four good men.' He looked towards the bedroom door with a frown.

'It wasn't his fault,' Bernie said quickly, surprised at her defensiveness.

'They were there for him.'

'Who were?'

'Who do you think? The soldiers. He turns up and just hours later so do the Brits.'

'It could have been a coincidence.'

'Some coincidence,' Connor said, raising his eyebrows,

'which makes it worrying for us. I don't know if any-where's safe now.'

'But we've still got to help him.'

Connor shrugged, examining the empty mug as if he was hoping to discover the answer in the cluster of tea leaves lying on the bottom.

'Four good men,' he muttered, looking at Bernie as she sipped her own tea.

'The thing is, I don't understand how they could have known he was there,' Bernie said.

'What do you mean?'

'How did they know he was in the house? He'd only arrived the day before.'

'Maybe they were following him?'

Bernie frowned.

'What?' Connor asked.

'If they were doing that, they could have got him at any time.'

'Maybe they wanted to see who he was meeting here. . . I don't know, Bernie. I don't know how they operate.'

'What if someone told them?'

'What do you mean?'

'You know what I mean.'

'No way,' he said, shaking his head vehemently. 'There are no traitors in our ranks. Who knew he was here? Half a dozen people at most and four of them are dead now. No way, Bernie.'

'I'm only saying,' she said, putting her mug down and placing a hand on his arm, squeezing it gently. 'I'm probably wrong anyway.'

'You are wrong.'

'Okay, I'm wrong then. I was just thinking aloud. I'm worried too, you know. I don't want soldiers turning up and shooting at us any more than you do . . . and they were my friends too.'

'I know,' Connor said, leaning over the table and kissing her forehead. 'I'm sorry. It's just . . . well, I should have been there.'

'What could you have done?'

'I could have helped. I don't know, maybe taken a few of them out.'

'And then what? You'd be dead too.' She grasped his hand. 'You can't feel guilty,' she said. 'It wasn't your fault and it's better for the movement that you're still alive. . . better for me, too.'

He leaned over again and kissed her, this time on the lips.

'Thank you,' he whispered, sitting back and glancing over her shoulder before moving in close again for a strong, lingering kiss that took her by surprise.

A man coughed behind her and she broke off from Connor, looking round to see Tom standing in the doorway. She stood up. She didn't know why. It was an automatic reaction though Connor remained in his chair, leaning back and folding his arms.

'Sorry for disturbing you,' Tom said.

'It's fine,' said Bernie.

He walked slowly towards her, his eyes remaining fixed on hers and she couldn't look away. It was a strange feeling, like she'd just raced up three flights of stairs and was feeling breathless and slightly dizzy as her heart raced at a frantic pace. If Connor was to place his hand on her breast at this precise moment, he would feel the pounding. Or what if it was Tom. . . The thought dragged her back to reality and she moved towards him in a more business-like manner.

'You shouldn't be on your feet,' she said, gripping his elbow and guiding him towards the table even though he tried to shrug off her attentions. He sat down with a heavy sigh and nodded towards Connor, who took off his glasses and rubbed his eyes before replacing them. He smiled at Tom, though it seemed to take great effort to conjure up even the mildest of grins.

'How are you feeling?' he asked.

'I'll be fine,' said Tom. 'The shoulder seems okay.'

'That's good.'

'And I owe my thanks to you,' said Tom, holding out his hand across the table. Connor stared at it for a moment before taking it.

'Only doing my job.'

'Well, you saved my life and I won't forget it.'

Bernie watched the exchange, standing in the middle of the room and holding the bandage she was going to have to use on Tom's wound. The doctor had explained to her how she should wrap it, and she was sure she'd remember what he'd said. She did know the bandage was to be tightly wrapped round the wound and that's what she intended to do, even though she knew it would hurt him. He might be sitting there proclaiming a miraculous recovery but she knew better. It was all for show, she realised, because Connor was there.

She continued studying the two men who were now sitting in silence. Connor had folded his arms again and sat wearing a smug expression like he knew something that no-one else did, and it was a secret he wasn't intending to share. Bernie recognised the look. It was one that always irritated her and she was sure Tom would find it equally objectionable. Connor hadn't always been like this. The job had changed him. Almost from the moment the news came from Ireland of his promotion to head of the Glasgow Brigade, he had assumed an air of arrogant superiority which Bernie was convinced would cost him one day.

When they had first met, it had been his gentleness and modesty which she had found attractive. In a room full of people he was quiet and shy, almost invisible at times, yet when it was just the two of them, he seemed to come alive, suddenly infused with a confidence and enthusiasm for the cause that was almost hypnotic. Still, she'd been as surprised as the rest of their group, including Connor, at his elevation, but more disappointed than any of them at what it had done to him.

Where once they had lain in bed, their bodies wrapped together, comfortable and warm and secure, and talked of the future – their future – now he only spoke about Ireland and what was going to happen when the war ended, as it surely would one day. She wondered about that too, and cared as much as any of them, but she also wanted to know what would happen to her – to them – in the future. Were they going to get married, as they'd talked about many times, and would they live in Galway or Dublin where Connor had grown up? It never seemed to be the right time any more to ask all these questions and so they remained floating in her head.

She looked again at Tom's torso, the wound fresh and raw and tender, and she wondered why her heart skipped another beat. That question remained unanswered too.

'Right, let's get you strapped up,' she said, stepping forward as Tom looked round. He started to get up but she stopped him and he sat back down with a shrug.

'This'll hurt,' she said, standing at his shoulder and taking a closer look at the wound to decide exactly how to start wrapping the bandage. She was also aware that Connor was watching her intently. She could feel her face beginning to turn the same shade as her hair, and she quickly began her task. She placed the bandage on top of his wound and began wrapping an end round the outside of his shoulder and down under his arm, and then back up over the shoulder again. As she repeated the process, she remembered to make it as tight as possible, but apart from an almost imperceptible flinch which Bernie wouldn't have noticed if she didn't have her fingertips on his other shoulder, Tom never displayed any other outward sign of pain. He obviously didn't want to show any trace of weakness, real or imagined, while Connor was there, and she smiled slightly at the stupidity of it all. Typical man, she thought.

'That's you done,' she said after tucking the edge of the bandage underneath the layers wrapped round his shoulder to keep it secure. Her hand rested on his left shoulder and he seemed reluctant at first to move. Connor's intense glare caused her to remove her hand, though it was also with a reluctance which momentarily puzzled her. She liked the texture of his flesh and the way his body seemed to relax at her touch as if she had the power to soothe his pain. She had to suppress a smile at the thought, realising how silly it sounded, even in her head, and she was glad Connor couldn't read her thoughts.

He'd taken off his glasses again and was rubbing his

eyes. He did that a lot now. The pressure of running the operation in the city, and the many hours it demanded of his time, was leaving him tired. If they could even get away for a couple of days it might make a difference. She'd be able to re-discover the real Connor, even if it was only for a brief spell, before he resumed his role in the city. She knew he'd never agree to any sort of break, however, and she wouldn't put him in the position of having to choose by asking him.

'Thanks,' Tom said, standing up and flexing his shoulders slightly. 'It'll soon be as good as new.'

He walked over to the bedroom and it took Bernie all her powers of self-restraint not to allow her eyes to follow him, knowing that her actions were currently under intense scrutiny. Tom re-appeared after a minute and this time she did look round. He had his shirt on and was buttoning it up.

'The Brits know I'm here,' he said.

'I know,' said Connor. 'You must have been followed from Ireland.'

Tom shook his head. 'I was fine until I got to Glasgow. It must have been someone here. Can you vouch for everyone in your group?'

'There are no traitors here,' Connor said, standing up and knocking over the chair which clattered noisily on the floor.

'Do you know that for sure?'

'Why don't you wait and I'll ask them all? Oh, that's right, four of them are dead now because of you.'

Tom stood, hands thrust in pockets and stared impassively at Connor who was now pacing up and down the room.

'How dare you accuse any of my men of being a traitor,' he said. 'They're good men, good Irishmen, and they were killed trying to protect you. I don't care who you are and whether Michael Collins sent you here, don't you dare come to my city and accuse my men of betraying the cause.'

'Your city?' said Tom.

'And don't you forget it.'

Tom smiled but Bernie could see, in his eyes, an ice-cold veil descending over them.

'You are an Irishman fighting for the freedom of our country,' he said. 'This is not your city and these are not your men. They are volunteers of the Irish Republican Army and don't you ever forget that.'

Connor stopped and glared at Tom. He was breathing heavily, his eyes narrowed and Bernie knew his teeth were clenched angrily together. He moved forward.

'Take another step and it will be your last,' said Tom. His hands remained in his pockets and his expression appeared neither angry nor annoyed but Bernie shivered inwardly at the voice which seemed to breathe a chilling menace across the room. She studied him closely, no longer bothered if Connor spotted her but knowing that his own attention would also be focused on Tom. He hadn't given her that impression before when she'd been treating him, but he was wounded and needed her help. She had felt relaxed, safe even, but now there was something different and suddenly she felt scared. Connor obviously did too because he stopped.

'We shouldn't be fighting each other,' Tom said. 'We're both on the same side.'

His voice now lacked the menace of a few moments ago and Bernie wondered how he was able to turn it on and off so quickly and effortlessly. He sat down and brought out a small green tin, taking out a cigarette and lighting it up. Bernie knew Connor would be annoyed – he hated smoking because it irritated his eyes – but she also knew that he wouldn't say anything.

Tom held the tin out to her and she hesitated, glancing at Connor who remained frozen to the spot, his face drained of all colour. He watched as her hand slowly reached forward, her fingers removing a white stick which she placed in her mouth, leaning forward and into the lit match which Tom held out for her. As the nicotine rolled down her throat, she felt the bitter taste of betrayal in her mouth and guiltily looked away from Connor who stared, unblinking, through the fog of their intermingled smoke.

No News is Good News

He knew she was in the room. He could see her standing in front of him, nervously hopping from left foot to right. He had heard her voice so he knew she was real and not some figment of his imagination. When he breathed in, he could smell strawberry shortbread, which should have made him smile but didn't. He couldn't look up because he knew if he stared into those green eyes which reminded him of an autumn Donegal field, his own would fill up with tears, and if that happened he was worried he wouldn't be able to stop. He could feel the tears hovering impatiently like a wall of water pressing on a flimsy sandbank. All they were looking for was one sign of weakness or a tiny gap in the defences through which they could flood out. He bit his tongue and breathed in deeply before exhaling, hoping that might compose him. He didn't know what to say. He didn't know if he could say anything anyway, and a quiver of emotion remained trapped in his throat whenever he tried to speak.

'I've got some bad news from Ireland,' Bernie had said, standing in front of him and biting nervously on her lip. 'It's your mum. . .'

As soon as she said that last word he knew what had happened and he'd held his hand up to stop her speaking. He didn't want to hear the news, and especially not from her. He was scared that, if he did, he would never be able to hear her voice in future without remembering what she'd told him.

He was clutching his father's medal. He wasn't sure whether the thoughts running through his head were prayers. Certainly, he would have struggled to recall the actual words, but at least in his mind he knew that what he was saying was genuine and heartfelt, and maybe even spiritual.

If there was a God he hoped that he'd look kindly on his mother, even though she had long ago abandoned any belief in his existence. Too many things had happened to her – all of them bad – for her to accept there was an all-loving God who was looking out for her. He hoped God would understand that. It was only natural to abandon a faith that seemed to have abandoned her, Tom thought.

What if they were to meet again now? His mother and Mick Costello. The thought was ludicrous. He knew that and he would never repeat it to anyone else, but it had still crept into his head like an unwelcome guest at a wake. Did that mean he believed in Heaven? And if he believed in Heaven, then did he also believe in God? There were too many thoughts jostling for space in his mind and he wished he could clear them all away and start afresh.

What he really wished for was that he hadn't been in the house when Bernie turned up with the news. Then he could remain oblivious to the reality of what had happened, at least for a while longer.

He was sure his mother would be in Heaven anyway, because she hadn't been a bad person. 'Good things happen to good people,' she would tell him when she was encouraging him to be well-behaved or warning him after he'd done something wrong. He believed her too. He had to. He wasn't so sure about his father, however. He didn't know him or very much about the kind of person he was, so there was just as much chance he was looking up at Tom as there was he was gazing down on him.

'Are you okay?'

Bernie's voice was no more than a whisper but Tom still heard it. He looked up, fighting the urge to blink because he knew tears would inevitably spill out. He nodded.

'Is there anything I can do?' she asked.

He shrugged. His mother was dead and there was nothing anyone could do to change that fact. Could he ask her to hold him? He knew that if he did, it would only embarrass them both. He wanted someone – Bernie – to wrap their arms round his shoulders and tell him everything would be fine. He'd close his eyes and imagine that was true while trying to forget that it wasn't. It was better she didn't touch him anyway. He knew he'd cry, burying his head in her comforting embrace and weeping like a baby. He could feel his face begin to burn even at the thought of it.

What he really wanted was five more minutes with his mother. He could have delayed leaving Donegal, though he doubted it would have lessened the guilt he was feeling now. He shouldn't have left at all, yet if he hadn't – if he'd turned down Michael Collins – then he'd have felt guilty about that too.

He remembered the last time he'd seen her. She was sleeping. Either that or the effort of keeping her eyelids open was too much for her. He hoped it was the latter because it meant she might have heard the words which floated across the cottage from the front door.

'I love you, mammy,' he'd said. His voice was soft and gentle, almost embarrassed at saying the words out loud. He was glad his Aunt Annie was at the other side of the door, standing outside in the light rain which had been falling unobtrusively all morning, giving him the privacy he needed. The words felt strange as they formed in his mouth. He hadn't told anyone he'd loved them since he was seven years old. It was his mother who'd heard the words then and he hoped she'd heard them now.

A mug appeared in front of his face. It was full almost to the brim with tea. He took the mug, feeling the heat against his palm, while steam wafted up from the surface of the dark brown liquid. There was a tiny pain in his shoulder as he held it like someone had nipped his skin, but he was relieved that was all he felt. The injury was clearing up well. He took a sip of the tea and screwed up his face.

'How much sugar did you put in this?' he asked.

'A lot,' Bernie said with a wary smile. 'It'll be good for you.'

Tom looked up and smiled back at her, realising immediately that it was a mistake. He suddenly felt in turmoil, like he was stuck on a fishing boat in the middle of the Irish Sea during a storm, carelessly tossed and turned by every angry wave. He was light-headed and his stomach was churning. A couple of stray tears seized the opportunity to escape from the corner of his eye and race down his cheek, but he managed to halt any more following in their wake.

He felt guilty too, because he knew it wasn't grief that was making him feel this way. He stared down at the mug of tea again, even though his heart continued racing and he couldn't stop thinking of her touch on his skin. He was wounded and she was helping him, but there was something else he felt too, though he realised it was a feeling he couldn't act upon. For one thing, Connor wouldn't be too far away. He'd probably done the right thing in staying out of the house when Tom was told the news, but it was only a matter of time before the two men would be in the same room again, and even with the best of intentions on both parts, there was no guarantee they wouldn't confront each other again.

He needed to focus on the task he'd been given and the reason he was here, at least once he'd time to adjust to his loss. Normally that wasn't a problem but something happened every time he saw Bernie. More than that, whenever she pushed her way into his mind – she was never far from the forefront, if truth be told – he felt a longing for her that was almost painful. It excited and worried him at the same time; he was even slightly scared as these unfamiliar feelings gripped his mind and body. Not that he hadn't been with a woman before. There were some he remembered and some he forgot, but none that he really cared for. Certainly, he knew there wasn't one who made him feel the way Bernie did. He didn't know why, which only made it all the more confusing.

He wanted to kiss her and he found his hand drifting towards his lips as if, by touching them, the imagined feeling of that would flow through his fingertips and he could savour the sensation. He stopped himself. It wasn't right and he knew that. At this moment his only thoughts should be of his mother because that's all he had now. Memories. His body shook suddenly at the realisation, like a tremor had struck, and he let out a sound that wasn't quite a full-blown cry, but it was something – a glimpse of how he really felt. He quickly suppressed it.

'Are you okay?'

He heard her voice though he didn't look up at first.

'Tom?'

'I'm fine,' he said, shaking his head as if that would dispel the grief which was spreading silently through his body, destroying his defences until he wouldn't be able to resist any longer. He heard a chair scraping on the floor and glanced up. Bernie had moved it next to him and sat down. A look of empathy which she strained to control flashed across her face. He swallowed hard.

'It's okay,' he said. 'I'll be fine.'

He knew she was staring at him. He gulped the tea which had now cooled down, hoping that the mug would hide at least some of his face. His mother had been the only woman he had ever told he loved – she was the only woman he ever had – and she had also been the only woman who had seen him cry. Even that had been years ago, when he was just a boy. The tears had dried up for good as the hairs began to appear on his body. Whether his mother missed the closeness they'd once had he didn't know. She never said anything, though he guessed she realised that it was inevitable, and a mammy's boy would never have survived two minutes in the company of any group of self-respecting Irishmen.

Now he was sitting here in front of a woman he barely knew and every second was a battle to control his emotions. What would she think if he started crying now? Would she show compassion or disdain? He bit his tongue, hoping the pain would push back the tears.

'I never knew my mammy.'

He looked up.

'She died when I was a wee girl.'

'I'm sorry.'

'I was only two,' Bernie said with a shrug. 'I don't remember her – well, you wouldn't, would you? I wish I did though.'

'What happened?'

'She died when she was having my sister. She started bleeding and they couldn't stop it. By the time they'd managed to get a doctor, it was too late.

'I'm sorry.'

'So am I. It would have been nice to have a mammy . . . just to brush your hair at night, or sing you to sleep or cuddle you when you were crying. . . My granny always used to say I was my mother all over. That's nice if it's true, isn't it?'

'It is.'

Tom's voice was barely a croak. He didn't really know what to say. He stared at Bernie's burning hair, shiny and smooth as a well-brushed horse's mane. He wouldn't tell her that because he knew it would sound like an insult when he meant it to be a compliment. She was staring into space now. Maybe, in the furthest recesses of her mind there would be a tiny memory of her mother that she'd be able to resurrect, faded and frayed at the edges like an old newspaper, but still recognisable. Tom knew that was unlikely, however. He didn't remember anything from when he was two – he didn't imagine anyone would – so there would be nothing to console Bernie. He wondered whether, when she stared into the mirror, she imagined that was how her mother looked.

He was lucky. He had a suitcase full of memories that he could unpack any time he wanted. He would never forget his mother and it was a much better position than Bernie, who would never remember hers. He wanted to focus on one memory that might make him happy or at least produce the faintest trace of a smile, but all he could picture was her lying in bed – her death bed – a frail and fragile shadow of her former vibrant self.

What had happened to that beautiful woman who had always been there to offer him unconditional love? He knew she turned heads, but her own was only ever focused on him. He wanted her back now, even in his mind, just so that he could hear her voice or see her smile which always made him feel safe, but she wouldn't return to his thoughts.

All he could hear was a cough, laboured and draining, and then a throat being cleared as another mouthful of blood was dispelled. He wanted to cover his ears with his hands in the hope it might drown out the noise reverberating through his mind, but he knew it was a futile gesture. The noise was already trapped there and nothing he did would get rid of it. Another tremor of grief rippled through his body.

'Are you sure you're okay?' Bernie asked.

Tom nodded.

'I never knew my father,' he said, not really sure why he was telling her. It just seemed to make sense, like they were trading secrets. So he told her what he knew about Mick Costello, most of it picked up from overheard conversations and discreet murmurings when adults thought he wasn't listening, while some of it was the product of his own imagination. What was true was that his father had died in this city, stabbed and left bleeding to death in his mother's arms. No wonder she had always hated Glasgow. He was glad she'd never found out he was over here, though now he was, he wouldn't be able to get back to Ireland for her funeral. It might have taken place already, for all he knew.

This time he let out a proper cry, though the noise startled him as much as Bernie, and he quickly pushed it back again. He should have been there with her when she died. He knew that, regardless of what he'd been asked to do by the Big Fella, his first thought should have been with his mother, because her first thought was always for him. As she breathed her last, it should have been his face her eyes looked upon. It should have been his tears that she felt falling on her. It should have been his voice she heard one final time. 'I love you, mammy,' he would have said, and she would have smiled.

'You know it's okay to cry,' Bernie whispered and he nodded without looking at her, blinking furiously, which only made the tears pour out quicker when he wanted to keep them in. He buried his head in his hands and started crying silently, his body shaking with every sob. He felt an arm rest on his trembling shoulders, the unexpected human contact only making him worse, though he didn't want her to let go.

'Please don't tell anyone about this,' he eventually managed to mumble through the tears. He didn't hear her reply, though he guessed from the gentle squeeze she gave his shoulder, that her silence was guaranteed.

Depths of Despair

Harrison knew he had hit the Irishman. He'd seen the way the body had been lifted off the ground by the force of the bullet and he had allowed himself a moment of self-congratulation, savouring another job well done. It had been easier than he had anticipated, the target stumbling straight into his path, and once he'd aimed his rifle, locked his sight on to the body and squeezed the trigger, he knew there could only be one outcome. That's why he was flabbergasted when he reached the end of the street and discovered there was no body. He fully expected the Irishman to be sprawled across the pavement, either dead already or slowly and painfully drifting inevitably towards his last breath while the grey cobbles darkened with his blood. Instead there was nothing. That wasn't quite true. There was blood, splashes of it dotted carelessly on the pavement and across the road as well where the wounded man had evidently stumbled, like someone had spilt a pot of paint, but there was no sign of a body.

One of the other soldiers had told him about the cart, which he had shot at, though it hadn't been enough to halt it in its tracks. He should have shot the horse, thought Harrison. He knew, however, that the Irishman's escape would only offer him a change of venue for his death. He was sure of that. He had hit the target, and there weren't too many who lived to tell the tale after feeling the full force of a bullet from a Lee-Enfield rifle slamming into tender flesh.

They had searched all the hospitals in the city, and raided another couple of buildings, but of the wounded man there was nothing. Even though Harrison was sure that his prey was dead or dying, he still wanted proof. He needed to see a body, grey and pasty and lifeless. That's what he had to report back to General Maxwell. Anything less was a failure. Anything less wasn't acceptable and Harrison refused to countenance any such thoughts. He had been chosen because he was the best and he liked to believe that success would be assured. He just needed to see that lifeless body and then he could leave this city for good.

The grumbling engine which had competed for his attention with his thoughts of dead Irishmen suddenly cut off and the car came to a shuddering halt. He glanced out through the window, clocking the grim facade of Duke Street Prison while the driver got out of the car and raced round to open the passenger door. He saluted as Harrison edged his way out of the car and returned the salute after he stood up and stretched himself to his full height.

Once the car coughed and spluttered its way back into life, it slowly pulled away from the front of the building, leaving Harrison standing outside, his six-foot three-inch frame suddenly seeming insignificant under the oppressive glare of the prison, which towered over him in imposing silence.

A small door at the side of the large, imposing entrance, through which trucks entered or exited, opened slightly and a head popped out.

'Corporal Harrison?'

'Yes.'

'We're expecting you. In you come.'

It was a Glasgow accent and the owner of it pushed the door until it was fully open, stepping out and standing at the side to usher Harrison in. He was a small man with a belly like a pregnant woman. His trousers couldn't stretch over it. Instead, they cowered under its shadow like a frightened child sheltering beneath a tree during a thunderstorm. He wore a navy uniform, though it was obvious that he wouldn't be able to fasten the jacket over his wide girth. Harrison also noticed that one of the buttons was missing.

The man liked a drink, Harrison thought, the smell of whisky fumes attacking his senses, so strong he felt his eyes stinging. He had to stop himself from saying anything. He didn't know the man, so he thought it best to avoid antagonising him unnecessarily.

Within seconds of stepping over the threshold of the prison, the door slammed shut and Harrison spun round automatically. The panic gripped him quickly and unexpectedly and he could feel beads of sweat forming uncontrollably on his forehead before they started to race down his cheeks. His shirt was already clinging to his skin and he wasn't sure whether he'd be able to put one foot in front of the other. His mouth was as dry as if he was stranded in the middle of a desert and his heart raced like he'd just completed a ten-mile training run. He was glad of the darkness that had engulfed them as soon as the door closed, offering him a cloak of secrecy he hoped would remain until he calmed down.

He closed his eyes as locks were turned and bolts drawn shut on the door. He remembered the way they would cower in the trenches when the German guns launched their bombardment. The first shell would approach unannounced until it was almost on top of them, then it sounded at first like a Catherine Wheel, whistling innocently before exploding with the ferocity of a thousand fireworks, though with much deadlier results. The sky still filled up with patterns, but they weren't pretty or luminous. Instead, a hideous collage of mud and water and blood and flesh scattered over them.

'This way, Corporal Harrison.'

The voice dragged him away from the trenches and he opened his eyes, though it was a wall of black which greeted him. He followed the heavy footsteps which resounded off the cobbled surface until a gloomy light emerged in front of him and he almost stumbled into a courtyard. It was surrounded on all four sides by the various buildings which housed the prisoners, and it felt like the concrete structures were huddling together conspiratorially in order to prevent the sun from shedding any light or warmth into the prison. It seemed to Harrison they were succeeding. Not only was it dark but it was cold too.

He followed the soldier who strode confidently across the empty courtyard to an opening at the far side which he immediately walked through. The soldier walked down two flights of stairs with Harrison at his shoulder, aware of the temperature dropping the further down they went. He shivered but said nothing.

At the bottom of the stairs the soldier stopped momentarily and glanced up and down the corridor before heading to the left. Lit candles which sat in small alcoves in the wall cast an eerie pallor along their path and Harrison found himself staring intently at the back of the soldier as if he was worried he was going to lose sight of him.

When they reached a plain grey door, the man in front stopped and banged on it with his fist. A small hatch opened and a pair of eyes peered out briefly before the hatch snapped shut. Harrison could hear various locks and chains clanking before the door was pushed open.

The soldier stood aside, gesturing with his arm for Harrison to step inside the cell. He nodded at the man, who didn't acknowledge him, before he entered. The door slammed shut behind him. It startled him again though the paralysing panic did not return. A single light dangled from the ceiling like an executed prisoner, casting a sombre glow across the room, and though it was too weak to illuminate the corners, Harrison could see all he needed.

The prisoner was slumped on a chair in the middle of the floor directly underneath the light. His head was bowed and the only thing that stopped him from toppling over was the heavy rope wrapped round his chest which bound him to the chair. A soldier was crouched beside him and Harrison realised, from the way he was examining the prisoner, that he was a doctor.

Another soldier stood leaning against the brick wall facing the prisoner. He was smoking and obviously enjoying the cigarette, taking long, heavy draws before exhaling with a satisfied sigh, filling the cramped space of the cell with smoke that only partially dispersed. Harrison could feel it tickling his throat and he had a sudden urge for a cigarette himself, though he quickly suppressed it.

'He'll not last much longer,' the doctor said as he stood up.

The smoking soldier, his shirt sleeves rolled up to his elbows, nodded as he finished his cigarette, flicking the end towards one of the dark corners.

'I'm nearly finished anyway,' he said, walking towards the door and opening it for the doctor who strode out the cell without another word.

'You must be Corporal Harrison,' the soldier said, closing the door.

Harrison nodded.

'I'm Buchanan . . . Sergeant Buchanan.'

Harrison immediately saluted and Buchanan laughed.

'No need for any formalities down here,' he said. 'I understand you want to ask Paddy here a few questions.'

'If he can talk.'

'Don't worry about that,' Buchanan said, picking up a steel bucket and throwing its contents – Harrison presumed it was cold water – over the prisoner. 'Wake up, Paddy!' he shouted, slapping the man a couple of times on the face as he groaned. Harrison didn't know what had already been done to the man and he didn't want to know.

The fact the man was still alive was a stroke of luck. The soldiers had laid the bodies on the pavement after the shoot-out, blankets taken from the house thrown over them as much to avoid any of the soldiers getting unnerved at the sight of a dead body as it was to pander to the sensitivities of the other residents in the street.

Not that the soldiers hadn't seen a dead body before. Most of them were veterans of the war and had witnessed more horrors than any man should see in a dozen life-times, but Harrison knew that it didn't lessen the effect of seeing a corpse. Any man who claimed it didn't bother him was lying, and any man who'd been responsible for ending that life and claimed the same was an even bigger liar.

Harrison had been striding back up towards the scene of the gun battle, convinced he'd shot the Irishman when he heard shouting outside the building. One of the dead bodies had moved. A private, who looked as though he'd seen a ghost – maybe he had – was stuttering and spluttering as he tried to explain what he'd seen. Another soldier dragged the cover off the body and knelt down, pressing his ear to the chest and then gently touching the neck.

'He's still breathing,' the soldier declared, and some of his colleagues automatically took an apprehensive step backwards.

'Get a doctor,' Harrison shouted, pushing his way past a couple of soldiers till he stood over the prisoner. 'Hurry up! I want this man alive.'

The prisoner was alive – just. Harrison knew that Buchanan would have inflicted some physical revenge for perceived grievances he held against the Irish. Harrison didn't want to contemplate what that might have involved, though the bruised and bloody face and the dark-stained shirt told their own story. Buchanan must be good, he thought, because he'd still managed to keep the man breathing. He'd have known that it would have been a bad career move to have let him die in his care before Harrison appeared. Now it was his turn to ask questions though he would do so without using any force himself. That would still be Buchanan's job.

'Can you hear me?' he said sharply at the prisoner, who tried raising his head at the sound of the voice but could barely muster any movement. Buchanan stepped over and stood behind him, gripping his hair and jerking the head back. The prisoner groaned.

'When is Costello going to do it?' Harrison asked. The prisoner frowned but said nothing.

Harrison plunged his hands in his pocket, his fingertips touching the lucky sixpence he carried everywhere with him. His mother had given it to him the day he'd enlisted – 'just in case you need it for anything,' she'd said, squeezing his hand as she wrapped it round the coin. He'd never felt the need to spend it but he did believe it had brought him luck. He also felt it meant that his mother was also there with him, looking out for him whenever he was in danger, which had been too many times to remember these past few years.

'When is Costello going to do it?' he asked again.

The prisoner shook his head. Harrison took the coin out of his pocket, holding it between his finger and thumb and lifting it up towards the ceiling where it sparkled when the light bounced off its edges. He remembered the day it saved his life, though it had cost Eric Ferguson his. One of them had to operate the machine-gun position that sat twenty yards in front of the main trench. It was a job no-one ever volunteered for; hours of monotonous inaction, punctuated by short, sharp bursts of machine-gun fire whenever any movement, real or imagined, was detected from the German side. It also meant you were a target for the enemy guns. The choice that day was between him and Ferguson.

Harrison tossed the sixpence in the air, watching its effortless twists and turns in the gloomy light of the prison cell, and he remembered doing the same thing in the trench, both he and Ferguson staring at the coin until it came to rest in his dirty palm. It was 'heads'. Ferguson would have to take up the machine-gun position. Just over an hour later, a German shell landed on top of him, blowing man and machine to smithereens. Life was that fragile. That's what Harrison had learned that day. Whether you lived or died was simply a matter of chance, as arbitrary as calling 'Heads' or 'Tails'.

'When is Costello going to do it?'

The prisoner looked up and opened his mouth as if he was going to speak and Harrison noticed that most of his teeth were missing. Instead of any sounds or words, however, the prisoner shook his head again. Harrison nodded at Buchanan who moved his left arm with an impressive swiftness while his right hand still gripped the prisoner's hair. His fist slammed into the man's back, jolting him forward, though Buchanan held on to him. A mouthful of blood spluttered out, landing on the floor and just missing Harrison's gleaming boots. He took a small step backwards as a precaution.

The prisoner was struggling to breathe, the blow to his kidneys knocking the wind out of him, and Harrison waited as the man fought to regain control of his breathing. His bullet wounds were still weeping blood. Harrison could see the dark stains on his shirt which clung to his body. They were slowly but inexorably getting bigger and he realised he didn't have much time left.

'When is Costello going to do it?' he asked for what he'd decided was the final time.

The prisoner groaned and moved his lips, though no sound appeared to come out. Harrison stepped forward and leant into the man until his ear was just inches from the man's mouth.

'What did you say?' he asked.

The man moved his lips again and this time Harrison heard the faint whisper.

'Red.'

'Red? Red what? What do you mean?'

The man whispered again. 'Red . . . men. . . '

The effort appeared to exhaust him and he slumped on the chair. No amount of encouragement, violent or otherwise, could get another sound out of him. Harrison could tell, just by looking at the man that his job here was over. He nodded at Buchanan as he stepped out the cell, knowing that the prisoner wasn't long for this world. He had minutes maybe, if he was lucky, or hours if he wasn't. Harrison had no idea what the prisoner meant. More than that, he was now back to square one in his search for the Irishman.

Casualties of War

Tom wanted to test his shoulder and to do that he'd need to use a gun. There were times when he forgot that he'd been shot though occasionally, when he'd move his body a certain way, a pain would surge through his shoulder to remind him. It wasn't so sore that he groaned out loud or even clenched his teeth. No-one would know from looking at him that anything was wrong at all, but he knew, and that was enough. He had to make sure that he was capable of using a rifle, and doing so accurately, before he undertook the mission he'd come here to complete. He'd only get one shot, if he was lucky, and it needed to be perfect. He couldn't predict the weather, or which way the wind was blowing, but he had to be sure that, physically and mentally, he was ready.

He'd mentioned it to Connor, who nodded and said he'd think of somewhere suitable where they wouldn't be disturbed or arouse any unwanted attention. It was a peace offering of sorts, giving the Dubliner his place even though Tom's preference would have been to use Connor as target practise. He also knew he couldn't do it alone. He didn't know the city or the surrounding areas, so he wouldn't even know where to start looking for a secluded area.

There was Bernie, of course. He could have asked her but he found it awkward to say anything coherent to her when they were in the same room, as if his tongue had suddenly swollen up and was too big for his mouth. She'd witnessed him at his weakest and Tom still felt vulnerable in her presence even though he sensed that she would take what she'd seen to her grave if necessary.

She knew anyway – Connor had obviously told her – and when she appeared at the house with him, Tom presumed that she would be accompanying them wherever they were going. Connor hadn't told him where that was. It was somewhere safe. That's all the information he volunteered, and Tom wasn't too bothered about finding out more. It didn't matter anyway. As long as it was quiet, that's all he was interested in.

The three of them walked down the stairs in silence, Connor leading the way and Tom at the back, his eyes almost magnetically drawn to Bernie's hair, and he hoped she wouldn't be able to feel his intense stare burning into her back. He could hear the rain even before they got to the mouth of the close and the three of them paused at the entrance, staring out at the dismal weather.

'It's like Donegal without the green,' Tom said. Connor just nodded. Tom suspected he'd never ventured as far north as Donegal, but Bernie smiled and that was enough for Tom to forget about the rain, at least for a moment. It was bouncing off the street which was already drenched black as if in mourning.

'It's not far to the tram stop,' Bernie said and her voice was a signal for Connor to step out into the rain. He began striding along the street. Bernie and Tom hesitated for a moment, glancing at each other before, almost in the same movement, plunging into the rain. Tom could feel drops hitting his cheeks and he was glad of the heavy coat Michael Collins had given him before he left Ireland. The cap that Connor had produced did provide some shelter for his head, though he could already feel the dampness coming through.

He looked at Bernie, almost having to peer through the rain to focus on her face which looked as though it was drenched in tears. She mustered up a weak smile of apology as if the weather was her fault.

'We'll get the tram at Crown Street,' she said. 'It's just round the corner,' she added, realising he didn't know where the street was.

Tom was relieved when they stopped walking, and the three of them huddled in the mouth of a close alongside several other drenched souls, the steam rising up off their wet clothes and chilled bodies, mingling almost incestuously with the clouds of cigarette smoke. He was even happier when the tram appeared in the street.

Connor led the way again, jumping on even before it had fully drawn to a stop and heading up to the top deck. When Tom appeared at the top of the stairs he noticed Connor was sitting beside a man and was talking to him. Bernie sat in the seat behind them and Tom dropped down beside her just as the tram began to pull away from the pavement, and he found himself gripping the edge of the seat to stop sliding off.

'This is Eugene,' Connor said, leaning round and nodding towards the man beside him, who held up a hand at the mention of his name without looking round. Tom noticed he had a scar on the back of his neck, a white gash that had been stitched in a hurry and left the skin uneven

'Eugene's a Derry man,' said Bernie.

'An Ulster man just like yourself,' Eugene said in an accent Tom would have recognised as pure Derry even in the middle of a thunderstorm. He guessed the man was not in possession of a full set of teeth from the whistling sound which accompanied some of his words and he grinned.

'Where are you from?' the Derry man asked.

'Gweedore,' said Tom, suddenly remembering his mother. He hoped there would be a good turn-out at the funeral. He was sure there would be – his Aunt Annie would see to that – though there would be one notable absentee – Kate Costello's only son. Tom sighed, hoping it would dispel the feeling of guilt which was attempting to take root in his mind again. He had other things to concentrate on today, however, and he couldn't afford his attention to be distracted.

'You'll know my uncle then,' Eugene said.

'What's his name?' Tom asked.

'Uncle Pat,' said Eugene. 'Do you know him?'

Tom looked at Bernie and shrugged. She grinned at him but said nothing to help.

'I don't think so,' Tom eventually said.

'You must know him. Everybody knows Pat Hanlon in Gweedore.'

'Pat Hanlon! Of course I know him.'

'See, I told you so.'

Tom shook his head and grinned while Bernie started laughing. He noticed Connor glancing round but only for a moment before he turned his head and continued staring out of the window which seemed to have a permanent coating of water. The weather didn't seem to deter the tram or, more precisely, the beast pulling it, and it seemed to build up speed as they reached the outskirts of the city. Tom knew they were heading towards the countryside. He could make out pale shadows of hills lurking in the distance through the rain and knew that fields of various colours sat in drenched silence below them.

He closed his eyes and imagined he was back in Donegal. He could see himself running through the fields near his cottage, fields that seemed to stretch as far as he could see. His mother was shouting him in for dinner but the fresh air held him in its thrall and he continued to ignore her shouts which were becoming more incessant and urgent. He was nine-years-old. He wasn't running anywhere in particular. Half the time it was only in circles and after he'd done that a dozen times on the trot, he'd collapse to the ground, lying flat on his back as the whole world seemed to spin chaotically around him, and he'd clutch the grass in case he fell off. He'd hear his mother's voice again as the earth slowed back down and then he'd get up and trudge home.

Tom felt a hand slip into his for a moment, just long enough to give him a comforting squeeze, though not long enough to be detected by anyone else. He looked round at Bernie in the same instant that he realised tears were running silently down his cheeks. He could feel his hand twitching to move towards his medals, though he preferred the consolation of Bernie's touch to any super-natural powers that might be attributed to the medals.

The rain had stopped by the time they reached their destination, though the sky still looked pregnant with water and ready to give birth at any moment.

'Where are we?' Tom asked as he stood at the opposite side of the road from the terminus where the tram had stopped. The driver was standing beside the horse, a cigarette in one hand while he patted the horse with the other.

'Bishopbriggs,' Connor muttered as he began squelching his way across the muddy field alongside Eugene, who was taking in the new surroundings, perhaps enamoured of the scenery which was so different to the grey and oppressive character of the city. More likely he was checking to make sure it was a safe location. Certainly, there was no sign of any other human life. A few cows were in the next field, some of them sitting lazily on the ground and chewing grass.

When they reached the edge of the field, Connor began to forge his way through a thicket of bushes, but stopped when Eugene began cursing.

'I've left the feckin' guns on the tram,' he said, shaking his head and trudging back over to where it was still parked. Connor shrugged his shoulders. Tom took out a cigarette and lit it but Bernie declined the offer of one when he held out the tin to her. He watched the Derry man through the cloud of smoke which now hovered in front of his face as he re-appeared out of the tram clutching a long black bag. Slinging it over his shoulder, Eugene retraced his footsteps while Tom flexed his own shoulder, pleased that there was no hint of any pain. Whether it would be able to take the strain of firing a rifle remained to be seen.

When Eugene was still a few yards away, Connor set off through the bushes again. Tom let Bernie go before him before he followed, having to duck occasionally to avoid any loose branches which sprang back towards him in her wake. After almost ten minutes, he began to think they were never getting out of the heavy woods and he wondered how Connor thought he'd be able to shoot anything in these dense surrounding.

It took him completely by surprise when they suddenly emerged into a clearing that stretched for at least one hundred yards. It was as if a giant hand had scythed an opening in the middle of the woods This would be a perfect place to practice his shooting. Connor had chosen well.

He could hear Eugene approaching, whistling *Dear Old Skibbereen*, and Tom was tempted to join in. It was his Uncle Peter's favourite song, and a hush would always descend on the room whenever he sang it, his voice drenched in whiskey but still powerful and perfectly in tune. It was a mournful sound, and Tom loved to sit in front of the peat fire, close his eyes and listen to the song while the heat waves floating out from the dancing flames caressed his cheeks.

Eugene stopped whistling as he emerged from the trees, dropping the bag heavily on the ground beside them.

'Careful,' said Connor, crouching down and opening up the bag. 'We can't afford any broken guns.'

Eugene shrugged and began whistling the same song again, though it was quieter and less obtrusive than before. Connor brought out a rifle and handed it to Tom who automatically began checking it, snapping open the bolt action and then closing it again. He repeated this a few times until he was satisfied the weapon was in good working order. Connor held out his hand and Tom took the bullets that rolled about in his palm, putting most of them in his pocket, but loading one into the gun. He held up the rifle, and took aim, as much to see how his shoulder felt. There was no pain, though he found it awkward to get the proper flexibility with the heavy coat on. Slipping it off along with his cap and dropping them on top of the bag, he repeated the motion of taking aim and this time he felt better.

He pressed the sight gently against his right eye and focused on a hole in the trunk of a tree at the far end of the clearing. His finger touched the trigger but as he began to squeeze it, there was another clicking and he broke off from his shot to look round. Eugene was loading an identical rifle.

'I could do with the practice,' he said.

Tom turned back and began the process all over again, aiming the gun at the hole, lightly touching the trigger... There was a roar behind him which rose up from the clearing and into the grey sky, scattering a few startled birds that had up to then remained hidden in the woods surrounding them. Tom let the rifle dangle at his side and glared at the Derry man.

'Sorry,' Eugene said with a sheepish grin.

'I need to practise,' said Tom.

'Sorry, sorry.'

Tom sighed and put the rifle down on top of his jacket, taking out his green tin. His concentration was broken for the moment and he hoped a cigarette would allow him to re-focus. Eugene went to put his rifle down as well but Tom stopped him.

'You may as well get another couple of shots in,' he said. 'I'm having a break.'

Eugene glanced at Connor who nodded, and the Derry man lifted his rifle up and stepped forward a few paces away from them. Loading the gun again, he took aim – at what Tom wasn't sure – and blasted off a shot which disappeared into the trees at the far side, staggering back a few steps from the force of the recoil on the rifle. Tom shook his head and turned away, taking a heavy draw on his cigarette.

'Don't mind Eugene,' Bernie whispered. 'He's harmless.'

Tom glanced round at the Derry man, who was reloading the rifle. He wanted to tell Bernie that Eugene wouldn't last five minutes with a flying column in Donegal but she'd probably know as much already. He wouldn't want someone like that alongside him anyway. 'Harmless' was just a polite way of saying useless, and he'd be a liability either way. Eugene held the loaded rifle – thankfully he wasn't pointing it in their direction – as he leant over and snatched up Tom's cap, pushing it on to his head. It was a tight fit.

'Now who's the best shot in the IRA,' he said, grinning as he offered a mock salute. Tom frowned but Bernie laughed.

'Take the hat off, Eugene,' Connor said, moving towards him.

Eugene turned and took aim. Tom still didn't know what he was trying to hit. Another roar filled the clearing but this time Eugene was blown off his feet, landing just beside them as the rifle flew into the air before twisting and turning as it plummeted to the ground.

The three of them didn't move. It was as if they'd all been frozen and had even lost the power of speech. Then

Bernie began screaming and suddenly Connor and Tom were scrambling to their knees, anxious to help Eugene. There was nothing they could do. Half of his head had been blown away by the force of a bullet which had slammed into his skull though Tom's cap still remained in place. Tom crawled across the grass and snatched up Eugene's rifle. It was still loaded.

'We need to get out of here,' he said, pointing the rifle towards the thick undergrowth, though since he had no idea where the shot had come from, it was a futile exercise.

'Quick,' he said with more urgency, getting to his feet and more or less pushing Bernie towards what he hoped would be the relative safety of the woods. At least it might provide them with some cover from the invisible gunman. Connor was still on his knees beside Eugene, staring blankly at the lifeless body of his comrade. Tom tugged at his arm.

'Connor, we need to go.'

'I can't leave him.'

'But there's someone out there. You could get killed.'

'I'm not leaving.'

'For feck's sake,' Tom said. 'Do you want to die?'

'Leave it, Tom,' Bernie said, touching his shoulder.

'But someone's just shot Eugene.' Tom could feel his voice beginning to get frantic and it surprised him. Normally, he was able to remain calm in the heat of battle but this had taken him by surprise and without an enemy to take aim at, he was worried. His rifle remained trained on the trees but whoever was lurking there could easily blow his head off the way he'd done with Eugene.

'We can come back for him,' he said, tugging at Connor's arm again.

'I'm not leaving.' This time Connor's voice was sharp and determined.

'We can't go,' Bernie said, kneeling down beside Connor and taking hold of his hand.

'Why not?'

'Because Eugene is Connor's brother.'

When they finally managed to negotiate their way back through the woods, Bernie leading the way while Connor and Tom carried Eugene, they laid the body down on the ground at the side of the road. Tom moved a few yards away, drawing heavily on a cigarette while Bernie spoke quietly to Connor before she joined him.

Tom had been thankful there had been no more shots fired but the one shot had worried him and not just because it had killed the Derry man. A nagging doubt gnawed away in his mind. He knew Eugene hadn't been the target and he wondered how the sniper had managed to make a mistake. He was grateful too, if truth be told, otherwise he'd be lying on the ground just now, though he suspected that Connor wouldn't have been so bothered about abandoning his body.

'I don't understand,' he said, nodding towards Connor while Bernie lit a cigarette. 'How can they be brothers?'

'What do you mean?'

'Well, Derry and Dublin are a bit far away from each other.'

'Eugene never left home. Connor did.'

'Connor's a Derry man?'

'Does that change your opinion about him?'

'What do you mean?'

'He studied for the priesthood at Maynooth,' she said, 'but it didn't work out. He just stayed on in Dublin after that, but he's an Ulster man just like you.'

She smiled and Tom frowned, looking over at Connor as he finished his cigarette.

The tram driver had taken some convincing before he'd agreed to let them take Eugene's body on his vehicle. Tom had thought of using his usual method of persuasion but Bernie talked him out of that. In the end they had been forced to cross the driver's palm with some coins, and Tom and Connor slowly carried Eugene on board, laying him down on the back seat. The driver agreed not to stop until they reached the Gorbals. Connor sat at the back, with Eugene's body stretched out across the seat, his head – the half that still remained – resting on his brother's lap. Occasionally, Tom would glance round but Connor never noticed him. His eyes were focused on his brother and Tom recognised the sense of loss in those eyes. It made him think of his mother again, and he looked away before his own eyes filled up with tears.

Song of Sorrow

A collection of shivering figures, all decked out in dark clothing of different shades and quality, huddled round the hole in the ground which had been hastily dug out of the soft earth by labourers who were comfortable working in the company of the dead. A priest stood at one end while the mourners gathered on the other three sides. They listened as the priest, dressed all in black too but with a regal purple sash draped round his neck, said prayers that most of them had heard before and would no doubt hear again. Some blessed themselves at random moments, while others moved their lips in silent accompaniment with the priest's incantations. Occasionally, a noise that was not one of grief – an angry shout or the impatient roar of a car engine – burst on to the scene from nearby, though these noises quickly evaporated, leaving only sadness; the strained sobs of grieving women a natural sound in such circumstances and surroundings, and one that nobody appeared even to notice.

Tom stayed on the fringes of the crowd, not wanting to intrude on a grief that he wasn't really part of. He sensed it would be better that he remain out of sight as much as possible. Connor had blamed him for the shoot-out which saw four of his comrades dead, and no doubt he'd blame Tom for the death of his brother too. Tom watched as

Bernie stood beside Connor, occasionally touching his arm or whispering words of comfort into his ear. She wore a black lace veil draped over her head which partially concealed her face so he couldn't see whether she was crying or not. Her hair still glowed beneath the veil, however, like a beacon demanding his attention no matter where else he tried to look.

It was a sunny day, though it was cold too, and Tom shivered with every invisible wave of chilled air that washed over him. He no longer had Michael Collins' coat to keep him warm. They'd laid it under Eugene's body in the tram and it bore the bloodied outline of the dead man. Tom wouldn't wear it again, even if it was to be scrubbed for days in the River Foyle, though he'd have been grateful for its protection at this moment.

It looked as though every mourner was puffing silently on an invisible cigarette, though the transparent clouds which floated up into the air were only the result of breathing in and out. Tom could have done with a cigarette, but he knew it was inappropriate. He wouldn't have long to wait, however, and the tin in his jacket pocket almost seemed to stir restlessly as if to remind him of its presence.

When the priest had finished his ceremonial duties, making the sign of the cross in a gesture that everyone else mimicked, there was silence and all eyes seemed to focus on Connor. After a few minutes which were punctuated by several uncomfortable coughs, he cleared his own throat.

'Eugene was my older brother and he was a good man, one of the best. . . He gave his life for our country, so that she might one day be free. I'm just sorry he won't be there to see that wonderful day. Rest síochána i mo dheartháir go hálainn.'

A lump of grief seemed to lodge in Connor's throat and he was barely able to finish speaking. Bernie clutched his arm as he sought to compose himself, not wanting to shed a tear in front of so many Irishmen, and comrades too. When it was obvious that Connor had finished talking, the six men who were holding the ropes which supported the coffin over the grave slowly began to lower it into the ground where it would soon become covered by the earth which was stacked up at the side of the grave.

Out of the depths of the crowd a lone voice began singing. It was a man's voice, and the words hung in the air while the tune would remain in every mourner's head long after they'd trudged home. Tom knew the song and as he discreetly closed his eyes, it seemed as if the man's voice faded away, to be replaced by a woman's lilting tone that sounded to him just like his mother's. The song was called *Dáimh Gaeilge Briste* but to him, and all his family when his mother performed it after everyone demanded that she do so, it was simply Kate's Song.

'I had a love, it made my heart beat stronger, but now it's gone I don't how I can go on much longer. . . I had a love, as bright as a Donegal morning, and then it darkened with no warning. . . Close your eyes and don't look back. . . 'Cause what you see would break your heart.'

Tom was one of the first to leave the cemetery and he found himself humming the tune in between drawing on a cigarette. Some people hurried past him, eager to get away from this place and try to shrug off the odour of death which inevitably clung to anyone who stepped through the gates.

Others huddled in small groups near him, content to pass a few more minutes in the company of friends they'd not seen for a while, sharing gossip or reminiscing over a cigarette. Occasionally, a laugh would escape from one of these groups, and everyone would stare at the guilty person as if it was an inappropriate action in these surroundings.

No-one acknowledged Tom. He was happy enough at that. Few of them would know who he was and he welcomed the anonymity. He finished one cigarette and immediately lit another as Bernie appeared beside him. He offered her one, detecting the hungry look she gave his.

'Where's Connor?' he asked.

She glanced back towards where they'd just buried Eugene, though it wasn't visible from where they stood, gravestones and statues concealing Connor.

'He's not ready to leave Eugene yet.'

'How is he?'

'He hasn't said much. I'm worried about him. I've tried talking to him but he doesn't want to say anything.'

'Give him time,' Tom said, dropping his cigarette end on the ground and crushing it with his foot.

'Come on,' she said with a sigh, taking one final look back towards the cemetery before walking away.

'Are you not going to wait for Connor?'

'He said he'll get us back at the house,' Bernie said, not turning round or stopping, and Tom had to break into a jog to catch up with her.

They walked in silence for a few minutes, with Bernie setting the pace. She was a fast walker, thought Tom, and he wanted to slow her down, if only because it would mean he'd get to spend a few more minutes with her.

Maybe she was hurrying up so that she'd get to spend a few minutes less with him?

'You know it was me they were trying to kill,' he said as they stood at the corner of a road, waiting until a tram slowly rattled past them before they crossed.

'I know,' she said, abruptly stopping halfway across the road to allow a horse and cart to trot pass. The driver tipped his cap, probably as relieved that he hadn't had to try and avoid anyone, or worse, that he hadn't hit anyone, as he was acknowledging the courtesy of giving him the right of way.

'Connor knows too, I take it?'

'Yes,' she said.

'Has he said anything about it?'

'I told you, he hasn't really said anything.'

They reached the opposite pavement and Tom tugged Bernie's arm, wanting her to stop.

'I'm sorry,' he said.

She shrugged.

'They knew I'd be there, just like they knew I was in the house. Somebody's telling them.'

This time Bernie nodded and he could tell from her face that the same thoughts occupied her mind as well.

'Do you have any idea who it could be?' he asked.

'No, but I'm sure Connor will try to find out. He'll want to know who was responsible for Eugene's death.'

'Even though it was me they were after.'

She nodded again and started walking away. He watched her until he had to run to catch up with her and they continued their journey to the house in silence.

Tom stayed in the other room even after Connor had arrived home. He didn't want to risk the Dubliner's grief turning to rage if he caught sight of him. As it was, there were still moments when he felt Connor's glare burning through the door and he was glad Bernie was out there to try at least to maintain a level of calmness. He knew he'd have to go out at some point but instinctively he sensed that it was best to delay the inevitable meeting in the hope that it wouldn't become a confrontation.

Five men had now died since his arrival in Glasgow and it was a grim tally he wasn't proud of. He knew that Connor blamed him for every death, and while he wasn't prepared to accept blame – he hadn't pulled the trigger which fired any fatal bullets – he still knew that it was his presence which had led to the five deaths. Connor had somehow accepted the reality of what had happened with the men who'd died in the shoot-out, but Eugene's death was different. He was Connor's brother and it was inevitable that would hurt more, much more, no matter how close he'd felt to any of his comrades.

Surely now Connor would accept there was a traitor in the ranks? How else could Eugene's death be explained? The killer had been waiting for them, hidden in the trees which not only provided camouflage to spy on them but, more importantly, it concealed the gunman even after he'd fired the fatal shot. He'd probably fled as soon as the bullet had blown off half of Eugene's head. Yet Tom was convinced the gunman had made a mistake. He was the target and it was just his luck that Eugene was firing the rifle at the time. He hoped the gunman hadn't realised what he'd done. If he thought Tom was dead, it would allow Tom to complete his own mission without having to worry about anyone trying to kill him. Still, while he continued with his plan for killing Maxwell, the task of unmasking the traitor was one that had to be carried out as well and he knew he'd have to speak to Connor. It was all in the timing, he realised, trying to imagine the other man's reaction when he raised the issue again.

The house was beginning to fill up with people. Tom could hear more voices that blended together to create a vaguely annoying drone beyond the door which he felt was now keeping him a prisoner. Different voices battled to be heard, some loud and some quiet. Tom would make out individual words or occasional bursts of laughter but it was difficult for him to differentiate between the voices – none of the owners he was likely to know – and he wanted to join the rest of them and escape this self-imposed prison.

A guitar was strummed loudly which seemed to introduce a hush to the room and Tom stood up. He wasn't going to miss the singing. A man's voice accompanied the guitar, while a penny whistle played the melody and Tom hesitated at the door, his hand poised on the handle as he listened to the song which he instantly recognised.

''Twas a day like no other, let me tell you right now. When I stood with me mother and our heads they did bow. The drum beat so slowly, the sky turned to grey, as they brought out Dan Foley for his own judgement day. . . 'Twas in Glasgow town for to take on the crown, Dan Foley he did go. . . But the traitors they sang and brave Dan did hang, and all Ireland she did mourn. . .'

He smiled as the singer continued with *The Ballad of Dan Foley*. It was one of his favourite songs and the man who was singing it had a good voice – he wondered if it was the graveside singer – and Tom could understand why he was able to command silence from his audience. He pressed his head gently against the door and listened to the song, waiting until it finished and the applause began before slipping into the room, hoping that his unannounced presence would also remain largely unnoticed.

Unfortunately he stepped into what felt like a stage with everyone staring in his direction and he wished he could slip back into the bedroom. It was too late for that, however, and it would only have made things worse. He caught Bernie's eye – she was sitting beside Connor – and she nodded towards a space on the floor near her where he was able to squeeze between two men who were leaning against the wall. The singer was enthroned on a wooden chair in the centre of the room, surrounded on all sides by an appreciative audience.

One of the men sitting beside Tom handed him a chunky black bottle. He immediately smelt the whiskey fumes escaping out the neck. He wiped the top with his sleeve and took a drink, just a small mouthful, and handed it back.

'Thanks,' he said, swallowing the liquid which scalded his throat. He searched in his pocket and brought out his green tin, offering it to the man with the whiskey bottle. He took a cigarette without saying anything and waited for Tom to provide a light.

Tom glanced round the room as the guitarist began singing another song, though it wasn't one he recognised. Apart from Connor and Bernie, there were only one or two faces he thought were vaguely familiar. Either they had floated in and out of the house over the past few days or it was just because he'd seen them at the funeral. There were three or four others, including the two sitting either side of him, whom he'd definitely never seen before. He didn't know who they were or what group they belonged to, but the fact they were all wearing red armbands indicated they were all together.

The wake continued without much enthusiasm for another three or four songs, all of which were performed with gusto by the singer, while the rest of the room joined in at various points, usually the chorus if they recognised it. Connor sat impassively, staring at the guitarist, though Tom suspected his focus was elsewhere, no doubt on his brother and images of the dead body which would haunt him for the rest of his life. Bernie remained by his side, though she would occasionally glance over and offer a weak smile in Tom's direction. Eventually, the guitarist put down his instrument, swapping it for a bottle of whiskey which helped to lubricate his throat after all his singing.

'What time are we going?' he asked, handing the whiskey to one of the men sitting beside Tom.

'There's been a change of plan.'

It was Connor's voice and Tom looked round, slightly surprised to hear it.

'But we need to see him,' the guitarist said. 'It's nearly time and we need his help.'

'He knows that.'

'Can we trust him?' It was another of the red armband men who spoke.

'I don't think you've got any choice,' said Connor.

'Is he for us or against us?'

Connor laughed.

'I don't see what's funny about that,' the guitarist said. 'We'd like to know if he is committed to our cause?'

'His politics are very simple,' Connor said, shaking his head. 'You pay him enough money and he'll be your biggest supporter . . . until someone else pays him more.'

'I don't know about dealing with someone like that.'

'That's fine,' said Connor, 'but you'll not get anyone else to help you.'

'That's a chance we'll have to take,' said one of the men sitting beside Tom.

'What do you think the British will do when you take to the streets?' asked Connor.

There were a few shrugs.

'I'll tell you what they'll do . . . they'll hit you with everything they've got – guns and tanks and anything else in their armoury, and if you're not prepared to fight fire with fire, then you're wasting your time. You'd be as well going home and forgetting all about your world revolution.'

A silence hung in the air as Connor's comments, dripping with scorn, were absorbed.

'We don't have a choice then?' It was the guitarist who spoke, and Connor nodded in agreement. 'So when are we going to see him?'

There was a knock on the door. It sounded like a hammer being banged on the other side of the wood and everyone turned round to stare at the door.

'Perfect timing,' said Connor. He stood up and walked over to the door, opening and standing aside. A man limped into the room. He was hunched over and used a thick, brown wooden walking stick to help his balance. When he got into the middle of the room, he stood up to his full height and Tom was sure he'd never seen anyone taller in his life. The man's bald head almost touched the ceiling. Connor closed the door, having also let in two of the bald man's companions. They both stood at the door, arms folded menacingly, their eyes scouring the room and staring suspiciously at everyone. Tom could sense a nervousness settle over the assembled group and he felt a little uneasy himself.

'For those of you who don't know, this is Mr Duffy,' said Connor, now standing beside the bald man, who towered over him. 'He's going to help us get some guns.'

Lonely Nightmare

Harrison didn't make mistakes. That had always been one of his strengths and it had given him a mental sureness he often had to rely on in the heat of battle. It had saved his life on more than one occasion, he was sure of that, and it also helped him deal with the reality of what he was doing. He was ending lives and he needed to be certain in his mind that it was the right thing to do. He didn't make mistakes and that had always consoled him when he thought about the person who had been the recipient of the bullet he'd fired. Now he had made two mistakes and it was unsettling him.

First there had been the shot in the street. He was still convinced that he had hit the Irishman – the blood on the ground had been real enough – but without a body he could hardly claim that effort a success. Added to that was the killing in the woods. The shot had been swift and decisive. He hadn't even had to wait and check that he'd been successful. As soon as he squeezed the trigger he knew the man was seconds from death; he thought it was Costello who was being despatched to meet his maker, and it made for a pleasant journey back to Glasgow as he basked in a self-congratulatory glow.

How was he to know that someone else was wearing Costello's hat? The news had deflated him quicker than a punctured balloon. He had to make it third time lucky though he hated the word 'luck'. He didn't want to leave anything to chance, yet chance was proving to be Costello's best ally. Harrison frowned. The Irishman couldn't rely on chance for ever – or even for much longer – and Harrison was ready to pounce when his luck ran out. The problem was, he no longer knew where Costello was and the more time that passed without him knowing, the more chance there was of Costello carrying out his own mission successfully.

The information which twice led him to the Irishman had suddenly dried up and now he was going to have to rely on his instincts, and maybe a little luck too. He took the sixpence out of his pocket and let it lie in the palm of his hand before picking it up and tossing it into the air. 'Heads' he would be successful in killing Costello, he told himself. He watched as the silver coin dropped back into his hand, smiling when he saw which side it had landed on. The door opened and Harrison quickly slipped the coin into his pocket before standing to attention.

'Sit down, Corporal Harrison,' a voice said and he looked round, startled. It was General Maxwell, who smiled when he saw Harrison's reaction.

'Are you surprised to see me in Glasgow or just to see me alive?' the General asked as he took a seat on the other side of the table to Harrison.

'Sir?'

'I'm being flippant, Corporal Harrison . . .'

The General produced a small gold case from inside his jacket and flicked it open, holding it out towards Harrison, whose eyes noted the perfect row of white cigarettes.

'Go on, take one. Don't be shy now.'

Harrison removed one of the white sticks with a respectful nod and quickly searched his own pockets for a box of matches, striking one and holding out the flame for the General to light his cigarette before he lit his own. The two men smoked in silence, though it was not an experience Harrison was able to enjoy. He was too nervous. He hadn't expected General Maxwell to appear, and not because he thought he might be dead. The original plan was for Harrison to kill Costello first before the General appeared in the city. It was the safest option. Something had obviously happened to change that plan but Harrison wasn't about to ask, certainly not without prompting.

'The Irishman is still alive?' General Maxwell asked, blowing a cloud of smoke in Harrison's direction.

'Yes, sir.'

'You've had opportunities to kill him?'

'Yes, sir.'

'Yet he's still alive?'

'Sir.'

The General took a final draw of his cigarette before stubbing it out in an ashtray.

'You won't fail next time?'

'No, sir.'

'Good,' said the General, 'because we can't afford any more mistakes, Corporal Harrison. Next time has to be the last time.'

'Yes, sir.'

Harrison knew that the General was talking about him as much as he was about Costello, and another missed opportunity would see him removed from the mission and probably banished to some God-forsaken outpost of the

Empire. However, his coin had landed on 'Heads'. He knew he wouldn't fail next time.

'These are turbulent times,' General Maxwell said. 'This city is a tinderbox, and the slightest spark could ignite it at any moment. I am here to try and ensure that doesn't happen, and if it does then I will fight the flames with every power at my disposal.'

'Yes, sir,' Harrison said as he discreetly extinguished his own cigarette.

'Damn communists,' the General said, shaking his head. 'It's a bad business that has happened in Russia.'

'Yes, sir,' Harrison said, his voice quiet, almost nervous. He had a vague understanding of what the General was talking about but he couldn't explain exactly what the 'bad business' was that the General had referred to. He didn't really want to know, if he was being honest, since politics held no interest for him, but he thought better than to tell the General that.

'We don't want that happening here now, do we?' the General said.

'No, sir.'

'And when they try, as they surely will, I will be there to crush them like the godless vermin they are,' he said, slamming his fist angrily down on the table.

Harrison jumped and silently tried to fight the panic that was suddenly threatening to paralyse him. He knew he shouldn't close his eyes but his brain was telling him to shut them tightly and then everything would go away. In his ears he could hear the explosions that felt like they were going off everywhere – above, behind, beside, in front of him – until it seemed like he was cocooned in a bubble of noise that fought for attention with the roar of his own voice which screamed in terror.

They said he was brave. He had the medals to prove it, but they were wrong. They hadn't been there.

Still his eyes stayed shut. He saw hands that gripped the machine-gun and pressed down on the trigger which released countless bullets into the air, the small but deadly pieces of metal immediately rushing off in search of bodies, drawn instinctively to the scent of human flesh like a pack of dogs out on a hunt. His body shook in time with the gun and he knew he had to keep on firing. He didn't know how many Germans he hit. The citation later mentioned twenty-five but at the time it could have been five or five hundred for all that he knew. He never told anyone that, even as he was firing, his gun the only thing that was preventing the Germans from over-running their trench, his eyes remained closed.

He couldn't have opened them, even if he wanted to. They were sealed by the terror of the moment, and nothing he could have done would have prised them open. He felt the soil bounce off him like hailstones, but still he kept screaming and shaking and firing, his gun rattling even after the explosions had ceased.

'Harrison.'

He just wanted to make sure he hit them all. Perhaps silencing their guns had simply been a ruse to trick him into stopping, so he kept his finger on the trigger.

'Harrison.'

Screaming.

'Harrison.'

Shaking.

'Harrison!'

Firing.

'CORPORAL HARRISON.'

He opened his eyes. The noise disappeared and General Maxwell stared at him.

'Are you okay, Corporal Harrison?'

'Yes, sir,' he said. 'Sorry, sir.'

Maxwell leant back in his chair and frowned at Harrison who could feel beads of sweat briefly gathering on his forehead before streaming down his face. He wanted to wipe them away but he was afraid to move. He was angry with himself, embarrassed too, and even a little worried. This had been the worst attack yet and it had come upon him so suddenly he had been unable to resist it.

'I'm fine, sir,' he said, trying to inject some conviction into his voice.

Maxwell shook his head after a few moments, clearly not convinced but evidently not prepared to delve any further into what had put Harrison into a momentary trance.

'This Costello business is a distraction,' the General said.

'Yes, sir.'

'Can I still rely on you to do this for me?'

'Yes, sir.'

'Well, sort it out, Corporal Harrison, and sort it now,' the General said, standing up.

'Yes, sir. I will.'

Harrison stood up and saluted as General Maxwell nodded and strode out of the room, leaving the door open in his wake. He listened as the General's footsteps became progressively fainter before he wiped his forehead with his sleeve.

A Family Affair

Tom pushed open the gate. It creaked noisily in the early morning air and he hesitated for a moment before closing it behind him. He could see the sandstone building at the end of the long gravel driveway peeking out shyly through the branches of trees and shrubbery which populated the large garden. He took one step forward and a man emerged from behind an oak tree that had sat impassively in the same spot for hundreds of years. He was pointing a rifle at Tom who stopped and automatically held his hands up.

'I'm here to see Mr Duffy,' Tom said.

'He never said anything to me.'

The man had a Glasgow accent and Tom struggled to make out what he was saying.

'I just want five minutes of his time.'

'If he doesn't know you're coming, then you've got no chance.'

Tom lowered his arms and slipped his hands in his pockets, hoping it would put the other man at ease.

'Can you ask him for me?'

The man took a step forward, still pointing the gun at Tom.

'Mr Duffy doesn't like unexpected guests.'

Tom studied the man who kept twitching his nose anxiously like a mouse. He had a thin black moustache that perched along his top lip and he'd occasionally run his tongue across it. Tom hoped the man wasn't too nervous because if he was to pull the trigger at this moment, he'd blow a hole in Tom's stomach and catapult his body back towards the gate. He kept his hands in his pockets, staying perfectly still and hoping that he looked relaxed and unthreatening.

'Tell him that Connor Daly sent me.'

'And who will I tell him is here?' asked the man, frowning.

'Father Costello.'

'Don't move, Father,' the man said, thrusting his gun warningly at Tom. A crunching sound behind him caused Tom to glance over his shoulder. Another man had emerged from the shadows. He was also pointing a rifle at Tom. He leant against the tree, his weapon still trained on Tom as the first man trudged noisily up towards the house. Tom watched until he disappeared round the back of the building.

'Do you mind if I smoke?' he said, looking round at the other guard, who shrugged. Tom slowly took his cigarette tin from the inside pocket of his jacket, though the man didn't seem unduly concerned at the movement. For all he knew, Tom could be gripping a pistol which he'd produce and blast a bullet into the man's brain before he even had time to register what was happening. Tom relaxed, knowing this guard wouldn't be worth worrying about. The man gratefully took a cigarette when offered and they both smoked in silence, Tom keeping a wary eye on the house for any sign of the first guard's return. He could tell he was a different proposition.

'Mr Duffy doesn't like priests,' the man said, taking a heavy draw on his cigarette and nodding towards Tom.

'Why not?'

The man shrugged. 'He says they're robbers and thieves, but they're not honest about it.'

'He's probably right,' Tom said with a smile and the man laughed. 'Why do you think we have all those collections at Mass?'

'Well, that's what Mr Duffy says too. You'll still be lucky if he agrees to meet you.'

'We'll just have to wait and see,' Tom said, finishing his cigarette and flicking it away.

The man rested his rifle against the tree trunk and folded his arms. He was happy enough to answer any of Tom's questions so that, within five minutes or so, he knew how many men Duffy had. It might prove to be invaluable information, though that was dependent on Duffy agreeing to meet him. If he wasn't, then it wouldn't matter that he knew there were half a dozen armed men hidden behind trees or bushes, or that another four were inside the house – two outside the door of whatever room Duffy was in and two at his side at all times, presumably except when he had to answer the call of nature.

'It must be your lucky day,' the first guard said as he returned, his rifle now dangling unthreateningly at his side. 'You've got five minutes – no more. So you better be quick with whatever it is you want to ask.'

He gestured with his head for Tom to follow him as he turned and headed towards the house again. The second guard melted back into the trees without another word and Tom trudged behind the first man, his own stride not quite in time so that it sounded like an echo of the man's steps on the ground as he walked. Duffy's house was stunning and as they reached the end of the driveway, the building emerged from behind the natural camouflage concealing it. Tom was impressed by the large sandstone structure and not even the man standing at the front door with a rifle aimed in his direction could spoil the picture.

'War has been very good to me,' Duffy said as he gestured for Tom to sit down on the armchair facing him. He had a voice that Tom knew from his earlier encounter could instil fear in many hardened souls, though it left him unmoved. It also bore traces of age, and its clear resonance would occasionally waver, after which he'd descend into a bout of heavy coughing before resuming his speech.

'There were plenty of people dying while I was making a killing,' he said with a cold grin. It obviously wasn't the first time he'd cracked that joke. Tom nodded with a polite smile.

Duffy sat back in his chair – it was like a giant black leather throne – and studied Tom. His walking stick leant lazily against an arm of the chair and he drummed the other arm with his long, skinny fingers. There were two other men in the room. One stood to Duffy's right, poised for a word or gesture from the leather chair that would demand an instant reaction. The other man stood behind Tom at the door, blocking any exit. His gun rested at his side though he still held it, ready to bring it into action at a moment's notice.

Tom looked at the man facing him, remembering the

name which would sometimes float discreetly, almost nervously in the air during his childhood. This was the man who had caused much misery to his mother. He remembered the way she would shudder whenever that name was mentioned. He'd been glad, sometimes, of the apparent invisibility his childhood provided him, or he'd have been none the wiser about the man who sat before him now.

'Now what can I do for you, priest?' Duffy asked, running a hand back and forth across his smooth, shiny head.

'I'm here to hear your confession.'

There was a moment of silence before Duffy started laughing, a callous sound that quickly became a heavy cough and he bent over to try and control it. The man beside him who had initially joined in the laughter now stepped forward warily, not wanting to intervene unless asked, but knowing it was best to be close enough to be able to do so instantly. After a moment or so, Duffy sat back with a deep sigh, clearing his throat a final time and spitting the contents of his mouth into a handkerchief one of the guards held out in the palm of his hand.

'Now that is funny,' he said, picking up his stick and pointing it at Tom. 'A priest with a sense of humour – I like that. . . You want to hear my confession? How many days have you got, Father?'

'It won't take long.'

'I'm not sure about that . . . and I don't think even God would be in the mood to forgive me after everything I've done.'

Tom continued watching Duffy as he settled back into his leather throne, his body almost writhing as it tried to find the shape it had indelibly left in the material over time, the leather creaking lazily with every movement. Tom joined his hands together, fingers entwined as if he was about to begin praying, though the tips of his right hand surreptitiously slipped into the left sleeve of his jacket until they touched the handle of the knife he'd taped to the inside of his left arm. He knew they'd search him – priest or no priest – but as he'd guessed, it was just a cursory check of his pockets and they were all empty. It would have taken a much more stringent search or a lucky break for them to have discovered the knife.

It ran from his wrist to the joint at his elbow, the sharp point of the blade occasionally nipping his skin if he bent his arm too much. He fully expected to discover blood later, knowing too that it would be on his shirt as well, but it was an annoyance he was more than willing to tolerate.

'Now tell me why you're really here,' Duffy said, holding the stick out steadily so that it seemed to hold Tom in its gaze. 'Why did Connor send you?'

'May I?' Tom asked, slowly beginning to move off the chair but stopping short of fully standing up until he got Duffy's permission. The bald man frowned but nodded.

'My mother died last week, God rest her,' he said, blessing himself in a gesture that seemed entirely in character with the outfit rather than his own personality. He wished he could hold the medals for support or strength, but he knew it would appear too much of a suspicious gesture.

'I'm sorry to hear that,' said Duffy.

'Her name was Kate Costello.'

Tom looked at Duffy, expecting some sort of reaction to the name but there was nothing, not even a flicker of recognition. Instead, it was Tom who frowned.

'I'm a busy man, Father,' said Duffy, picking up his stick again, evidently on the point of standing up himself, 'and this conversation is now beginning to waste my time. . . Tell Connor to come himself the next time he wants to speak to me.'

'You killed my father.'

'What?'

'Mick Costello. You murdered him here in Glasgow. He was stabbed to death in the street in front of my mother. Her name was –'

'Kate.' Duffy said the word slowly, allowing it to swirl around in his mouth like something he'd not said for a long, long time and he was tasting it again to see if he still enjoyed its sound. He nodded and a gun catch clicked behind Tom.

'So you're Kate's son?' He smiled grimly. 'Who'd have thought a two-shilling whore would have produced a priest? I didn't even know she was pregnant.'

'Neither did my father.'

'Are you sure he was the father? She got around did our Kate. . . Like throwing a sausage up a close, I would say. No offence, Father.'

Tom's fingertips touched the handle of the knife.

'None taken,' he said.

Duffy sat back and laughed, shaking his head.

'Kate's son . . . a priest . . . Now I've seen everything. . . So what do you really want, priest?' he asked, the last word sizzling in the air like an extinguished flame.

'She wanted me to tell you that she forgave you.'

'For what?'

'For killing my father . . . Her husband.'

'Her husband?' Duffy laughed again, a cackling sound

that once again descended into a violent cough. 'Kate was never married,' he spluttered through continued bursts of coughing and laughing. 'So I'm afraid that makes you a bastard. No offence, Father.'

Tom tried to hide the shock from spreading across his face though without much success, and the obvious surprise etched in his expression was causing Duffy to laugh and cough even more violently.

'She forgave you anyway,' Tom said, having inched his way forward until he was just a couple of feet away from Duffy.

'Kate's little bastard is telling me she forgave me,' he said with a sigh. 'I don't need her forgiveness and I don't want it,' he said, his tone suddenly serious and menacing. 'You're either a brave or a foolish man to have come here, Father, but for old time's sake, I'm going to let you leave here in one piece. After all, I might be your father for all you know,' he said, sneering at Tom and licking his lips like he'd remembered some long-forgotten memory.

Tom stepped forward, snatching the knife from his sleeve and thrusting it against Duffy's exposed neck, pressing hard with the sharp blade until he was sure it touched the leather of the chair. Duffy's head wobbled though it still remained precariously attached to the rest of his body and Tom withdrew the knife, allowing Duffy to topple forward and crash noisily on to the ground like some giant oak tree that had just been felled, blood gushing out from the deep wound and quickly forming a dark puddle on the floor.

He snatched the walking stick and threw it towards the guard at the door who still looked stunned, his brain not quite registering what had just happened in the blink of an eye. He reacted automatically to the object flying towards him, trying to bat it away with his rifle and pressing the trigger in the same instant, firing a bullet into the ceiling. As plaster began to rain down, Tom was upon him, stabbing him three times in the chest with short, sharp punches. The man staggered back and fell against the door.

Tom grabbed the rifle and spun round, immediately racing towards the other guard who was desperately trying to get a pistol out of his jacket pocket. In his nervousness, the weapon remained stuck in the material and Tom flattened him with the butt-end of the rifle, the man tumbling to the floor and hitting his head on the edge of a glass table that sat against the wall, knocking him unconscious. Tom removed the pistol from the man's jacket with ease and headed over to the door where other guards were desperately banging on it and trying to open it, though the dead weight of their colleague slumped at the door was keeping them out.

Tom cocked the pistol and fired one shot through the door. There was a moment of silence, as the roar of the gun subsided, on either side of the room before a man started screaming, filling the air with panic-stricken obscenities. Tom quickly stepped across to the window as a volley of angry bullets burst back through the door, many of them ending up imbedded in the dead guard. He waited for a minute before scurrying over to Duffy, turning the body over and staring at the face of the man who'd killed his father and who had caused so much pain to his mother. Duffy's eyes were open and his mouth seemed to be frozen in a permanent sneer as if, even in death, he was still laughing at Tom . . . bastard Tom.

There would be time enough to think about that later, he realised. He rummaged in Duffy's pockets, finding a rolled-up bundle of notes. He couldn't even begin to imagine how much it would amount to. It was more money than he'd ever seen in his life before. Probably some of it had recently belonged to Connor and the communists. He put the bundle in his own pocket.

Duffy had a gun too, which Tom quickly checked. It was loaded. He turned back towards the door, a pistol in either hand. The shooting had stopped now, though he was sure it was only a temporary respite, and he crept to the door, pressing his ear gently against its scarred surface. There was noisy activity outside in the hall, and the wounded man still moaned painfully, though either by choice or order, it was a less desperate sound. He then moved to the window, and looked from behind the lace curtains into the garden. There was nothing that he could spot though he suspected all the guards had raced into the house at the sound of the gunfire. Either that or they still remained hidden, ready to pounce should he suddenly appear in their midst.

Tom stepped away from the window and leant against the wall. His mind was racing, coming up with various plans of escape before quickly dissecting them and realising they wouldn't work. There were still eight armed men – or seven-and-a-half if you took into account the wounded man – ready and resolved to kill him and he knew he'd be lucky to get out of here unscathed.

A low, agonised moan in the other corner of the room alerted him to the fact that one of the guards was still alive. He stepped across and stood over the man who was bleeding heavily from a wound at the side of his head. He was moving – just – and Tom gently prodded him with the toe of his boot to see what resistance was offered, but the man didn't seem to acknowledge it. Putting both pistols on the floor out of reach of the man, just in case, Tom dragged him towards the door, then skipped over to Duffy's leather chair. He could hear voices outside the room and realised another assault on the door was imminent.

He pushed the chair over towards the window. It scraped noisily on the polished wooden floor, marking the perfect surface, but still he kept pushing. It took him three attempts to lift the chair and he staggered back, briefly worried he was going to end up with the piece of furniture on top of him. Instead, he managed to muster up a final burst of strength and lunged forward, thrusting the chair at the window. It exploded through the sheet of glass like a blast of dynamite, and Tom admired his handiwork even as he rolled the dead man aside from the door, hearing footsteps racing down the hall towards the garden.

He picked up the pistols, keeping one in his hand and slipping the other inside the waist of his trousers. Then, with some difficulty, he manoeuvred the groaning guard into a standing position. He held the man up, gripping his trousers as the man swayed like a tree in a breeze, and he slowly opened the door with his other hand, which also held the pistol.

As the door opened wider, he fired the gun blindly out into the corridor and then pushed the guard ahead of him. A volley of gunfire blasted into the man, sending him crashing off the walls. When the shooting had ceased, Tom stepped out into the doorway, grabbing the other pistol from his waist, and firing at the two guards to his left who had inadvertently killed their colleague. They were still trying to register what they'd just done, staring dumbly at the body of the dead guard slumped at their feet, when the bullets slammed into them. One was hit in the head while the other took a bullet to his chest. Both men were dead in an instant and Tom ventured into the corridor, glancing either way before deciding to head in the opposite direction from the garden which would now be covered with shards of glass and patrolled by anxious guards.

He let off another shot, this time into the body of the guard he'd wounded earlier when he'd fired through the door. It looked from the blood stain on the main's trousers that he'd been hit in the groin and he'd been drifting in and out of consciousness. He was dead now.

Tom raced down the corridor towards the back of the house, knowing that the gunfire would quickly draw the rest of the guards back into the building. He'd have to be quick – and lucky – if he was going to get out of here in one piece.

Caught in the Middle

The front window of the house seemed to explode and Bernie staggered back, almost falling on the pavement. She crouched down and peered through a gap in the hedge which surrounded the garden, spotting the gaping hole in the building where once there had been glass. Voices were shouting in a blind panic and then they tailed off, no doubt heading towards the gunfire which had suddenly broken out from within the house. She kept her head down, eager not to be spotted, though it was unlikely any of the men inside the property would have their attention drawn towards anything outside the house or garden. Slowly, she stood up, her knees clicking as she did.

She was worried for Tom. Was he firing the shots or was he taking the bullets? She'd have to tell Connor. At least he might know what to do next. She only hoped that it wouldn't prove too late for Tom. She took an unsteady step back and collided with a solid object. Startled, she looked round to find herself facing a soldier who stood, hands on hips, frowning. Three other soldiers were behind him. All of them were armed, though none of the guns were pointed at her.

Miss O'Hara?' the first soldier asked.

Bernie nodded warily.

'Can you come with us, please? There's someone who'd like a little chat with you, if you don't mind.'

'And what if I do mind?'

The soldier shrugged as Bernie glanced back towards the house.

'Don't worry,' the soldier said. 'We'll be sorting that out soon enough.'

Now it was Bernie's turn to shrug, and she followed the soldiers away from the house as another burst of gunfire from the house reached her ears.

Bernie slumped in the chair, her elbows leaning on the table in front of her. She had been in the room for over an hour at least and she was restless. She'd sat for a while, then stood up and walked round the table before sitting back down again, but nothing could alleviate the frustrating boredom which seemed to be taking greater root in her mind with every passing minute. The room was empty save for the table and two chairs. Four grey walls surrounded her and even the inside of the door had been painted the same dull shade. If there had been a window at least she'd have been able to stare out and imagine she was back home in Galway, but there was nothing to help encourage her imagination.

She had sat in the back of an army truck along with two soldiers. The soldier who had spoken to her was in the front of the vehicle along with the driver. She didn't even waste her breath asking either of the soldiers facing her if they knew where she was being taken. She guessed they wouldn't tell her if they knew, so it was better she conserve her energy till later when she might need it.

She wondered again about Tom. Was he dead or alive?

She hadn't planned to follow him. She'd been walking back to the house when she spotted him on the other side of the street. She'd shouted his name as he reached the corner of Portugal Street but her voice was drowned out by the traffic as he disappeared out of sight. She wondered where he was going, particularly given his lack of knowledge and familiarity with the city. More than that, she was curious as to why he was dressed as a priest again. Careful not to be noticed, she followed him as he strode along Main Street, heading towards the Clyde.

She held back as he headed across Victoria Bridge; there weren't too many people on the bridge and she knew that if he were to glance over his shoulder, he'd spot her right away. Still, it meant that once he was almost at the other side, she had to break into a run so as not to lose him, which was a danger as he darted through the throng of people in the centre of town. She sensed he was heading east, and he soon settled into a steady stride along Duke Street. She didn't know where he was going but it seemed to be with a determination and purpose which puzzled her.

Red sandstone tenements were quickly left behind and he turned off Duke Street, heading up the hill into wider streets that divided larger houses on either side. When he turned into Broompark Drive she knew whose house he was going to and realised, even before the shooting began and windows suddenly exploded, that he was in danger. Duffy was not a man to be messed with. Everyone knew that and, whether brave or foolish, Tom was stumbling into something terrible and not even a fake clerical collar would be able to provide him with the protection he'd undoubtedly need.

She also wanted to know what Tom's business was

with Duffy. He was already supplying guns to Connor and also to the communists, which Connor had arranged for them. They kept talking about uprisings and revolutions but to Bernie they just sounded like a bunch of idealistic and naïve youngsters.

There would also have been a gun for Tom when the time came for him to carry out whatever it was he'd been sent to Glasgow to do by Michael Collins, so why was there any need for any separate deals with Duffy, not unless he was providing something that Connor couldn't. At least, she'd thought that until the house seemed to explode with anger and she realised that it wasn't a courtesy call Tom had been making on Duffy.

The grey door opened and the soldier who'd spoken with her outside Duffy's house walked in, followed by another soldier. The first man pulled out the empty chair for his colleague, who sat down noisily. He placed a pale blue folder on the table in front of him.

'This is Corporal Harrison,' the first soldier said. 'He has a few questions he'd like to ask you.'

Bernie shrugged as Harrison opened the folder, turning over a couple of loose sheets of paper and studying them intently.

'I'll be outside if you need me, sir,' the soldier said, saluting briefly before marching out the room, closing the door behind him.

Bernie kept her eyes focused on the wooden surface of the table, sensing that Corporal Harrison was staring at her. She could feel her heart pounding though she kept telling herself that she hadn't done anything they could pin on her. She knew that didn't really matter to the Brits, though it wasn't the fact she'd been caught outside Duffy's house which worried her. They knew her name so it probably meant they knew what or who she was involved with. Her heart beat a little faster.

Harrison cleared his throat and she heard him rustling his papers again. She wanted to prepare what she was going to tell him but she didn't know what he was going to ask so that was impossible. Thoughts of Tom and Connor jostled for space in her mind along with ones about her own situation. Tom could be dead now for all she knew. What was he doing at Duffy's house? She might never find that out now, and even if he was still alive, would she ever get the chance to ask him? Would he tell her even if she did? It still seemed strange to her that the soldiers were happy to ignore what was going on behind them in order to arrest her. She wanted to ask about that too but she wasn't going to be the one to break the silence in the room.

She wished she could let Connor know what had happened to her. She hadn't told him where she was going – the opportunity to follow Tom had happened so quickly and unexpectedly that she hadn't the chance to say anything to anyone, though she doubted that she would have told Connor even if she'd bumped into him while she was tracking Tom. She knew he didn't like the Donegal man, blaming him for Eugene's death; she suspected he was also nervous of the fact Michael Collins had sent him to Glasgow and for reasons that had not even been explained to the head of the movement in the city. There was something else too – a trace of jealousy which hung in the air like a bad smell – and it was something she instinctively didn't want to dwell upon.

'What can you tell me about Tom Costello?' Harrison suddenly asked and Bernie looked up quickly as if he'd just read her mind. He sat with his arms folded, his face impassive.

Bernie wanted to shrug nonchalantly like she didn't care what he'd just asked and was letting him know she was in no hurry to give him any answer, but she'd reacted too quickly to his question and her face was turning bright red despite her best efforts to stop it. Harrison picked up a sheet of dull yellow paper and cleared his throat.

'Tom Costello was born in eighteen ninety-two in Donegal. His mother is Kate Costello – sorry, was Kate Costello. She died a couple of weeks ago. Nothing is known of his father. He became active in the republican movement from an early age and joined the Irish Republican Brotherhood sometime between nineteen twelve and nineteen fourteen. He was in Dublin two years later and was captured after the uprising and sent to a military camp in Wales, where he remained for nine months. He was released in late nineteen seventeen and returned to Donegal where he became a prominent and active republican in the area. He is one of the IRA's best marksmen – if not the best – and has been responsible for the deaths of many British soldiers over the past two years.

'Two weeks ago, he arrived in Glasgow on the orders of Michael Collins to assassinate General Sir John Maxwell. He was staying at one hundred and twenty-five Abercrombie Street but, as you know, there was an incident there and he is now hiding elsewhere in the city planning, with the help of his republican friends. . .' Harrison looked up and nodded at Bernie, '. . .to carry out the assassination.' He put down the sheet of yellow paper. 'That, Miss O'Hara, is what I know about Tom Costello.'

Harrison sat back and folded his arms again. He wore a self-satisfied expression that Bernie knew was a result of her reaction to what she'd just heard. Her face no longer burned. Instead, she imagined it had quickly drained of colour and was now as pale as the walls which surrounded her. It wasn't so much the shock of finding out what Tom had been sent to Glasgow for – that was stunning enough and she knew that if he succeeded, it would deliver an incredible boost to the movement, while also settling a few scores from nineteen sixteen. She also understood now why he hadn't told anyone and why Michael Collins hadn't even informed Connor.

What shocked her more was the fact they had so much information about him. It was as if they'd been spying on him for almost as long as he had lived. And how did they know about his mother? The earth had barely been piled up on top of her coffin, yet her passing was registered in black and white on a sheet of paper in an army folder.

Harrison picked up another sheet of yellow paper.

'Bernadette O'Hara. Born on the eighteenth of April, eighteen ninety-six, the fourth child of Denis and Mary O'Hara from Oranmore, County Galway. Your mother died in eighteen ninety-nine. You came to Glasgow in nineteen fourteen, working as a domestic maid for the Lyle family of Pollokshields. In nineteen sixteen, you became involved with Connor Daly and, from there you joined the Irish Republican movement, which you continue to be involved with, though as yet you have faced no criminal prosecution for any of your activities within the city.'

Harrison let the sheet of paper float gently to the desk and tapped the folder with his fingers.

'Would you like to hear any more? Perhaps there's something about Connor Daly that you don't know about?'

Bernie stared at Harrison but said nothing.

'So you see, Miss O'Hara, your secret organisation is not so secret after all. We know who you are, we know what you're up to and we could crush you any time we want.'

Bernie grinned.

'What's so funny?' asked Harrison.

For the first time since she'd been arrested, Bernie found herself relaxing. Harrison was trying to intimidate and frighten her and he'd almost succeeded, but his grand boasts were without substance. If he knew all he said he did, then there would have been no need to arrest her or question her. If the Brits knew everything, they'd know where to find the safe house Tom had been staying in, and they'd also know where and when he planned to kill General Maxwell. Certainly, Bernie knew none of that information but, unlike Harrison, she wasn't pretending that she did.

'You're in a lot of trouble, Miss O'Hara,' Harrison said, leaning forward, 'so there's nothing to laugh about.'

Bernie shrugged, no longer worried by Harrison's voice and immune now to his implied threats. Let them try and find Tom if they could – she hoped at least he was still alive so that he could continue to evade capture. She wasn't going to help Harrison or any other Brit by telling them where the house was.

'So how is your family back in Ireland?' Harrison asked.

'What do you mean?' Bernie said warily.

'Your brother, John? How is he?'

Bernie frowned as Harrison lifted another sheet.

'John O'Hara, aged thirty-one. Arrested last week on suspicion of being a member of the IRA and of being actively engaged in acts of treason against his majesty's forces, the penalty for which, when found guilty, of course, is death.'

'That's a lie,' Bernie shouted, snatching the sheet of paper which Harrison held out for her. She quickly scanned the type-written words, absorbing the details of what had happened to her brother which Harrison had omitted to tell her.

'But he's not guilty,' she said, her voice now beginning to tremble. 'He's not even involved in anything to do with the war.'

'That's not what it says there.'

'But it's a lie,' she said, though this time her voice was no more than a quivering whisper. She pictured her brother. He was a giant of a man, broad-shouldered and bulky, but he was also the gentlest human being she'd ever met and when he smiled, it was the biggest and warmest grin imaginable and it always made her smile too.

He wasn't involved in anything to do with the war, not even hiding weapons or offering a safe haven for any volunteer on the run. He had Noreen and their three children, and they were the only cause that he would ever consider worth fighting, or dying, for. He wasn't happy about what she was doing either. They'd had long arguments about fighting and freedom – well, she argued while he responded in the same calm and measured tone he always did. They would never agree, but it didn't mean she thought any less of him just because he'd chosen a different path, nor him of her.

She had no memories of her mother – she was only two when she'd died – but she remembered her brother kneeling at the side of her bed and stroking her hair as he sang to her until she stopped crying for her mother. He was only eleven but he instinctively knew what to do to make his wee sister feel better and got her to sleep and it was something she had never forgotten.

'My brother is innocent,' she said

'Well, that's for a court to decide, Miss O'Hara, and in a time of war, it is only by dealing harshly with those who would oppose us that we can be assured of victory.'

'I know him and I know he wouldn't be involved in anything like this. This is just wrong.'

'What can I do?' Harrison said with a shrug. 'You, on the other hand, might be able to help him.'

Bernie looked up as a solitary tear fell on the sheet of paper she was holding, immediately smudging some of the words.

'How?' she said quietly.

'You can start by telling me where I can find Tom Costello.'

An Uneasy Peace

Tom quietly closed the front door and turned round. A fist slammed into his face, sending him crashing off the door. As he stumbled forward, the fist hit him again and he collided with the door again, a sharp pain shooting across his shoulder as his wound, which had just about healed, took the brunt of the collision. A heavy boot smashed into his groin and he bent over in agony, his face now at the perfect height to connect with a knee which smashed into his nose. He knew instantly that it was broken. He heard the crack, and the searing pain made his eyes water, temporarily blinding him. He toppled to the ground, landing heavily on the wooden floor and he felt a few blows as he began scrambling desperately for breath like a drowning man.

There was a lull in the attack and he groaned, spitting out a mouthful of blood and what he presumed was a tooth. He couldn't really move and when he tried to, the pain which surged through his body instantly warned him to stop. Even breathing through his nose was now an agonising task, but one that he was unable to cease.

Angry footsteps circled him, the boots no doubt waiting for another excuse to rain further blows on his already broken body. He was determined not to provide that opportunity. He could feel hot breath against his cheek as a face leant in close to his.

'Is that it?' the voice whispered, spraying tiny drops of spit on Tom's cheeks. 'Is that how easy it is? The IRA's top man floored by a couple of punches. I was expecting more of a fight from you. I'm really disappointed.'

Tom remained as still as he possibly could, refusing to react to the taunting voice. He had a knife in his jacket and a pistol stuck into the waist of his trousers, but he was unable to get to either, at least for just now. One false move and the attack would begin again. Tom knew that and was prepared to bide his time, hoping an opportunity to fight back would arise at some point.

'Get him up.'

Other footsteps shuffled towards him before hands grabbed him roughly and hauled him to his feet. He groaned intermittently but it didn't make them treat him any gentler. He was finding it difficult to remain steady on his feet and he was grateful for the physical support of the two men. They dragged him across the room and dumped him roughly in a chair. One of the men gripped his shoulders to prevent him falling over. He looked up through blurry eyes and tried to focus despite the sharp throbbing on the bridge of his broken nose which was competing with the sporadic shots of pain that convulsed his body.

'What the hell have you done?' Connor said.

He was pacing up and down the room in front of Tom, who started coughing and dredged up a mouthful of blood which he spat on the floor. He ran his tongue across his teeth, locating the gap that had just appeared. He tried not to breathe in too deeply. It was sore every time he did so and he suspected he might have broken a rib as well.

He wondered how he looked at this precise moment,

wishing for a mirror so that he could check out the damage Connor had inflicted on him. It was best to assess that first before he decided what the reparations would be. He thought it strange if Connor hadn't anticipated the possibility of revenge, and he wondered how he imagined he could avoid it. Tom wasn't going to let this pass – he couldn't – but for now he wasn't in a position to do anything other than sit and suffer in silence.

'They've got Bernie,' Connor said.

'What?'

'Bernie's been caught. They took her in.'

'Who did?'

'Who do you think? The Brits.'

'The Brits have Bernie?'

Connor stepped forward as if he was going to hit Tom but he stopped, sighing deeply and turning away with a shake of the head.

'I didn't know,' Tom mumbled. 'Is she okay?'

'How the hell do I know,' Connor said, spinning round to face Tom again.

'But what's that got to do with me?'

'They caught her outside Duffy's house while you were inside shooting the feckin' place to bits.'

'What was she doing there?'

'You tell me.'

'Tell you what?'

'What the hell you were doing at Duffy's and why you dragged Bernie into your crazy scheme.'

'But I didn't. I was on my own. I never knew she was there.'

'So what was she doing outside his house then?'

'I don't know.'

'This is a mess,' he muttered, shaking his head. 'A bloody mess.'

Tom shrugged. He didn't know Bernie had been outside Duffy's house and he was as keen as Connor to find out why. More than that, he was worried now because the Brits had her and he knew what they were capable of doing when they caught republicans. He could feel his anger rising at the thought and he clenched his fists. If anyone hurts her . . . the feelings which suddenly surged through his body surprised and confused him. Why did he feel like it would be the worst thing in the world if he didn't see her again? More than that, he was angry and frustrated at his helplessness, not only because there was nothing he could do for Bernie, but also because he was battered and bruised and stuck in this room with three men, one of whom had already proved his enthusiasm for attacking him. If he couldn't even get out of here, then what use was he to Bernie?

'Duffy was important to us.'

Tom spat out more blood, which just missed Connor.

'Is that what Michael Collins sent you over here to do? Was it?'

Tom shrugged.

'Well, what a pointless, stupid mission if it was. Duffy helped us and now you've gone and ruined that.'

'Michael Collins sent me to do a job here and your orders were to help me, nothing more and nothing less.'

'But you don't just turn up in my city and kill our main source of weapons without telling me.'

'This is not your city and you would do well to

remember that. And the Big Fella will not be happy when he hears what you've done to me.'

'He'll not be happy when he hears what you've done.'

Tom knew Connor was right about that. The Big Fella would be furious when he found out what happened, which he surely would because he seemed to know everything that went on.

'So why did you kill Duffy?

'It was personal,' Tom said.

'What?'

'It was personal.'

'Personal? Are you kidding? You can't go about my city killing people and then just say it's personal. Nothing you do here is personal, and don't you forget that.'

'I told you before that this is not your city,' Tom muttered.

'What?'

Tom's voice remained no more than a whisper as he repeated the words to Connor, drawing the other man towards him as he strained to hear what had been said. Tom moved his lips again and as Connor stepped into range, Tom's leg shot up, his boot catching the other man between the legs. The surprise of the attack, and the instant pain caused him to bend over and Tom was immediately on his feet, shrugging off the grip of the guard and crashing his own knee into Connor's face. As he fell back, Tom grabbed the chair and smashed it across the guard's chest, flooring him instantly.

He spun round, ready to resume his attack on Connor but was barged to the ground by the other guard. He threw himself on top of Tom, who struggled to wrestle the man off. His opponent was strong but seemed more content to try and subdue Tom rather than deliver any punches himself. Tom was in pain – his nose, his ribs and his shoulder – and there was a temptation to relax and accept defeat, but he knew Connor was getting to his feet, his face bloody and his temper roused, and it was unlikely he'd escape further physical punishment.

Rolling on to his side, Tom saw a hairy arm and sunk his teeth into it. The guard screamed and released his grip for a second, which was long enough for Tom to smash his fist into the man's face and push him off. Scrambling to his feet, he kicked the man on the chin, knocking him out cold, and then he turned to face Connor who was now on his feet but he seemed to be swaying. His mouth was red and his glasses hung precariously on his face. He looked as if he was deciding whether or not to muster up the strength for another attack on Tom though the element of surprise had gone now, as had the superiority in numbers.

Tom heard a noise to his right and saw the first guard whom he'd struck with the chair standing up and glaring at him. He pulled out the pistol from his waist and cocked it.

'Don't even think about it,' he said and the man took a nervous step back.

Connor too, slowly began to shuffle back towards the door, his eyes staring at the gun.

'I'm not going to feckin' shoot you,' Tom said, clicking the safety catch on and putting the gun back in his waist. It was enough to embolden the other man who suddenly burst forward. Tom stepped to the side as the onrushing body reached him and in the same instant snatched his pistol out again and smacked the handle across the man's skull, sending him crashing to the ground.

'At least there's no brain to damage there,' Tom said, shaking his head. He looked down at the man who lay prone on the floor, blood beginning to trickle out the wound at the side of his head.

'What the hell's happened here?'

Connor and Tom both spun round as Bernie stood in the doorway, arms on her hips. Tom guiltily stuck the pistol back in his waist, suddenly feeling bloodied and bruised and embarrassed. Connor looked as though he was feeling the same way, taking off his glasses and rubbing his eyes nervously.

'Typical bloody Irishmen,' she said, shaking her head. 'You should be fighting the Brits instead of each other.'

She walked into the room, slamming the door behind her and stood between the two men.

Tom sat at the kitchen table and peered through eyes that were slowly closing as the swelling from his broken nose got worse. Connor continued to dab at his own wound with the wet cloth Bernie had given him, but he did so gently, anxious to avoid hurting himself any more than he had to. Tom was glad that he'd stopped spitting blood. Bernie had bathed his wounds too, but none too gently, and it seemed to him that she took a strange pleasure from inflicting pain on him. In truth, there wasn't too much she could do except to clean him up, though he did ask for strapping for his ribs. That was a job for a doctor, she'd said, and suggested he try not breathing in and out so often if it was hurting him. Connor grinned when she'd offered that medical advice and even Tom had to smile.

She glanced over towards the bedroom where one of

Connor's accomplices lay nursing a bloodied and swollen head and not really aware of where he was. They'd had to help Bernie carry him in there, even though every movement was painful for Tom. He was sure Connor felt the same. Bernie had packed the other man off, telling him to get his wife to mend him, but Eddie was in a bad way. The blow of the pistol to his head had been a severe one and Eddie was definitely in need of proper medical attention. Tom wasn't that sorry – he knew if he hadn't fought back then they'd probably have continued beating him – but he still hoped that Eddie wouldn't suffer any lasting damage.

Tom fished out his cigarettes and lit one. He blew the smoke over his left shoulder, away from Connor, though he was sure the other man didn't appreciate or even notice the gesture. If Connor smoked, it would have been easier simply to slide the tin across the table to him, and he could have taken a cigarette as a peace offering; their silent smoking might have at least represented a truce, but instead Tom knew he was wasting his time trying to be considerate.

Bernie picked up the packet and lit a cigarette, not bothering where she blew the smoke.

'A pair of eejits,' she muttered, shaking her head, though Tom was sure he could detect the faintest sign of a smile flickering across her face.

'You're probably right,' he said.

Connor looked up but said nothing.

'No hard feelings,' Tom said, holding out his hand. Connor stared at it, frowning like it was something he'd never seen before in his life. He glanced up at Bernie. He shook his head but still took the outstretched hand, though Tom could tell from the weak grip that it was a reluctant gesture.

'That's better,' said Bernie, sitting down at the table. Both men looked at her.

'So what happened to you then?' asked Tom.

'Nothing.'

'What do you mean, nothing? The Brits had you.'

Bernie shrugged.

'What did they do to you?' Connor said.

'I told you, nothing.'

'So what did they ask you?' Tom asked, lighting another cigarette.

'They just wanted to know what I was doing outside Duffy's house.'

'And what were you doing outside Duffy's house?' asked Connor.

'I was following this eejit,' she said, nodding at Tom. 'And they picked me up while he was starting a bloody war in the house.'

'Duffy's dead,' Connor said, glancing at Tom.

'Why did you kill him?' asked Bernie.

'It was personal.'

'What does that mean' she asked as Connor snorted.

Tom shrugged and drew deeply on his cigarette before filling the air with smoke. Bernie stared at him while Connor sat back and folded his arms, knowing there would be no answer forthcoming.

'So the Brits didn't do anything to you?' Tom eventually said.

'They just asked me a few questions – who I was, where did I stay, what was I doing there. And then they let me go.'

'And are you okay?' Tom said as he flicked some ash on the floor.

'Of course. It would take a lot more than a few questions from a Brit to get me upset.'

'What if they've followed you?'

'They haven't.'

'How do you know?'

'I would have spotted them . . . and anyway, do you think I was daft enough just to walk straight back here and lead them straight to us?'

'Okay, I was just asking.'

'Well, they didn't follow me. Trust me.'

'That's good then.'

Bernie smiled as Connor stood up, scraping the chair noisily off the floor. He walked over to the window and stared out for a few moments before turning round to face them. He leant against the sink and folded his arms.

'I still want to know what happened with Duffy,' he said. 'Why did you do it?'

'Look, he's dead and that's the end of the matter,' said Tom. 'You'll just have to find someone else to get you the guns. He can't be the only man in Glasgow who'll do that for you.'

'But he was the best.'

'Exactly. He *was* the best but now he's not so get over it.'

'You're a feckin' liability,' said Connor, shaking his head again.

'And you've got too much to say for yourself.'

'Stop it, the pair of you,' said Bernie. 'You're acting like a couple of daft boys. Look at the state of you. Honestly, bloody men!'

'I still need your help,' Tom said after a few minutes of smoky silence. Connor pushed the broken glasses back up the bridge of his nose but said nothing.

'What do you want?' Bernie asked, blowing smoke into Tom's face and he blinked, suddenly appreciating Connor's irritation.

'It's a reconnaissance job,' he said. 'I just need to check out a couple of locations.'

'For killing Maxwell?' Bernie asked.

Connor glanced from Bernie to Tom.

'I'll tell you later,' Tom said. 'I just need you to show me a couple of places.'

Connor and Bernie looked at each other for a few moments before Connor nodded.

'Okay,' he said with a sigh. 'We'll help you.'

Reds and Greens

Connor stood leaning against a lamp-post at the end of Cadder Street. His arms were folded and he looked, from a distance, like he was sleeping, his head pressed against the metal pole. Tom kept his eyes focused on the motionless figure as he and Bernie walked slowly towards Connor. Her arms were linked in his and he found the close contact soothing. That probably wasn't the right word, though he didn't want to think of how it excited his mind, which was already full of images of the two of them in bed together. He knew Connor wasn't happy. He felt he could see the rage emblazoned across the other man's face as they approached him and it took all his best efforts not to start grinning. He had insisted on walking up and down the street with Bernie rather than on his own.

'It would be too suspicious otherwise,' he had said to a reluctant Connor, who had eventually agreed, though he had opted to stay in the street himself and not round the corner as Tom had suggested. He knew the Dubliner wanted to keep an eye on him. The animosity between the two men was still there – he could almost touch it as a tangible presence in the air whenever they were in the same room – and as they nursed their respective wounds, they both sensed that the war wasn't over. This was only an uneasy truce brought about by the intervention of Bernie. Neither of them wanted to disagree with her.

She was humming a tune as they passed the house and Tom glanced again at the sandstone edifice. There was no sign of life either in the house or in the grounds and this was the third time they had walked past. He was glad of that otherwise someone might have stopped them with some awkward questions.

He let his fingertips linger over the shape of the pistol which was still lodged in the waist of his trousers and hoped it wouldn't come to that. There was also the knife in his jacket pocket. That was usually his weapon of choice for this type of mission, though he knew he was unlikely to get close enough to Maxwell to be able to use it. He'd probably have to use a rifle, training the sight on the British officer's head and then pulling the trigger, watching the trajectory of the bullet as it whizzed to its target, blowing apart Maxwell's skull on impact so swiftly and silently that he wouldn't feel a thing.

'What song is that?' he asked as Bernie continued humming.

'*The Banks of Roses.* Bronagh used to sing it when she was cooking.'

'Who's Bronagh?'

'My sister.'

'Was she a good singer?'

'She still is hopefully. She said my mammy sang it when she was at the stove and she always felt she should too, like she was passing something on for the rest of us.'

'That makes sense.'

'It's nice, though, isn't it? So it's always been one of my

favourite songs because it's like I'm remembering my mammy, even though it's really only my sister I can picture.'

Tom nodded and smiled as Bernie seemed to take a tighter hold of his arm. This could almost be a perfect afternoon, if it wasn't for the fact Connor was watching them with an intensity which belied his languid pose. If anyone did notice them, they would simply think it another courting couple walking through Glasgow's streets, looking enviously at the buildings and dreaming of the big house that would be theirs when they got married, though knowing that reality always took precedence over romance and there was little chance of that happening in this lifetime, or probably even the next.

They had walked up Cadder Street on the other side of the road and Tom studied the houses facing the one where he knew Maxwell would be staying. One of them would be his hiding place. He'd crouch at an upstairs window, his rifle resting on the window sill, and wait till his target came into sight. He would require more help when the time came. Other people would have to accompany him to subdue the occupants of the house and he knew he'd need some extra fire-power when the Brits came after them, as they surely would.

He'd been surprised to discover this was just a residential street. He had presumed Maxwell would be staying in an army barracks, which would have been impossible to attack or break into, and he'd figured on having to come up with a more elaborate ambush, but when they'd turned into the street, he was taken aback. It was definitely the right address – Michael Collins didn't make mistakes like that – and it also probably made sense too. Who would ever think a top-ranking army general would be living here, while the Brits would hope that the man sent by the IRA was now dead with no-one to replace him.

They were almost back at the lamp-post now and Connor was standing waiting for them.

'Have you seen everything you need to then?' he said impatiently, his hands now in his pockets.

'I think so,' said Tom with a shrug. 'But I'll have one more look, just to be on the safe side.'

Connor sighed impatiently as Bernie slipped her arm out of Tom's and edged over to him, lightly touching his jacket with her hand.

'I just need to be sure of everything in my mind,' Tom said. 'It's too big a job to mess up.'

'We'll not be long,' Bernie said, kissing Connor's cheek gently. He frowned but nodded in agreement and Tom looked away, concealing the sudden flash of jealousy which burst across his face. It was only momentary, and it was unlikely either of them would have noticed, but it happened nevertheless, and it took Tom by surprise. With Bernie now holding on to his arm again, he looked at Connor.

'We'll be ten minutes at the most,' he said and the other man stared coldly at him before resuming his position against the lamp-post, ready, Tom hoped, to shout a warning should any soldiers suddenly appear.

As they walked, Tom could sense that Bernie's grip wasn't as tight as before and he wondered whether a sense of guilt was to blame. But what had she to feel guilty about? They were out on a mission, and the fact she was walking arm-in-arm with another man while her boyfriend watched from afar was neither here nor there. He thought of telling her that, but sensed it was better to say nothing.

They were just passing the house where Tom would hide out and wait for Maxwell when they heard a shout, followed swiftly by a rumble like approaching thunder. Tom glanced over his shoulder as Connor started walking away from the lamp-post towards Albert Road, nodding as he did so at the source of the noise, which had now come into view. An army truck turned the corner and slowly rumbled up the street, followed by a shiny black car.

Tom knew the vehicles were going to stop outside the house across the road and he realised they'd be there before he and Bernie could get to the other end of the street. He didn't know if anyone would stop him – he thought it unlikely but he couldn't take the chance – and someone might wonder why such a modestly dressed couple were in this plush avenue in the first place. He stopped and spun Bernie gently round to face him.

'Sorry,' he muttered before leaning in and kissing her. His hand was on the back of her head, stopping her from pulling away. That would certainly have caught someone's attention. So he continued kissing her, his mind slowly beginning to believe that she was no longer trying to break away from him as her surprise gave way to an acceptance of what he was doing.

'Lucky bastard,' a voice shouted, followed by a few wolf-whistles and cheers. It was soldiers from the truck. He could hear boots crunching on the cobbles and still they kept kissing. Voices were barking orders but he didn't want to look round. The truth was, he didn't want to stop. Suddenly she pulled her lips away from his though, in the same moment, she wrapped her arms round his neck and hugged him, moving her face closer to his until they were almost cheek to cheek.

'If you ever try pushing that tongue of yours into my mouth again, I'll bite it off,' she whispered, pulling roughly on a couple of hairs on his neck, which made him flinch, though he couldn't help grinning at the same time.

'We should go now,' he said and they turned back. Most of the soldiers had disappeared inside the house, but a couple of men were standing at the back of the truck smoking. Both of them grinned enviously at Tom as they passed. No wonder, he thought, allowing himself a quick glance at Bernie, who was once more holding on to his arm though she kept running her tongue across her lips.

The journey back to the house was a silent one, Bernie having transferred to Connor's arm as soon as they had met up with him. He'd slipped away as soon as the soldiers appeared, which Tom was glad of. He didn't think the other man would have appreciated his impulsive gesture, and it would probably have caused another fight. His injuries were still healing from the last one, so he thought it best to avoid any physical confrontations if possible.

The house was busy when they arrived though Tom realised it was mainly full of communists rather than republicans. A few of them threw disdainful glances in his direction and he guessed it was because of what he'd done to Duffy.

Red flags were propped up against one of the walls, while two crates were lying opened in the middle of the room. A young man was sitting beside them, rummaging through the straw and producing a pistol every few moments which he would hold up to the light and inspect before checking the mechanics of the weapon. When he was satisfied it was in good working order – no-one ever really knew for sure until a gun was fired – he placed the weapon on the floor. There were already half a dozen in plain sight and still he kept producing more.

He didn't look any older than twenty, if that. His light-brown hair was closely cropped – like an army haircut, thought Tom – and his blue eyes had an intense focus, whether on the guns or on any of the other people in the room.

'Where did these come from?' Connor asked, kneeling down beside the blue-eyed boy.

'Duffy.'

'But Duffy's dead.'

'A parting gift,' the young man said, looking straight at Tom, who stared back without blinking.

A pistol was held out to him and he took it warily, letting it roll back and forth in the palm of his hand. It was an Enfield revolver, British Army issue, and he wondered again if this young man had military connections, though it could just as easily, or more likely, have been Duffy who had stolen the weapons from an army barracks. Still, it made Tom wary of this stranger, indeed, of all the strangers in the room.

He clicked the catch on and off a few times before handing the gun back with a nod of approval. It was placed on the floor with its companions.

'Jimmy Dougall,' the young man said, holding out his hand. Tom shook it firmly and nodded.

'Tom Costello.'

'So you're the man who killed Duffy then?'

Tom stared at the young man but said nothing.

'That wasn't exactly helpful to our cause.'

'And what exactly is your cause?' Tom asked.

'We're fighting for the rights of our fellow workers against the bourgeoisie who have exploited us for far too long now. We have to rise up and overthrow them like our comrades in Russia and let the workers take control of the means of production so that we can establish a dictatorship of the proletariat which will eventually lead to a classless community society – a workers' paradise.'

There was some applause from the rest of the room.

'Well remembered,' Tom said with a smile. 'What book did you read that in?'

'Marx's Communist Manifesto,' Jimmy said, pulling a battered paperback out of his jacket pocket and brandishing it in front of Tom. 'You should read it sometime. Maybe you republicans could learn something from it.'

'I was born a republican and I'll die one too, and I don't need any book full of fancy language to tell me how to overthrow anyone. Just give me a loaded gun and I'll do fine.'

'Hopefully it won't take us seven hundred years to still not win,' Jimmy said as he put the book back in his pocket.

'You've got a sharp tongue for a young man,' Tom said. 'That could prove a hindrance as well as a help.'

'Sharp tongue, sharp feet,' said a voice from the couch. 'That's Jimmy for you.'

'What are you talking about?' Tom said, looking round.

'Wee Jimmy Dougall was the best player Celtic never had,' the voice said.

'Away you go, Neilly,' Jimmy said with a shake of the head. 'You're just a blether.'

'I'm telling you. What a player he was. What a player.

Better than Patsy Gallacher and that's the truth, as God is my witness.'

'I thought none of you communists believed in God,' Connor asked and the whole room laughed, even Jimmy, who had now stood up.

'That boy would have been a great player,' Neilly said, pointing his finger at Jimmy, 'if it wasn't for some big balloon out in Dumbarton who smashed his knee up. I can still hear that noise even now,' he said, shaking his head.

'Yesterday's news, Neilly,' Jimmy said, shuffling over towards the red flags. Tom noticed the young man walked with a slight but noticeable limp and glanced back at Neilly who was still proclaiming Jimmy's footballing genius to the room. Jimmy was counting the flags and as he flicked through them, one or two fell noisily to the floor.

'Is everything nearly ready?' Connor asked.

Jimmy nodded.

'When is it going to happen?'

'This Friday,' the young man said. 'In George Square.'

A nervous hush suddenly seemed to fall over the room and Tom glanced at each face in turn, eventually stopping when he came to Bernie.

'What's happening on Friday?' he asked her quietly, though he knew the rest of the room heard.

'The revolution,' Jimmy said, taking one of the flags and waving it wildly above his head. 'Up the revolution,' he shouted and the rest of the men cheered, some of them stamping their feet noisily on the wooden floor. They were like excited schoolboys, Tom thought, realising some of them, including Jimmy, still looked young enough to pass for such. He glanced at Bernie, who shrugged.

'There's a rally in the Square,' she said. 'Something to do with the shipbuilders' strike.'

'It's more than just a strike,' said Jimmy, placing the flag against the wall and turning to face them. 'The workers have had enough and they're ready to rise up.'

A few voices murmured approvingly.

'It's happened in Russia and it's going to happen here,' Jimmy declared.

Tom decided not to say anything as the spirit of revolution swirled around the room. Ireland had been fighting the British for hundreds of years and yet they were still entrenched on their island. He hardly imagined the might of an empire that had just won a world war would be trembling at the thought of a few idealistic youngsters waving red flags and brandishing pistols. He would give George Square a miss, he thought. The revolution could do without him.

Running out of Time

'The way to treat these people is to be harsh but fair . . . though you can do without the fair if you have to.'

The room erupted in laughter which seemed to mingle with the clouds of smoke in the air and General Maxwell sat back with a contented smile. He was holding court with his fellow officers, telling grand tales of his time in South Africa and Egypt and, of course, Ireland.

'There is only one thing the Irish understand, and that's force,' Maxwell said, leaning forward and waving his cigar above his head, leaving a trail of smoke in its wake, 'When they look down the barrel of a gun, a British gun, they know then who are their masters and if they don't. . . well, just bloody well shoot them.'

There was more laughter and backs being slapped appreciatively. Maxwell lifted up his glass of whisky, holding it to the light and admiring the sparkling golden liquid.

'Superstitious too,' he continued, taking a sip of his drink. 'They bless themselves every time they sneeze. God help the man with a runny nose. His arm never gets a moment's peace.'

Harrison stood at the doorway, content to be on the periphery of the conversation. His fingers clasped the sixpence in his pocket as Maxwell spoke about luck and he realised he always felt better knowing it was there with him. If the tiny silver coin his mother had given him played any part in his continued survival, then he would be happy to proclaim himself as superstitious as the next man . . . or the next Irishman.

'They breed like bloody rabbits too,' Maxwell said.

'I've half a mind to become a Catholic myself if I end up getting it all the time too,' said one of the other officers.

'I think it's a miracle you need for that, Charles, rather than a change of religion,' Maxwell said and the rest of the room, including Charles laughed. 'I mean, look at that couple going at it out in the middle of the street... in the middle of the street, for goodness sake. And at this time of the day too. Have they no self-control?'

'How do you know they were Irish?' one of the officers asked.

'Because they bloody looked like it,' Maxwell said and the room erupted in laughter again.

Harrison's thoughts turned to the kissing couple outside the house and he was sure he wasn't the only one who'd cast envious glances towards the man who was embracing the red-haired girl. He was already inside the house when he thought of Bernadette O'Hara and he raced back downstairs and out the front door, sprinting to the front gate, having to weave in and out of the other soldiers who were carrying boxes into the house. When he got to the gate he looked up and down the street but there was no sign of the couple and after a few minutes he trudged back up the gravel driveway. He convinced himself it wasn't her. This wasn't her part of the city and, besides, they had an arrangement. He would have been informed if she intended to bring him here, and he'd have been waiting for their arrival.

'To business, gentlemen,' Maxwell said, draining the last few drops of whisky from his glass and slamming it down on the table as if trying to attract the attention of the barman who would glide silently towards him, bottle in hand to replenish the empty glass. Instead, the other officers followed suit and soon there were five empty glasses on the table.

'There's a rally planned for Friday in George Square,' said the officer called Charles.

'A rally!' Maxwell spat out the word venomously. 'More like a bloody revolution.'

'There will be women and children on the march too.'

'That's the coward's way, Charles. Trust me, I've seen it before. Hiding behind the innocent because they think we won't act.'

'They say it's a workers' protest,' said Charles. 'Something to do with their working hours.'

'They should be bloody grateful of a job,' said Maxwell with a dismissive shake of the head.

'What are we going to do?' one of the other officers asked.

'We are going to meet fire with fire.'

'What do you mean?'

'These people, be they Irish or Scottish or communist for all I know or care, only understand one thing – force. And they will soon discover the error of taking on Britannia's guns.'

'Well said, John,' said Charles, and everyone nodded in agreement.

They all shuffled forward until they stood round Maxwell's desk like errant schoolboys called to the headmaster's study, and the General spread out a large white map that Harrison presumed was of Glasgow. As he pointed out various landmarks, occasionally barking orders or suggestions to these senior officers who were still evidently his subordinates, Harrison wondered again why he'd been summoned.

The General wanted an update on his mission – he'd said as much earlier on in the car – and Harrison continued to go over in his head an explanation that would be palatable to his senior officer when the reality was that he still hadn't killed Tom Costello. He'd been close and he was getting closer still, and he was confident the girl would eventually lead him to the Irishman. He saw how she spoke about her brother and there was no way she'd put anything, or anyone, before her family. It was just a matter of waiting but he knew the General wasn't patient. For one thing, he knew Maxwell was anxious to return to England and once the so-called revolution had been crushed then there would be little reason to remain.

He knew his turn to speak would come soon enough, once the officers had been briefed, and he could only imagine that the General wanted Harrison to see him in full flow. To be fair, it was hard not to be impressed. The stature of office, and his physical presence, made him stand out, and he spoke with the confidence of a man who never believed he was wrong and couldn't countenance such an eventuality occurring.

Harrison didn't know too much about what was happening in the city. He wasn't interested either, since after he'd finished his mission here he hoped never to set foot on Scottish soil again.

'Field Marshall Robertson is in charge of the whole operation,' Maxwell was explaining to the other men, 'and he has given explicit orders that we are to assist the local constabulary. They will call upon our services as and when required, but they are responsible for policing in this city and our presence is to assist them and not incite the crowd. However, when we are called upon, we must act decisively and without mercy.'

The briefing continued for another ten minutes before Maxwell called it to an abrupt halt, obviously content that he had delivered all the necessary information to the men who would orchestrate operations on the ground. Cigars were reluctantly stubbed out in the crystal ashtray on the desk, and cursory farewells were offered before the officers all filed out, leaving only Harrison in the room. The General nodded and Harrison closed the door.

'Sit down,' the General ordered as he took a deep draw on what remained of his cigar, blowing a cloud of smoke carelessly towards Harrison, who breathed in deeply. It was an aroma he'd always enjoyed and he hoped Maxwell might offer him a cigar, while knowing that was unlikely.

Harrison was aware of eyes staring through the smoke at him and he kept his own focused on his feet, though he would occasionally glance up, immediately realising the other man hadn't looked away. He felt uncomfortable under the spotlight of the General's gaze and he thought it better to wait until he was spoken to before even venturing to engage his commanding officer in any way. He saw the fading embers of the cigar as it was extinguished in the ashtray and he looked up again.

'We have a problem, Corporal Harrison.'

'Yes, sir.'

Maxwell sat forward, leaning on his elbow and joining

his hands together. He sighed deeply and frowned, his eyebrows knitting together and Harrison had the feeling they were about to have the same conversation as before, though this time his assurances that he would kill Costello were bound to ring hollow in the General's ears.

'You were chosen because you were the best,' Maxwell said. 'That's what I was told and I expected you to have shown me that by now.'

'Yes, sir.'

'So what am I to do?'

Harrison didn't know the answer to that question. The truth was, he was as bemused as Maxwell about his lack of success. He'd arrived in the city fully expecting to have quickly despatched the Irishman to meet his maker and take the plaudits that would undoubtedly have come his way after the completion of another successful mission, but instead he was still here and Costello was still alive and there was no praise coming his way. Instead, he felt he was floundering like a horse stuck in mud, desperately trying to extricate itself and the gun wagon attached to it. At any time a shell was liable to explode, shredding beast and cart to smithereens, and Harrison felt that way too.

He still had confidence in his own ability, and he knew, given enough time, that he would kill Costello, but he was no longer sure Maxwell believed that. Generals didn't want excuses or promises. They wanted results and how those results were achieved was not of any interest. Harrison thought again of the girl, and another fleeting image of the kissing couple outside the house flashed into his mind.

'Three days, Corporal Harrison.'

'Sir?'

'I am giving you three days to kill Costello which, in the circumstance is very generous don't you think?'

'Yes, sir.'

'As you heard, there are other, more pressing matters that I have to deal with so I am giving you one final chance to redeem yourself.'

'Thank you, sir.'

The General puffed on his cigar, looking abstractly at the map which was still sprawled across his desk, occasionally tapping a spot on it and muttering a few words as if he was still going over the instructions he'd given his officers, though Harrison couldn't make out any of it.

Harrison was surprised he'd been given any more time, never mind three days, and he knew this really was his last chance. He could understand why the General wanted the matter sorted once and for all. Costello was in Glasgow to kill him, after all, and if he didn't kill the Irishman, and do it soon, there was a good chance that there would at least be an attempt on the General's life. Three days he had, and he would get Costello within that time. If he didn't, then he didn't deserve the mission, or, indeed, the reputation which preceded him, and he would accept whatever fate lay in store for him.

'We've brought reinforcements in from other parts of Scotland,' Maxwell said, looking up. 'Don't want to rely on the local troops. They might jump ship and we couldn't have that.'

'No, sir.'

'Soldiers fighting fellow soldiers. Heaven forbid,' he said. 'We're not savages, you know.'

'Yes, sir.'

'I feel we've been here before, Corporal Harrison, and I don't want to be here again. Are you clear about what you have to do?'

'Yes, sir.'

'Three days, Corporal. Not one minute more. Three days and I want to see Costello's cold, dead body with my own eyes.'

'You will, sir.'

I hope so,' said Maxwell. 'I certainly hope so.'

In the Heat of Battle

A weak sunlight was trying valiantly to push its way through the grey clouds that hung ominously in the air and it cast a gloomy pallor over the city, while a vicious winter chill scuttled up and down every street, attacking anyone who wasn't well protected against the elements. It was the last day of January and it seemed like everyone had somewhere to go, with people scurrying in all directions, many heading towards the city centre, while others swam against the tide, often muttering warnings as they passed by, though their words were ignored. It was the distant roar, like incessant waves crashing off a cliff face, which was drawing crowds hypnotically towards it. No-one knew what the source of the noise was, but curiosity had gripped many souls; some might have guessed it was connected to the shipbuilders' strike but they wanted confirmation with their own eyes.

Occasionally, an enthusiastic runner would sprint by holding a red flag which billowed in their wake, and several people had to duck or step aside to avoid being hit by the material.

Bernie led the way, followed by a reluctant Tom. He hadn't wanted to venture out, and it had taken all her powers of persuasion to drag him from the house, which had woken to a hive of activity, the hustle and bustle of

Jimmy Dougall and his group strangely alluring, and Bernie found herself caught up in the nervous excitement of the moment.

Connor had left with the communists, arranging with Bernie a time and a place to meet up. He didn't want her venturing into George Square on her own, and she thought better than to mention Tom would be with her. It would certainly have provoked a jealous reaction and she knew Connor had been given some important tasks which were vital to the day. If he were to withdraw now, and Bernie sensed that he would do just that rather than see her on her own with Tom, then everything would suffer, and she knew Connor would feel guilty about that too. He'd find out soon enough when she met him who had accompanied her but by then it would be too late anyway.

She glanced at Tom who was walking beside her. He shivered every couple of minutes as the cold nipped at the bare flesh of his face and neck but he didn't complain. He was wearing a spare jacket that had been left in the house. It fitted, more or less, but it was thin and flimsy, and without a hat or scarf to call upon, Tom was exposed to the elements. She saw him shiver again and impulsively she grabbed hold of his arm, slipping her own in between his and squeezing it sympathetically. She couldn't make him any warmer but at least she wanted to let him know she realised he was cold.

He offered a brief smile in return and she kept hold of him as they continued walking. It wasn't quite as relaxed as when they'd been strolling up and down the posh street, but she still found the physical contact comforting. She'd tried to push that day to the back of her mind, not least because of the kiss. In truth, it was only because of the kiss. It had taken her by surprise, but what left her shocked and continued to prey on her mind was the fact that she hadn't hated it. More than that, she had liked it, enjoyed it, been thrilled by it almost, and her stomach danced erratically whenever the memory of it emerged vividly in her mind, though she quickly tried to submerge these feelings under a tidal wave of guilt.

'I still don't know why we're going here,' Tom said in a shivering voice.

'I said I'd meet Connor in Virginia Street.'

'But what are we meant to be doing?'

'Nothing. Just showing solidarity.'

'With a bunch of daft boys who have no idea what they're getting into or who they're taking on.'

'With our fellow workers and working class comrades.'

Tom stopped suddenly and Bernie almost stumbled, though his free arm provided a welcome barrier and he held on to her until she steadied herself.

'You don't believe all that nonsense, do you?'

'If they win, then maybe we'll win too.'

'They won't win,' Tom said quietly, shaking his head. 'Will we?'

He looked at her and she held his gaze, trying not to look startled as one powerful thought kept racing through her mind in those few seconds. She wanted him to kiss her again.

'I don't know,' he eventually said, and she let out a deep sigh like she'd been holding her breath in for too long.

'Come on,' she said, tugging his arm until he reluctantly began walking again. She wanted to keep moving, as much to avoid succumbing to any temptation to kiss him which she was sure would surprise him as much as the urge shocked her.

As they got closer to the city centre, the streets seemed to be even busier, with people filling up every available space of pavement and road, making the journey of horses and carts, trams and even the occasional car, a slow and arduous one, though none of the drivers wanted to risk the wrath of the crowd by reacting angrily to their presence. It was noisier too, like they were approaching the source of some great waterfall and she felt her step quicken.

She could see a few more red flags in the distance now. They towered above the bobbing heads of the crowd, swaying almost hypnotically in the air. She knew this was a protest about workers' hours. That's what the strike at the shipyards had been called for, but she'd sat in enough smoky rooms on the periphery of conversations that Jimmy Dougall and his comrades had with Connor to know there was a grander plan.

Would they succeed? She hadn't really thought about it before, but Tom was adamant they wouldn't. Certainly, many of them seemed so young and idealistic, as Connor had once described them, comparing their fanaticism to his – their – own for the republican cause. She thought of them as innocent rather than idealistic though she hoped they wouldn't lose either trait when they came up against the Brits. She'd already seen what it had done to Connor, and she suspected it had made Tom the way he was. She didn't want to see that happening to Jimmy and the rest of the communists.

They turned into Ingram Street, Bernie nudging into Tom to guide him that way when they were blasted with an almighty roar which almost knocked the two of them off their feet. They both stopped, stunned at the scene of chaos developing before their eyes. People were running in every direction, some shouting angrily while others were screaming frantic warnings. Sporadic groups of men would gather together and then charge in the same direction, propelled by deep, aggressive shouts, towards the line of policemen strung across the road. The officers moved to meet them, swinging batons and dodging punches or improvised weapons aimed in their direction.

One policeman crumbled to the ground as a long piece of wood – it looked like it had previously held a flag – cracked his skull and the attacker immediately began kicking the prone body before other officers came to their colleague's aid, bundling the attacker over and launching their own assault on him as he tried vainly to scramble to his feet. All over the street, there were mini battles going on, with bodies writhing on the ground, trading blows and shouting what Bernie was sure were furious swear words, but the sum of all these cries simply gathered into one collective din which rose up into the air, buffeting the buildings on either side of the street which almost seemed to visibly tremble.

'Come on, let's get out of here,' Tom said, turning round and grasping her hand as the sound of a charge raced along the street towards them. Bernie glanced over her shoulder as a long line of policemen sprinted towards them, crushing anything that stood in its path.

They began running, re-tracing their footsteps as they turned into Glassford Street, which was a similarly chaotic scene of fighting and screaming and shouting, and Bernie tried to keep as close as possible to Tom as he cleared a path for them to race through.

Suddenly a hand gripped her arm and she screamed out as the fingers squeezed tightly on her flesh. She looked round as a policeman started dragging her back towards the noise and the crowd and, she presumed, a waiting van which would cart her off to jail. She let go of Tom's hand and swung her arm at the officer, slapping him hard on the face. She was twisting her body frantically, trying to escape the vice-like grip, and she aimed a few kicks at the man, though none managed to connect.

A sudden blow crashed down on her shoulder and she sagged to the ground, the strength temporarily sapped from her legs. The policeman kept a tight hold of her arm, preventing her from falling and she glanced up as he brought the chunky black baton down angrily towards her head. She flinched and closed her eyes, anticipating the inevitable blow which she was sure would crack her skull and knock her out cold but it never came.

Instead, her arm was suddenly freed from the officer's grip and she was being dragged in the other direction, Tom's rough hand clutching hers and propelling her along the street. She managed to glance back and saw the policeman on his knees, holding his face in his hands as blood dripped through his fingers, his baton rolling aimlessly across the cobbled street in front of him.

There were plenty of other people racing in the same direction, some in silence while others shouted and screamed with an urgency borne out of fear. There were many policemen in the street, pursuing them all and attacking people with a random viciousness that shocked her. Two of them stopped at their kneeling colleague and began examining his bloodied face, though one of them continued to swing his baton at any passers-by within reach, felling an old woman who was shuffling along as fast as her weak feet could carry her, clutching her shawl tightly to her chest. She fell instantly, cracking her head off the ground and she lay perfectly still. Most people side-stepped her, while one or two tripped over her, falling down and then springing back up to continue their frantic escape without concern for their own injuries.

Bernie turned away and stared at Tom's back. He kept a firm hold of her hand as they ran, occasionally bumping people out of the way, after which he'd glance back at Bernie, offering a smile of reassurance which she gratefully accepted. A policeman suddenly stepped out from the side of a building, brandishing his baton and spreading his arms to block their way. Tom's head smashed into the man's face, immediately flooring him, and they kept running without breaking stride.

Her shoulder was aching now like a crushing weight had been placed on it and a couple of times she tugged on Tom's hand, trying to get him to slow down but he either didn't feel it or was ignoring it because they continued running at the same pace. She was out of breath too and it was as if someone was sitting on her chest, trying to crush her rib cage. She shouted on Tom to stop but her cry was quickly lost amidst the shouts and screams already tearing the air all around them.

Whether he suddenly sensed that she was struggling or it was just God answering her prayer, he suddenly slowed down to a brisk walk and Bernie was grateful of the respite. They were now almost at the water and as they crossed Jamaica Street Bridge, she could sense Tom relax slightly and she did too, as if they'd now put enough distance between themselves and the riot, though the bedlam of the ongoing chaos still floated in the air after them, an audible reminder that they had to keep moving. They would only really be safe once they were back in the house, with the door securely locked behind them.

Tom lit two cigarettes, handing one over to her, and they sat smoking in silence, both of them digesting what had just happened. Bernie kept adjusting her position on the seat to try and ease the pain which at times seemed to stretch across her shoulder and down her back, but any relief she enjoyed was only temporary and the pain soon returned, at times even more painful than before.

'Let me a have a look at your shoulder,' Tom said, finishing his cigarette.

'It's fine,' she said, shaking her head, though she flinched as she tried to move her arm to prove to him that she wasn't hurt.

'Look, it's not fine,' he said as he stood beside her.

'You're not a doctor, so what can you do to help?'

'Well, you're not a nurse but I still let you treat my wounds.'

She shrugged, which sent a burst of pain shooting down the left side of her body, and she didn't have the strength to keep arguing with him. He seemed to detect the change of attitude and leant in closer to her.

'What are you doing?' she said.

'I'm having a look at your shoulder.'

'I take back what I said.'

'What?'

'You'd make a great feckin' doctor, so you would.'

'And you make a feckin' terrible patient, so you do.'

He stood back and folded his arms, a sudden yawn breaking out across his face which he didn't try to suppress.

'Sorry, am I boring you?'

He shook his head and frowned, but said nothing.

'I told you, I'll be fine,' said Bernie, stubbing the cigarette out in a small saucer already filled with dead cigarette ends.

'You'll need to take your blouse . . . can you take it . . . even just to. . .'

'Just spit it out! You want me to take my blouse off?'

'No, I mean . . . well, I need to have a look. Even if you just slip your blouse off your shoulder?'

'Fine.'

Slowly she began unbuttoning her blouse until she was able to slip it off and she shivered as her bare shoulder was suddenly exposed. She shivered again as his fingers cautiously touched her flesh. It wasn't that they were cold, or even that the roughness of his skin was uncomfortable. It was the feel of an unfamiliar hand on her that unnerved her.

'Can you lift your arm?'

'Not really.'

She tried moving her arm up and down. It was painful, though with each movement it became slightly easier.

'Is it sore here?' he asked, squeezing the edge of her shoulder.

'No.'

'What about here?' He squeezed a little further in.

'No.'

'Here?'

'YES!'

'Sorry.'

'That's sore.'

'Sorry.'

Her shoulder throbbed where he'd squeezed it, though she felt another touch on it. She froze and it was as if all air had suddenly been drawn right out of her and she could hardly breathe. Her stomach began churning and her heart thumped wildly.

'What did you do there?' she asked nervously.

'What?'

'Did you kiss my shoulder?'

There was silence behind her though she could feel his breath gently caressing her skin. Then there was the same feeling again. This time she was sure. He'd definitely kissed her. Still she didn't move, though her stomach was doing somersaults now. He kissed her again. His lips seemed to be targeting the source of her pain and she realised that she hadn't noticed it for a few moments. She knew she should tell him to stop but she could barely muster up a breath never mind a word.

His lips continued to touch her skin, and she closed her eyes, letting out a low moan that startled her and made open her eyes again, though almost immediately his face was in front of hers, his lips pressed hard against hers, his tongue in her mouth – she wasn't going to bite it off now – and she was responding to his kisses, wrapping her good arm round his neck and pulling him even closer to him.

Suddenly she felt like she was floating and she kept a tight grip of his neck as he slowly shuffled to the bedroom, instinctively knowing where he was going and all the while continuing to kiss her. His leg kicked open the door and then she was back on solid ground as he lowered her gently on to the bed, immediately following suit and lying on top of her. She dragged her skirt up until she could wrap her legs round his waist, realising as she did so that she hadn't thought of the pain in her shoulder. It was still there, she knew, but she no longer cared.

She lay on her front and peered through the strands of sweaty hair which had fallen across her face and stuck to her skin. Tom was sitting up in bed, his back against the wall, smoking a cigarette.

'You know you took advantage of an injured woman?' she said.

'How's your shoulder?'

'Bloody sore,' she said and he grinned.

'Sorry.'

'I'm sure there must be something about doctors sleeping with their patients. I don't know if that's allowed.'

'Well, you did say I'd be a feckin' rotten doctor.'

Bernie laughed and buried her head in the pillow, letting out a tired but contented smile. She wished she could lie here all day, just the two of them; what she really wished for was that they could repeat exactly what they'd just spent the past half-hour doing, but that urge shocked her, and she realised too, that there was a tiny warning sounding in the back of her mind that Connor might return at any moment and she didn't want him to walk in on this.

She could feel Tom running his finger gently up and down her spine and she groaned again. It felt somehow smoother and colder too, even though her body wasn't that familiar with his touch, but it was still soothing and she didn't want him to stop.

'So how do you know about Maxwell?'

This time she did stop breathing. In the same instant so too did the caressing of her back, though it halted at the base of her spine and she could feel pressure slowly pressing down on her flesh. It was still cold, though now she realised it was as cold as steel and she felt like she dare not breathe. His voice was different too, emotionless, and she still wondered how he was able to switch so quickly and effortlessly from his previous gentle tone.

'Are you the traitor in the camp, Bernadette O'Hara?'

The pressure on her back increased a little more and she sensed that any sudden movement would be a bad idea. She shook her head and whispered 'No,' but her reply was lost, smothered in the pillow which her face rested on. A hand roughly gripped her shoulder and she screamed out in pain. He pushed her over until she was on her back. Her hands searched for the edges of the cover so she could pull it up and hide her nakedness. She was scared, terrified even, and her vulnerability was multiplied by the fact he knelt above her, a knife in his hand and the expression of a dead man on his face.

He now ran the tip of the blade up and down her body from her throat to her waist, dragging it gently back and forth several times across her flesh and she hardly dared shiver. She'd stopped grasping blindly for the cover but instead lay frozen, though she continued staring at Tom, hoping to re-connect with those eyes which had previously soaked up every inch of her body appreciatively as she'd straddled his waist.

'Who told you about Maxwell?' he asked in the same cold tone, the knife coming to rest on her throat. She felt that, if she tried to speak, the tip of the blade would pierce her skin though she also realised that silence wasn't an option.

'There are only two people in the movement who know about Maxwell, and neither of them is you, so how do you know?'

'They told me,' she mumbled weakly.

'Who?'

'The Brits.'

Tom's expression was suddenly confused rather than cold, but still she didn't want to nod confirmation to his question because the knife remained pressed against her throat.

'What do they know?'

'Everything.'

'What do you mean, everything?'

Bernie let out a tiny cough, affected enough to let him know she wasn't comfortable with the knife on her flesh.

'Sorry,' he muttered, placing the weapon down on the pillow and grabbing a handful of the cover from under him and tugging it up until it concealed the lower half of her body. She took hold of the material gratefully and kept pulling until it was up at her neck, a more soothing feeling against her skin than the cold steel of the knife.

'What do they know?' Tom asked, his voice suddenly quieter, and almost back to the way it had been before.

'They know you're here to kill Maxwell, and they want to kill you before you do.'

'When did they tell you that?'

'When they took me in for questioning. They want me to tell them what's going on.'

'With the movement?'

'No, with you. I've to tell them where they can find you and then they'll. . .'

'I know, they'll kill me. . . So, what did you say?'

Bernie looked away, biting her bottom lip guiltily.

'I'm sorry, Tom,' she whispered as tears began streaming down her cheeks. 'I had no choice.'

'You were going to betray me?'

'They threatened to shoot my brother. What could I do?' She stretched out an arm – it was her sore one and the pain in her shoulder was almost bad enough to make her scream, but she managed to hold it in. Her fingertips lightly brushed his arm, but he flinched and immediately pulled away.

'I'm so sorry,' Bernie sobbed, burying her head in the cover. Tom hadn't moved from the bed, which was good, and he hadn't taken up the knife again, which was even better, but she didn't know what else she could say.

'So who did you speak to?' he eventually asked.

She peeked out from the edge of the cover. He stared at the bare wall in front of them.

'Harrison,' she mumbled.

'Who?'

'I think his name was Harrison. Corporal Harrison.'

Tom repeated the name a couple of times, nodding his head, but saying nothing else. She continued looking at him, though out the corner of her eye she caught sight of the glint of the blade and she said a silent prayer that he wouldn't pick it up again.

Nerves of Steel

When Tom left the room, Bernie continued lying in the bed, wrapped up in the cover that was still damp from the collective sweat of their bodies that had not long before been wrapped around each other, but which were now as cold and distant as strangers. The sound of the bedroom door closing seemed to be a trigger for her emotions to be unleashed and she cried; tears of relief, fear, guilt and longing all poured down her cheeks.

She could hear him moving around the other room, though she still didn't get out of the bed. She knew she should, and get dressed quickly too. What if Connor did come home at this very moment? There could be no explanation that would make any sense other than the obvious one, and she didn't want to hurt him like that. She also didn't want Tom to hurt him either, and if Connor found out, then she knew there would be trouble; she didn't think, in a straight confrontation between the two, that Connor would come off best.

Bernie sat up and pulled her knees to her chest, hugging them tightly and still crying, though her sobs were quieter now as her body drained itself of emotion. She roughly pushed the hair away from her face and made a half-hearted attempt to wipe the tears off her cheeks, but they were quickly replaced by others still spilling from her eyes, and she realised it was a futile task. Her clothes were scattered all over the floor and she slid to the side of the bed, lowering her feet on to the cold floor. She still kept the cover wrapped round her bare flesh just in case Tom should suddenly burst back into the room.

She suspected he wouldn't, however, and that feeling was confirmed when she heard the front door opening and then being slammed shut. That sound seemed to blow away the heavy weight resting on her shoulders and she could feel herself relax as she picked up the various garments that had been so urgently removed, Tom becoming increasingly excited as more of her flesh was revealed.

It didn't take her long to get dressed and after making the bed up as best she could to disguise what had just happened – she retrieved an old jumper from a drawer and threw it across the cover to hide the tell-tale creases that she believed would scream out her guilty secret – she walked over to the sink. The cold water she splashed on her face was like a slap, though it seemed to sharpen her mind. Connor would be back, whether in the next few minutes or next few hours, and she had to act as though nothing had happened. Gathering up her hair, she quickly fastened it back with a white ribbon that she retrieved from her pocket.

Tom had left his cigarettes lying on the table and she took one out and lit it with trembling fingers, inhaling it gratefully and finding the nicotine filling her lungs strangely soothing. She didn't know where Tom had gone, though she hoped he wouldn't return any time soon. She tried to push to the back of her mind what had just happened, though he'd made that slightly easier with what he'd asked her to do.

'I want you to go to Harrison and tell him where I'll be,' he had said to her as he gathered up his clothes in the bedroom.

'What?'

'I'll give you a time and a place and you let him know.'

'You're crazy.'

'Just do it.'

'No, I will not! He'll kill you and I don't want you to die.' The last word caught in her throat and she almost began crying at that point, though she managed to push the sobs back down into her stomach like she was swallowing poison rather than spitting it out.

She'd thought that, if someone had asked her at that precise moment whether she loved or hated Tom, she would have instantly chosen the latter emotion. She definitely didn't love him. That much was true. How could she? She barely knew him, but she knew deep down she didn't hate him. How could she after what had just happened? She knew for sure that she didn't want him to die.

'He's not going to kill me,' Tom said. 'I'll be waiting for him and when he turns up, I'll kill him.'

'What if you don't?'

'I'm better than he is,' he said.

'He might suspect.'

'Not if you convince him. Besides, he's a Brit so he'll not be that smart.'

He held the bundle of clothes in front of him casually,

though it did provide a tiny shred of decency which she was grateful for. She wouldn't have known where to look otherwise. He was staring at her, waiting for her answer. It was impossible to figure out what he was thinking. Those eyes, which had been alive as he'd lain on top of her, the pupils dancing excitedly with each thrust, were now chillingly still, like they'd just been painted on. She didn't even think he was picturing what lay under the modest cover, though the images would still be fresh in his mind.

'I don't know,' she eventually muttered, shaking her head, a stray bead of sweat escaping from her hair and running down her forehead. She wiped it away with a tiny edge of the cover.

'It'll be fine,' he said. 'Trust me.'

She looked up at his face as he spoke, knowing in her heart that those two words were difficult to associate with him. She nodded slightly, which was enough confirmation for him to turn and head out the room, his backside the last thing she saw before the door closed.

The thought of his bare arse brought a tiny flicker of a smile to Bernie's face for a moment, though she quickly shook her head to dispel it. There was really nothing funny to the situation, either about what she'd done, or what he'd asked her to do. And what of John? Her brother's life was still in danger and if she betrayed Harrison to Tom, then he was liable to face a firing squad, and she couldn't bear the thought of that. What if she betrayed Tom to Harrison? Then he would be dead, and she didn't want that either.

She continued sitting at the table, working her way through the rest of Tom's cigarettes, oblivious as to how long she remained there, though it was an hour at least. Her daydreaming was abruptly interrupted by the sound of urgent footsteps approaching up the stairs and then the door being noisily thrown open.

Connor led the way, followed by Jimmy Dougall, who was propped up by two of his comrades, one on either side of him. His arms were draped across their shoulders as they carried him into the house, his feet dragging heavily across the floor.

'What's happened?' Bernie asked, standing up.

'It's okay. Jimmy just struck his head on a police baton, that's all.'

Jimmy managed a weak laugh as he was lowered on to a chair with a groan.

'We'll need to clean him up and bandage that,' Connor said, looking at Bernie, who waited a few seconds before realising she was being asked to undertake this task. She hurried from the sink to the bedroom and then to Jimmy, having managed to conjure up a basin of tepid water and an old towel which she ripped in two, one half to bathe the wound and the other half to dry it. Each touch seemed to bring a fresh groan from Jimmy, though he immediately tried to offer a reassuring smile so that she would continue; it was a painful attempt, however, and it merely made his face look contorted.

'That was crazy out there,' Connor said, taking a seat beside Jimmy and watching Bernie as she worked. 'The police were out of control.'

Jimmy nodded, and then groaned.

'Don't move your head, you eejit,' Bernie said.

'Sorry,' whispered Jimmy.

'Where were you?' Connor asked. 'I waited for a while in Virginia Street but we had to get away when they charged.'

'I was heading that way too but we had to run away. One of them got me on the shoulder,' Bernie said, shrugging her shoulder slightly, suddenly aware that it was sore again.

'Who's 'we'?'

'Me and Tom,' she said, hoping her voice didn't sound too shaky.

'Tom?'

'He fought off the policeman who was trying to arrest me.'

'So where is he now?'

'I don't know. He just went out.'

'He left you here on your own when there are policemen on the rampage all over the city?'

'He's not long away,' Bernie said defensively, feeling her face beginning to burn as she did so. Connor didn't notice, his eyes remaining focused on Jimmy's head, which displayed an impressive gash where the baton had connected, though she could see he was frowning.

'So he brought you back here safely?' he eventually asked.

'Yes,' she nodded.

'And then what?'

'What do you mean?' She could sense a trace of panic now laced in her voice.

'What did you do then?'

'We just sat smoking and waiting for you to come back. Why? What do you think we were doing?'

'Nothing,' Connor said with a laugh, holding his hands up defensively. 'I was only asking.'

'Well, that's all we did.'

'So where did he go?'

'I told you, I don't know. He just went out without saying anything.'

Connor shook his head as Bernie finished bathing Jimmy's head and stood up.

'I'll need to get a bandage for that,' she said. 'You don't want any dirt getting into the wound.

'Thanks,' Jimmy said.

The door clicked open and Tom walked in. The three of them turned round though Tom never said anything as he closed the door. He walked over to the table and picked up the cigarettes, examining the packet and raising his eyebrows as he looked at Bernie.

'Sorry,' she muttered.

'It's fine. I've got another packet,' he said, patting his pocket.

He strode over to the far wall, sitting down on the floor and lighting up a cigarette, blowing clouds of smoke out in front of him that he evidently wanted to provide a degree of camouflage or privacy from the other three people in the room. No-one said anything, though they all studied the silent smoking man.

There was little in the way of conversation filling the room. A brief discussion on what had happened earlier in the day quickly petered out – Bernie figured they were all too exhausted and shocked to really talk about it – while a chat about what they would do next ended even quicker. Bernie stood at the sink and then she sat down, tapping her foot nervously on the floor.

'That's not annoying at all,' Connor eventually said.

'Sorry.'

'What's up with you?'

'Nothing. I'm fine,' she said, though she was sure, even as she offered such reassurances, that Connor could see through her lies and into her black soul. Maybe he could smell Tom on her, she thought, edging back on her seat to put a tiny bit of distance between them, though she realised that thought didn't make sense. All the while, Tom sat against the wall, smoking quietly and staring aimlessly ahead of him.

There was a knock on the door and heads spun round in unison to face the wooden frame. Connor slowly got up while Jimmy slipped a hand inside his jacket, no doubt taking a grip of the revolver Bernie guessed was in his pocket. She hoped it wouldn't see the light of day. The last thing they needed was another shoot-out, especially with the army crawling all over the city. They might be looking for communists but she was sure that a few dead Irish rebels would be viewed as an added bonus.

'Who is it?' Connor shouted and a muffled voice replied. Evidently satisfied with the answer, Connor unlocked the door and pulled it open. Pat Devenney rushed into the room, almost breathless.

'What's wrong, Pat?'

Pat panted a reply that no-one in the room could understand and Connor told him to slow down and start again.

'They've – killed – Father – McNeill,' he said.

'Who has?'

'I don't know. The Brits?'

'Why would they kill an old priest?' Connor asked. 'That doesn't make sense.'

'All I know is that they found him in the church and he'd been murdered.'

'It can't be the Brits,' said Connor, shaking his head. 'They wouldn't just kill a priest.'

'Maybe they thought he was helping us?' Jimmy said.

'A man of God helping a communist? I told you, it doesn't make sense.'

'Maybe they thought he was helping you?' said Jimmy with a shrug.

'No, that makes even less sense,' said Connor. 'Father McNeill wasn't like that.'

'He wasn't into politics?'

'No, he hated the Irish,' Connor said. 'He would as soon see us hang as help us.'

Bernie glanced over to where Tom sat, his head pressed against the wall. A cigarette hung lazily out the edge of his mouth which he puffed on without ever taking it out. He must have sensed she was looking at him because he looked over and his eyes, cold and calculating, caused her to look away. Where before he'd sent shivers of pleasure through her body, now there was fear. She slipped her hand into the pocket of her skirt and her fingers grasped the piece of paper she'd retrieved when it had fallen out of Tom's jacket.

She'd memorised what was written on it and those words jangled in her head now. It had read *Father Angus McNeill, St Francis' Church*. It was the name of the dead priest and Bernie now wished, as she stole a quick glance at Tom, that she'd destroyed it. She could feel Tom's eyes boring into her and she wondered whether he knew what had happened to the piece of paper? He had never once asked about it.

She wanted to feel sorry for Father McNeill, though the only thing running through her mind was a memory of Tom's knife slowly snaking its way up and down her body before resting on her throat, and she knew she was lucky to be alive, though she was confused too. Her stomach continued to churn every time she looked at him, and she realised, guiltily, that only part of that was due to fear.

Secrets and Lies

'Tanks!'

The shout startled everyone in the house and heads turned in the same instant to face the excited voice. Tom guessed the boy was about ten-years-old. He wore a grey jumper that looked as though it had been through several previous owners. It was at least two sizes too big for him and hung down well below his waist, while he'd had to fold the sleeves up several times until there was a thick chunk of material at either wrist. His grey trousers were dirty at the knees, and out of one of them peeked the tiniest trace of flesh through a hole in the material that would only keep getting bigger. He wiped his nose casually on a sleeve, mopping up stray traces of snot with his hand which he then ran through his unkempt hair.

'What's up, Jackie?' Connor asked, standing up and walking towards the boy.

'There's tanks out there.'

'Where?' Jimmy Dougall said with a derisory laugh.

'In the streets. I seen them. They're massive, so they are.' Jimmy laughed again.

Connor crouched down until he was head height with the boy.

'Are you sure, Jackie?' he asked.

'Cross my heart and hope to die,' the boy said, making

the sign of the cross. His face had an innocent intensity that seemed to convince Connor, who straightened up and went to ruffle Jackie's hair, but thought better of it.

'Where are the tanks, Jackie?'

The boy turned his head and pointed at the door.

'Are they in the town?'

Jackie nodded.

'What are we going to do?' Connor said, turning towards Jimmy.

Jimmy shrugged.

'I can't believe they've brought in the tanks,' Connor said, standing up.

'I can,' said Jimmy. 'Any excuse to try and crush us.'

Tom was tempted to say 'I told you so,' but thought better of it.

'If it's a war they want, then that's what we'll give them,' said Jimmy, standing in the middle of the room. A few cheers from some of his comrades greeted his words, though Tom felt like groaning.

'You did good, Jackie,' Connor said, patting the boy on the shoulder and slipping what Tom presumed was a small coin into the youngster's hand. The boy glanced down at his palm, a grin suddenly breaking out across his face. It was so wide Tom thought it might crack the edges of his mouth. Jackie quickly plunged his hands into his pocket, eager to hide his sudden treasure, while also enjoying its reassuring touch.

'Remember, if you see anything at all just tell me,' Connor said and the boy nodded, no doubt imagining the future financial rewards that would come his way in return for fragments of information. The boy quickly skipped out of the house, eager to get back on the streets. The sooner he got there, the quicker he'd be able to return with more news.

The rioting had continued throughout Glasgow for most of that day and into the next. There were regular visitors to the house, some reporting on the latest skirmishes, while others stumbled through the door in need of medical attention or even just a place to rest weary limbs for half an hour.

Jimmy Dougall had assumed command of the house, something Tom thought he did with far too much ease for a young man, though Connor didn't seem to mind. Certainly, the blue-eyed boy, once he'd got his head bandaged up, had restricted his orders to his fellow communists. The republicans, Tom included, remained silent spectators, though occasionally Connor and Jimmy would disappear out the front door, no doubt to whisper secrets in the dull shadows of the close. Tom didn't care, just as long as no-one organised him into doing anything.

Jimmy evidently sensed that reluctance which almost seemed to shimmer from Tom's body like heat waves off the ground on a summer's day. The communist leader had wanted to go back on to the streets as soon as his wound had been treated, but the multitude of voices protesting at the prospect of him returning to the fray were loud and powerful enough to dissuade him, for a few hours at least.

It had seemed like there was a never-ending flow of people in and out of the house, and Tom soon stopped paying any attention to who they were or what was being said. Jimmy's voice, which continued to bark orders, soon blended into the background, while the voices of those who reported on what was happening out on the streets in excited, agitated or even weary tones, became like the drone of a distant engine that never quite came into view.

Tom sat at the kitchen table nursing a cup of tea that had long ago gone cold, though he was still reluctant to drain the last few drops of liquid. His hands were wrapped round it and his eyes lazily studied its white surface, which had been chipped and stained through time.

A stream of steaming liquid suddenly began to trickle into the cup and he looked up, startled. Bernie smiled at him as she filled the cup with fresh tea and then glided back over to the stove where her own cup lay, proceeding to fill that one too. Tom was aware that the sound of the tea splashing into the cup was the only one he could hear and his eyes quickly scanned the room.

'Where is everybody?'

Bernie didn't answer as she put the teapot down and picked up her cup, taking a gentle sip out of it. Tom frowned. It seemed like the whole house was empty. A couple of red flags lay on the floor with a few stray strands of straw scattered on top of them, the only traces from the crates which held the guns Duffy had supplied. There was no sign of the crates or the weapons, and Tom feared they were now out on the streets, ready to be used by callow youths who would face at least the equivalent firepower – he suspected it would be much more – and a vastly more experienced enemy.

He watched Bernie as she continued drinking her tea. She would catch him occasionally when she glanced over, though he didn't bother trying to hide the fact he was staring at her, his eyes running up and down her body, remembering every naked inch that he'd committed to memory. Yet, he kept being drawn back to her hair, red and fiery and hypnotic, and he wanted to grab on to it again as she arched her back, tugging harder with every thrust, their grunts and groans mingling into one frenzied noise.

'Are you okay?' she asked as he shook his head to try and dispel the images, though he knew the best he could hope for would be that they sank to the back of his mind for a while at least. He couldn't afford to get distracted now, not when there was so much at stake. He'd decided on a time and place to confront Harrison, and had already carried out the necessary reconnaissance though he'd still to tell Bernie, and he had to focus on that. It was a life or death issue, and if he wasn't ready and prepared, then his death would be the issue. Yet, whenever he caught the outline of her breasts pressing against the material of her blouse, he immediately licked his lips as he remembered running his tongue over them.

'Tom, are you okay?'

'What?'

'You seem miles away.'

'I'm fine.'

'Are you sure?'

He nodded, though in the same instant he almost groaned as she leant across the sink to put her cup in it, and her breasts seemed to hypnotise him once more. He ran his hand through his hair and nipped the back of his neck to try force himself to concentrate on anything but Bernie's body.

'I've got the information for you to give Harrison,' he said.

'I'm still not happy about it,' she said, folding her arms.

'I told you, it'll be fine.'

'He wants to kill you and –'

'I know, but I'll kill him first,' he said with a smile.

She shook her head angrily but didn't say anything else. He could tell she was agitated, her eyes scanning the room looking for tasks to keep her occupied, and he liked watching her as she moved, marvelling to himself how clothing could hide such a wonder as her body, giving little in the way of clues as to what lay beneath the layers of material. He was glad he'd managed to find out and once again he found his mind filling up with images and sounds that thrilled and excited and frustrated him at the same time.

There had been few words between them since it had happened, though he guessed the fact that it had finished with him running the tip of a knife up and down her flesh wasn't an ideal starting point to any relationship. And then there was Connor. He was still her . . . Tom didn't really know what he was. Her boyfriend? Lover? He knew they weren't married, and he'd seen little sign of affection between the two of them; what there was he knew had mainly been for his benefit.

'Where's Connor?' he asked.

'He's away with Jimmy and the rest of them.'

'Why aren't you with him?' he asked.

'Because I'm here with you,' she said.

She had stopped moving about and stood, hands on hips, staring at him. He felt like she was challenging him in some way – he didn't know for what, though – but still he stood up slowly and walked over to the sink. Her eyes never strayed from his and her arms were already wrapped tightly round his neck as their lips met. He spun her round and shuffled towards the table as her kisses became more urgent. They stopped moving when she bumped into the kitchen table and she sat up on the edge of it, wrapping her legs round his hips and drawing him in even closer to her.

He pressed against her, drawn on by each eager groan and suddenly he felt like he was tumbling forward as she lay back on the table. His braces hastily unhooked and his trousers dropped to his ankles, he clambered up on top of her as she hitched her skirt to her waist. Their lips met again and she bit his tongue as he moved gently back and forth, his knees balanced on the edge of the table, though his movement quickly became more urgent as he forgot his precarious position.

There was another groan, louder and more high-pitched than before, which Tom took as a sign of approval and he thrust himself forward with a groan of his own, though in the same movement, the legs of the table collapsed and they crashed to the ground. He still lay on top of her, but didn't move.

'Are you okay?' he asked nervously as she buried her head into his chest, her sobs enough to make him run his hand soothingly back and forth over her red hair, the frenzied urge to continue what he was doing now gone; he was suddenly aware of a draft on his bare arse and he wished he could pull his trousers up, though he didn't want to stop consoling Bernie. Gently moving back so that he could see her face, he spotted tears streaming down her cheeks.

'What's wrong?'

She shook her head.

'Bernie, are you okay?'

Suddenly she was howling, and it took him a few

moments to realise that she was laughing; not just laughing but shrieking, and soon he was joining in.

'I thought you were hurt,' he eventually said but she shook her head. Slowly he pushed himself off her as she wiped the tears from her cheeks and sat up.

'What will we do about the table?' she asked as they both got to their feet.

Tom studied the broken piece of furniture as he slipped his braces over his shoulders.

'I don't know.'

The table was beyond repair. One of the legs had broken in two under their collective weight while the other three legs had snapped off at the base of the table on impact with the floor, making them almost impossible to fix.

'I don't know,' he muttered again.

He felt a hand slipping into his and he looked down.

'It'll be safer in here,' Bernie said as led him towards the bedroom. He glanced back at the broken table one final time before stepping into the bedroom, kicking the door shut with the heel of his boot.

She lay with her back pressed against him and he draped his arm across her body, every now and then kissing her flesh, making her shiver each time he did so. They were both naked though the cover he'd pulled over them provided a degree of warmth, and the heat transferring from her body to his was enough to keep him excited, though she'd shrugged off his renewed advances with a lingering kiss and a warning that they'd have to get dressed soon and try to do something about the table before anyone returned to the house. He'd been content enough with the close contact and she had, as yet, shown no great urgency to leave the bed.

He tried again, kissing the nape of her neck as his hand gently caressed her breasts. Encouraged by her deep sigh, he began moving his hand down her stomach towards her waist, all the time his lips covering her back and shoulders with kisses. Suddenly she pulled away from him.

'Did you hear that?' she whispered urgently.

'What?'

'That noise?'

'Where?'

'In the next room. There's someone out there.'

'I didn't hear anything,' he said, his hand trying to resume its journey down her body. She slapped it.

'We need to get up. There's someone in the house.'

She sat up and quickly slipped out of bed, gathering up her clothes which were scattered across the floor. Tom leant on his elbow, content to watch her moving quickly round the bed.

'What if it's Connor,' she said, suddenly groaning. 'Tom! Hurry up and get dressed.'

He shrugged, but got out of bed as she glared at him and threw some of his clothes at him, hitting him in the face. He laughed.

'Ssh!' she hissed. 'They'll hear you.'

Once they were both dressed, they stood at the foot of the bed and stared at each other.

'We can't go out together,' Bernie said.

'Well, you go out first.'

'Me?'

'Okay, I'll go first.'

'No!.'

'Bernie!'

'Okay, you go first. . . but what if it's Connor? He'll know something's happened if I come creeping out behind you.'

Tom shook his head and walked over to the door. He'd intended to pull it open aggressively, but as his hand touched the handle, instinctively he turned it gently and slowly opened the door, peeking his head out.

'It's fine,' he said after a few moments, opening the door wide so that Bernie could see out into the room.

'It's only Jackie,' he said and Bernie sighed, her shoulders visibly relaxing.

The boy sat, cross-legged, on top of the broken table, munching on a slice of bread that he clutched with a dirty hand.

'Are you okay, Jackie?' Bernie asked as she brushed past Tom and headed towards the boy.

'How long have you been here?' she asked.

Jackie shrugged.

'That looks like a nice piece,' Bernie said, nodding at the bread.

'Where's Connor?' Jackie asked.

'He's out fighting the soldiers.'

Tom leant against the door frame, arms folded, and studied the boy whose own concentration was directed towards the bread which was diminishing in his hand every time he took a bite.

'When will he be back?' Jackie asked.

'Soon, I think,' Bernie said, glancing to her right as she sensed Tom now standing beside her.

'Have you got any more information, Jackie?' Tom asked.

'It's Jack.'

'What?'

'My name's Jack,' the boy mumbled, his mouth now full of the remainder of the bread which he'd stuffed in.

'Okay, Jack,' said Tom. 'Do you have more information for Connor?'

The boy nodded, standing up on the table as the bread crumbs on his clothes tumbled to the floor like tiny specs of snow.

'I'll come back later,' he said, walking to the door, and neither of them made any attempt to stop him. When he'd closed the door behind him, Bernie looked up at Tom.

'Do you think he heard anything?' she asked.

'Probably.'

'Oh God,' she said, putting her head in her hands.

'He won't understand,' Tom said, prising her hands away from her face.

'I hope you're right.'

'I am,' he said, leaning in and kissing her slowly and gently, though he sensed she wasn't convinced.

'You need to go and see Harrison now,' he said, kissing her again to stop her protesting. They remained standing in the middle of the room, kissing for a few minutes until he led her towards the door, which she opened hesitantly. It had to be done, thought Tom, and the sooner the better.

Battle Stations: Part I

Tom set the revolver down on the table and stared at it. He'd checked it several times and it was in good working order. He didn't want to say 'perfect' since he knew there was always the slim chance that it would jam at precisely the wrong moment. If that was to happen today, then he knew what in all likelihood the consequences would be for him, but he didn't dwell too long on that prospect. The gun would work and it would do its job. It was fully loaded and he had spare ammunition in his jacket pocket just in case it was required. He picked up the revolver and checked one final time that every carriage held a bullet, then clicked the safety catch off and on again. He smiled briefly, satisfied that the weapon wouldn't let him down, and placed it on the table again.

He brought out the knife which he kept in the inside pocket of his jacket. Its steely blade, cold and deadly, sparkled in the weak dawn sunlight hovering shyly in the room and he turned it round in the palm of his hand. If he was as sure as it was possible to be about the gun, then he was absolutely certain the knife wouldn't let him down. It had never done so in the past and, if called upon today, it would do what was required once more. He wasn't sure whether he'd have the opportunity to use it, however. That would depend how close he got to the Brit, but if he did get near enough to smell his breath, then the knife would slice through the other man's skin effortlessly and with fatal consequences.

Tom touched the tip of the knife with his forefinger. He wondered how it had felt when he'd dragged its sharp point up and down Bernie's skin. He knew she was scared – terrified even – as he towered over her. He saw her body shiver and felt the tremors as she lay on the bed. She knew that one false move and the blade would cut her open. He'd wanted her to be scared but at the same time he felt guilty, having lain naked with her just minutes before. He had needed to discover how she knew about Maxwell, though even as the knife ran across her body, his mind was in turmoil. What if she was the informer? He'd have to use the blade on her and that would have been a terrible, if necessary thing for him to do.

He wasn't sure if her story was plausible, or if it was just because he wanted to believe her. It hadn't dampened the desire which now seemed to infuse every cell in his body, and he'd convinced himself of her innocence when they'd been alone in the flat. At least if it was to be his last time with a woman, then it would be a fond memory to take with him to his grave, though he wasn't intending to occupy his final resting place just yet. Whether it would be his last time with Bernie was another matter, regardless of how this day turned out. That would depend on her – and Connor – and they'd not spoken about anything beyond the moment.

It would have been a waste of time and effort anyway. A conversation of 'what if' and 'what could be' had no place in their lives right now, especially not when he was preparing to meet the man who'd been sent to Glasgow to kill him.

'I don't want you to die,' she'd whispered in his ear as he sat on the edge of the bed, pulling up his trousers. He'd started to speak, ready to offer the same reassurances as before, but she planted her lips on his, silencing him with a kiss that was more than just passionate. He knew, as their lips moved gently in perfect synchronicity, that she cared about him, and he realised he felt the same way about her too.

There would be plenty of time for conversations later, he thought, even though in his mind he pictured scenes of tortured silence when the things that they both wanted to say remained unformed words in their mouths. If only she could read his mind, then it would save him a lot of emotional turmoil.

Tom slipped the knife back into his jacket, blade first, and took a deep breath. He was going to kill a man today and it wasn't something he took lightly. It was his job, and he was good at it, and if he didn't do it, then he'd soon be lying with a bullet in his body and his blood moistening the ground. Still, he acknowledged that the Brit – Harrison – might be a husband and a father; he was certainly somebody's son and his mother would mourn the death of her son, if no-one else did.

His mother wouldn't mourn his death, he thought, sighing deeply as he realised it had been a couple of days since he'd thought of her. A quick wave of guilt washed over him and he wondered whether, one day, some years down the line, he'd forget about her completely. He shook his head as if trying to dispel the thought from his head. He knew that would never happen. His mother was the only woman he'd ever loved and she had loved him absolutely. If she'd been alive, she would have mourned him with a pain that only a mother could feel for her child; her wails would have been heard from Donegal to the ends of the earth and her tears would have drenched the mound of earth covering his coffin.

Instead, it was she who was lying in the ground, the soil heaped up in a pile which was dry and thirsty from the lack of tears shed at that graveside. One day he would stand in front of her and say a proper goodbye, though he didn't know when that would be.

The house was quiet, still in a state of slumber along with the various bodies scattered in the living room. Exhaustion from the constant fighting and tension on the streets had ensured that most of those who'd staggered back last night quickly and gratefully grasped the opportunity to shut their eyes and rest their bodies, even if it had meant lying on the floor. Several of them took it in turns to stay awake and reasonably alert, just in case any unwelcome visitors suddenly arrived at the house, taking up vigil on the landing outside the front door. Tom had opened it slightly and peeked out. A black-haired youth sat at the top of the stairs smoking a cigarette and staring aimlessly ahead of him. He didn't appear to hear the door open and Tom quietly closed it again.

He lit a cigarette himself, holding his breath as he struck the match, but no-one seemed to stir, and he sat down at the table, content to smoke in silence, his eyes locked on to the revolver. His free hand drifted aimlessly to the medals round his neck and instinctively he clutched the medal of Our Lady that had once been Danny's. If he hadn't thought about his mother for a couple of days, it had been much longer since he'd given any consideration to his cousin.

He closed his eyes and remembered the wet hills of Donegal and the dark stained ground where Danny fell. He shuddered and squeezed the medal harder, and Danny's face was there before him. Tom smiled and it was as if his cousin saw him, a grin breaking out across his face as he winked at Tom, and he opened his eyes again with a smile, immediately locking on to the gun. He picked it up and stuck it into the waist-band of his trousers.

He knew Bernie was sleeping in the bedroom, lying side by side with Connor, or perhaps they were wrapped together. He didn't even want to imagine that was the case. She had asked him to wake her before he left.

'I just want to say goodbye,' she'd said.

'But I'm coming back.'

'I know.'

'I'll be home before you know it,' he said, kissing her forehead as she sighed.

'I just want to say –'

'Not goodbye.'

'Okay, good luck then.'

He'd agreed, knowing as he did so that he'd leave her sleeping. It was better for both of them that there were no goodbyes. There was nothing more to say, not now at any rate. When he came home – and he was sure now that he would, his confidence soaring after Danny's wink – it would be a different matter. Of course, there was still his main task to complete, but that too would be easier once Harrison was out of the way.

How did the Brits know he was here? That thought

kept gnawing away at the back of his mind. Only he and Michael Collins, as far as he was aware, knew about this mission, though he had to presume that the Big Fella had told someone back in Ireland. He'd have to get word home that there might be a spy in the camp, just as he suspected there was one in Glasgow too.

He finished his cigarette, taking one final deep draw until the tips of his fingers began to feel the heat and then he dropped the end into the saucer and let it fizzle out itself. He stood up, his mind beginning to narrow its train of thought and focus on what he was about to do. He had to concentrate now. When he was part of an ambush there was a sense of detachment; he was just one of a group and he would generally not get close enough to any of his victims to even give them a moment's consideration.

This was different, however. It was one man against another and the best man   or the luckiest   would win. He wanted to give himself every advantage and the fact he was able to choose the time and setting for their showdown would, he hoped, provide the crucial differ-ence. This wasn't a fair fight but he made no apologies for that. Since when had the Brits ever fought fairly in Ireland anyway? This was a fight to the finish. One of them would walk away while the other would be lying dead. He had no intention of suffering that fate.

Tom opened the front door of the flat and gently closed it behind him, walking to the top of the stairs where the black-haired boy looked up with a nod before resuming his vigil, staring with a tired focus down to the next landing, a cigarette hanging lazily out the corner of his mouth. Tom stepped past him – he couldn't have been much older than eighteen at most – and walked down the stairs, feeling the cold air from the street slowly creeping towards him the nearer he got to the mouth of the close.

He shivered as he stepped out into the early morning, a grey pallor hanging over the street, which was deserted except for a scruffy black dog drinking from a puddle at the side of the pavement. It looked up briefly as Tom walked past, before continuing to lap the dirty water. Tom patted his jacket, feeling the outline of the knife under the material and he did the same thing with the gun.

As he reached the end of the street, he turned the corner and heard a bark. He glanced back and saw the black dog looking towards him. He smiled, taking the solitary noise from the animal as a final message of good luck, and he quickened his stride, a sense of determination and urgency now beginning to surge through his body.

Battle Stations: Part II

Harrison nestled the rifle in his arms like a father with his newborn son, and gazed down at in fondly. There wasn't much he trusted in this world, not after all that he'd seen and done these past few years, but he had absolute faith in this weapon. It never answered back and it never let him down; he knew it would never lead him towards his own end. Instead it was his biggest protector. In turn, he cared for it with a paternal love that he didn't think he would be able to conjure up even if he was ever to produce a son and heir. That was an unlikely prospect and it wasn't one he wished to dwell on, reminding him, as it did, that he was alone in this world.

That wasn't quite true. His parents were still alive and staying in the same house in Coventry that he'd grown up in. It had been a while since he had visited them, though if asked, he couldn't give one genuine or acceptable reason why this was the case. Weeks had become months, which had turned into years, and the longer he went without seeing them, the harder it felt for him to turn up at their doorstep.

Not that his mother would complain. She'd welcome him home like the prodigal son, smothering him with hugs and kisses and preparing a huge feast to celebrate the occasion, sending his father out to proclaim to the world that their son was home again. He imagined his father's face, traces of disapproval managing to escape from an otherwise brow-beaten expression.

Harrison gently laid the rifle down on the camp bed in front of him as if it was a sleeping baby and he was wary of waking it, before taking out the sixpence from his pocket. He wondered if his mother still remembered that she'd given it to him all those years ago. It was just a tiny piece of silver yet he felt invincible with it in his pocket. He thought about tossing the coin in the air and calling 'heads' or 'tails' to see if he would be successful this morning, but he decided against it. He wasn't keen on leaving anything to chance today. There was too much at stake. Possibly General Maxwell's life. Definitely his own, along with his career if he managed to survive this encounter with Costello but failed to kill him.

He'd been surprised when the girl had come to him with the information from the Irishman and he eyed her suspiciously, immediately suspecting a trap. He might have persuaded the girl to work for him after threatening to execute her brother, but that didn't mean she wouldn't have gone straight back to Costello and revealed everything, vowing to work against her blackmailer. If that was the case, she was prepared to risk, in her own mind at least, her brother's life. The truth was, Harrison didn't even know if the authorities back in Ireland had John O'Hara in their sights, but since information was power, he'd been able to present a convincing case to her, knowing she had no way of checking the veracity of the story.

'Are you setting me up, Miss O'Hara?' he'd asked, leaning forward in his chair.

'No,' she'd said, shaking her head.

'He wants a meeting, just the two of us?'

She nodded.

'And when you say 'meeting', what exactly does that mean?'

'It means that one of you is going to die.'

'So why should I believe you?' Harrison had asked with a frown.

'Because it's the truth. He knows about you. He threatened to kill me if I didn't tell him.'

'So he knows I'm here to kill him.'

'Yes.'

'Well, he's making it easy for me if he really does want to meet up.'

'I told him he was stupid and he'd end up getting killed, but he wouldn't listen.'

The girl had sighed deeply, almost mournfully at that point, and Harrison sensed then that it wasn't a trap. She seemed genuinely worried for the Irishman, and so she should be.

He glanced at the rifle again, imagining it in his hands, the butt pressed tightly at his shoulder as he stared through the sight and focused on the target that was still moving and breathing until he squeezed the trigger. The first time he had shot something, he'd felt exhilarated. It had been a deer, a small, scrawny creature which had strayed from its parents and was standing, alone and lost in the middle of a clearing amidst the small cluster of trees near his home. His father had nudged him gently, nodding towards the animal, and Harrison quickly looked through the sight of the rifle.

'Take your time,' his father had whispered in his ear and he'd composed himself, taking a deep breath and studying the animal for what seemed like an eternity but was probably only about thirty seconds in total. All the instructions his father had given him now reverberated in his mind about keeping his head still, his hands steady and his eyes focused. His fingertip touched the trigger and he could feel his heart racing. The deer was still rooted to the spot. Only its head moved as it scanned the area for any sign of its companions.

'Steady,' his father's voice counselled. Harrison closed his eyes for a second, then opened them and stared at the animal, squeezing the trigger and feeling the harsh recoil of the rifle as it slammed into his shoulder – he'd later admire the bruise it left as a badge of honour.

The roar of the rifle filled the air, scattering birds into the sky with a frantic flurry of wings, though he could never ever figure out if the deer managed to hear the noise before the bullet slammed into the side of its head. The animal dropped instantly to the ground as Harrison continued looking through the sight that now focused on some shrubbery which had previously been hidden by the deer.

'Well done, son,' his father had said, patting his shoulder as he got to his feet. Harrison remained lying on the ground for a minute or so until he felt his heart-rate return to its normal pace. He could feel himself smiling, however. No, it was more than that. It was a massive grin and he felt the happiest he had ever done in his life at that point.

Harrison realised now, as he remembered the moment, that he'd never been able to recapture that feeling, no matter how many men he'd gone on to kill. With each one, there was only a sense of relief that it had been them and not him. People fell around him. Some of them were strangers but others were men who had become like brothers to him through their lives – and ordeal – in the trenches – and he mourned each one like he had lost a member of his family. Even then, he was always glad it was them and not him.

Standing up, Harrison dropped the sixpence back into his pocket and stretched before glancing down automatically at his feet. His boots, as ever, were parade-ground gleaming. His mother would be proud.

He picked up the rifle and slung it over his shoulder, walking briskly out of his room and down the corridor, not concerned that his footsteps were echoing off the walls noisily and liable to wake some of the other soldiers who were sleeping in the dormitories. He'd been afforded his own room for the night and he was grateful for the privacy, though he'd not slept much.

He'd lain staring at the white ceiling, his thoughts fluctuating between killing the Irishman and kissing the red-haired girl. It was her hair which dazzled him. He'd never seen anything which seemed to burn so brightly, and when she was sitting across the desk from him he was tempted to reach out his hand and touch her hair, like a curious child whose fingertips couldn't resist the dancing flames of a coal fire. He was glad he hadn't, however. It would have alarmed her, though given the fact she'd been arrested, there wasn't much she could have done. He didn't want to scare her, so he'd fought the temptation, trying not to let his eyes linger on her hair.

He wondered what it would feel like to kiss her. It had been a long time since he'd kissed a woman, at least one that he hadn't paid for. That was different. That was a business transaction and he could sense the lack of response to his promptings. He wanted to feel his heart soar as lips met and know that her heart was feeling the same way too. A name crept into his ear, whispered quickly by the ghosts of his past, before disappearing again, leaving him with a memory that was both fond and painful at the same time.

'Hannah.'

The ghost whispered again, just in case he hadn't heard the first time. It needn't have bothered. He was already thinking of her while trying not to. He knew he couldn't afford to clutter his mind when he had to focus on killing Costello. Her hair hadn't been red. It was blonde. That was how he remembered it when he'd gone off to war, vowing to return to her while she promised to wait for him. He knew that she was waiting. Every letter told him the same thing. He wrote back to her, hoping that his words offered the same pledge to her.

It was a letter from his mother which told him the news. No-one really knew how it happened; a careless stumble most likely, a clumsy everyday movement normally never remembered, but which, in this instance, had projected her, fatally, into the busy road. 'A terrible tragedy,' his mother called it. He kept that letter even after he burned all the other ones which had promised hope for the future. She had been waiting for him, but then she was gone. Hannah.

Harrison reached the front door and stepped briskly out into the early morning chill. He found the slap of the cold air on his cheeks strangely refreshing and he breathed in deeply. He began to empty his mind of any thought except that of the Irishman. He remembered the photograph General Maxwell had shown him and he closed his eyes to conjure up a vivid image of the man. He was confident now that he'd be able to recognise Costello in the middle of a snowstorm, and imagined standing over the dead body of the Irishman, satisfied that he'd completed his task, at last.

'Are you alright there, Corporal Harrison?'

The voice startled Harrison. 'Just focusing my mind,' he said with an awkward smile.

'Whatever keeps you happy. Are you ready to go?'

Harrison nodded and walked across the courtyard, his boots crunching on the hard tarmac surface.

'How long will it take us to get there?'

'Not long,' the voice said. 'It's a strange place to choose.'

'I think it's perfect,' Harrison said. 'Very clever. I'd have done the same thing myself. And it's always an advantage when you choose the battlefield.'

'Well, we've got strength in numbers,' the voice said and Harrison nodded.

'I hope that'll be enough,' he said.

'Don't worry,' the voice said with a laugh. 'Tom Costello is going to meet his maker this morning and what better place to do so?'

Harrison didn't say anything else, wary of over-confidence, which was as much of a danger as any lack of preparation might prove to be in any operation. He knew Costello was good – the IRA wouldn't have sent just anyone to kill Maxwell. They'd chosen their best man, and Harrison was well aware that he would have to be at his best if he wanted to make the return journey to the barracks. He discreetly slipped his hand into his pocket until his fingers touched the sixpence and he smiled, knowing his mother would be looking over him again.

The Killing Fields

Tom stood at the foot of the grave and stared at the small granite headstone. His hands were in his pockets, which he realised was probably a bit disrespectful, but it was still cold at this time of the morning so he kept them where they were. The world was beginning to wake up as he'd walked purposefully towards the cemetery, keeping his head down and tracking his own footsteps rather than catch anyone's eye or attention; he looked, to the casual observer, like a labourer scurrying towards his place of work, or at least to where he'd heard there might be some on offer, and he wanted to get there ahead of the other desperate souls also searching for work in the city.

In this place, however, there was no sign of life, an irony that almost forced a smile on Tom's face. Sunlight was trying to stretch itself out across the grounds, but it was struggling to achieve any success, and a gloomy light like a gas lamp in thick fog hung over the cemetery, as if it couldn't decide whether to be day or night.

Sporadic patches of mist silently rolled across the grass; underneath lay the dead of the city, most long buried, though a few were not long deposited here, going by the mounds of freshly stacked earth and bundles of flowers covering them. Tom shivered as the mist hovered round his knees and he knew trying to kick it away would be a futile gesture. He shivered again and pushed his hands deeper into his pockets looking at the names on the headstones.

Harrison went over everything one last time with the men and they nodded in silent agreement, though whether they were actually taking everything in remained to be seen. They would split into two groups and enter the cemetery at different points. It was important to engage Costello as soon as possible in order to identify his position and trap him.

His final instruction was short and to the point, though his whispered words seemed to hang chillingly in the early morning air.

'Shoot to kill.'

Tom knelt and wiped at the granite with his bare hand. His palm quickly became dirty and he switched hands, though the same thing happened to the other hand. After a couple of minutes he stood up, his knees cracking as he did so. He looked at the stone and the lettering, which was now discernible.

Instinctively he clutched the medals round his neck as he stared at the words which told him that this was where his father lay. He didn't think of his father, though. How could he when there were no memories to conjure up save for a few fragments of overheard conversations? Instead, it was his mother's face which appeared before his eyes and he realised the next time he'd see her would be in a place like this, standing over her graveside in Donegal.

It had been surprisingly easy to locate the grave. Admittedly, he'd required some help from the Church, but the Highland priest had been most co-operative. Tom found that a sharp knife pressed firmly against the quivering flesh of an exposed throat was a particularly persuasive argument, and Father Angus McNeill had gone out of his way to check Church records for him.

He'd been another involved in delivering Dan Foley to the Brits all those years ago though, like Walsh, had probably thought his part had been forgotten, but the Irish Republican Brotherhood hadn't forgotten. Michael Collins hadn't forgotten. It might have been twenty-seven years since Dan Foley had been captured in this city and sent back to Ireland to be executed, but time did not lessen the treachery of those who had betrayed him.

Whether the priest thought his willing assistance now would spare his life or not, Tom didn't know, but once he had found out that his father lay in St Peter's Cemetery, he despatched the priest to meet his maker, though not before he'd found out that his other clerical target, Archbishop Eyre, was already dead. Tom was relieved. It meant one less person to kill.

He'd sliced through Father McNeill's throat and let the body fall to the ground, not waiting until the priest had breathed his last. He knew, as the desperate gurgling grew fainter with each stride away he took, that it wouldn't be long.

Harrison had sent three of the men to the far side of the cemetery, telling them one final time to spread out. At least if Costello shot one of them, the other two would have a better chance of returning fire and hopefully killing the Irishman before he could get off another shot. Harrison and two of his soldiers were going to climb over the wall.

One of the men was already sitting on top of it and was taking his colleague's rifle before the other man quickly scrambled up the bricks. Handing his own rifle up to the first man as the second one dropped down into the cemetery, Harrison hesitated. He put his hand in his pocket and touched the sixpence, closing his eyes for the briefest of moments.

When this was all over he would go home to Coventry and visit his parents. It had been too long an absence and he suddenly looked forward to sitting in the front room, a coal fire providing a welcoming heat, while his mother hurried between the living room and the kitchen, fussing over her only son. His father would bury his head in his newspaper, pretending not to care, though Harrison knew he'd be secretly delighted.

He held the coin tight for a few more seconds until he could feel himself relax, a sense of reassurance washing over his body because he knew his mother would be there with him when he entered the cemetery, and she would keep her son safe, and alive.

Tom let go of the medals and touched the headstone one final time. As he did so he heard a faint crash behind him and he was suddenly alert. Something, or someone had fallen to the ground. There was a larger headstone four plots down from his father's grave and Tom took up position there, crouching down on one knee behind it and peering out from the side towards where the noise came from as clouds of mist continued to roll across the ground in front of him.

He could feel the dampness soaking through the material of his trousers but it didn't bother him. This was nothing compared to lying on a wet and cold Donegal hill for hours at a time. He took out the revolver, and as quietly as he could, clicked the safety catch off. He knew that even the faintest of sounds would travel in the eerie silence of a graveyard and he didn't want to give up his position so easily.

Harrison landed beside the other two men, a sharp pain instantly slashing through his knee as he hit the ground. He shrugged it off, though it appeared again when he moved forward to take up his rifle. He gestured for the two men to spread out, one going to the right, about ten yards away, while the other did the same thing on his left flank. Crouching low, Harrison began moving forward slowly, aware of the pain in his knee, though there was nothing he could do about it. His two colleagues took up similar positions and the three of them began moving slowly into the cemetery.

Harrison's eyes scanned the area in front of him, looking for any sign of Costello, but all he could see were shadowy outlines of gravestones through the mist.

After advancing a few yards, he gestured for the two men to halt, and they all took up positions behind gravestones, their rifles pointing out nervously. Harrison waited for a couple of minutes, his eyes scanning the terrain in front of them, before slowly, and painfully, getting to his feet. His men followed suit and they resumed their slow advance.

Tom waited and watched. Patience was one of his great strengths and he was prepared to stay in this position for as long as was necessary, though he suspected that it wouldn't be a long wait.

A lone cry from a crow hidden in the branches of a tree behind him echoed across the graves and when Tom stared through the faint mist again, he spotted a movement. It was as if the crow had been shouting a warning to him and he nodded gratefully towards it. He was tempted to join the bird in its high vantage point and take out Harrison from there, but if he wasn't successful with his first shot, then he'd be a sitting target. He preferred to be on the ground where he could utilise the protection of the dead and their stone memorials. Besides, he had made preparations for this and it wouldn't work if he was perched up a tree. He pointed the revolver at the moving shadow and waited.

Harrison's knee was sore. He hadn't been able to shrug off the pain and he really wanted to stop and sit down so that he could rest for a few minutes. He gestured for the men to halt and they did so instantly, taking up positions behind gravestones again.

The man on Harrison's right took off his cap, placing it precariously on top of the gravestone and wiping his forehead with a white handkerchief. A sudden roar seemed to rise up out of the ground and the man disappeared. It took a moment, as the sound reverberated through the air, before Harrison realised the man had been shot. He dropped to the ground and began crawling towards his colleague, while the other soldier fired a couple of shots towards an invisible target.

He knew straight away the man was dead. The legs were still twitching but there was a gaping hole in the man's face. Snatching the cap from the gravestone, Harrison hastily placed it on the man's face before grabbing the spare rifle and crawling back to his previous position. A shake of the head told the other man the bad news.

Tom didn't wait to see whether he'd hit his target. He was already sprinting away to his right as the bullet sped towards the man. It had been a good shot and he was confident it had been a successful one as well. It had been the white cloth which had given him his first clear sighting. Until then he had only made out dark shadows, created by the mixture of weak sunlight and sleepy mist.

A couple of shots were returned as Tom ran, though he had no idea where they landed. He skidded to a halt behind another stone – a grey Celtic cross that didn't offer perfect concealment, though it was ideal for shooting through.

Harrison remained behind the large stone, leaning against it until he'd regained control of his breathing. He'd accepted in his mind the inevitability of losing someone on this mission. The Irishman was good – he already knew that – and he realised that he might have to sacrifice a man or two in order to find out where Costello was hiding. Now he did, and he told himself that the man hadn't died in vain.

He took out his own handkerchief and hung it on the end of his rifle which he then dangled out from behind the gravestone. He did this several times without provoking any response, and he eventually decided it might be safe to move forward again. Slowly standing up, he began moving out from behind his hiding place, with the man to his left following his lead.

Harrison's own rifle was poised and ready to use, while the dead man's weapon was slung over his shoulder. His knee still hurt and he limped slightly, though it didn't stop him. It couldn't.

All he needed was one sighting of the Irishman and he would be able to do what he was best at. Failing that, of course, there were three other men approaching from a different position. The numbers were stacked heavily in his favour and he knew Costello didn't have long to live.

Tom peered through the Celtic cross, the revolver in his hand and ready to be called upon at a moment's notice. He'd quickly managed to control his breathing, which was rapid and, if not subdued, threatened to reveal his hiding place.

The roar of the gun continued ringing in his ears and it felt like it still hung in the air as well. It had shattered the morbid tranquillity of the cemetery, scattering all the resting birds. The watchful crow had also gone, flapping its way towards the clouds without any sense of what was going on.

The Brit now knew for sure that Tom was here, and he also knew it wasn't a game. For all Tom knew, it could well have been Harrison that he'd just shot, but something told him that wasn't the case. He'd guessed that Harrison wouldn't have come alone.

That would have been a fatal error and his adversary was smart enough to realise that. It might have been the more honourable thing to do – certainly the message he'd asked Bernie to pass on had said he would be alone – but Harrison wanted him dead no matter what.

There was no honour in keeping to the terms of the challenge if you ended up with a bullet in your brain. Tom didn't begrudge Harrison for bringing back-up. His plan had anticipated such an eventuality.

He didn't know how many men Harrison had, however, and he realised that if it was too many, then no amount of preparation was going to be enough to keep him alive.

Harrison stopped again, though they'd only gone a few yards. He told himself it was because of his knee which was now throbbing. He half-expected to look down and see that it had ballooned to twice its size, though when he did glance at his trousers, there didn't seem to be anything untoward.

He was wary of being out in the open where he would be a target for Costello. It could just as easily have been him who'd been the recipient of the Irishman's bullet, and if he had been, it would have been all over for him. He still had the sixpence in his pocket, however, and that was keeping him safe. He touched it again for reassurance before moving forward again, still slowly and still in pain.

Tom could see shadows moving again and he aimed his gun at them. Just have a little patience, he told himself, resisting the urge to squeeze the trigger. One of the shadows was beginning to take shape as it got nearer. A man was emerging out of the mist. He was wearing dark clothes, while his cap was pulled tight on his head, making it difficult to see what he looked like. That was probably better, thought Tom. He preferred not to put a face to any man he killed so that they remained a mere statistic.

He took aim, ready to stop the man in his tracks, and his finger had started to press the trigger when he heard a noise like a chicken's neck being broken. He realised it was a heavy foot snapping a loose branch on the ground. There was someone behind him as well.

Harrison could see the Celtic cross standing tall and proud above the flat headstones. It was obviously the grave of someone important because the monument would have cost a lot of money. He adjusted the rifle on his shoulder while keeping his own weapon trained on the open ground ahead of him.

He spun round suddenly and automatically fired a shot towards the rustling sound which had caught his attention. He saw the long tail of a rat scurrying away towards the bushes and he realised he'd just wasted a shot for nothing.

Tom looked round as a single gunshot blasted out but he was relieved that it didn't appear to have been aimed at him. A second silhouette was pointing his rifle towards a cluster of bushes away to Tom's left and he wondered who was there. He heard another footstep behind him and realised the owner was getting closer. He had to move away to his next position quickly before he became trapped.

Falling on his stomach, he began crawling across the grass, on top of the dead, no longer concerned that it might be disrespectful. The damp dew of dawn quickly clung to his clothes and he felt its touch seeping through the material and chilling his flesh. It only made him crawl even faster towards the white marble headstone with a statue of Our Lady standing on top of it, looking down benevolently on what Tom presumed had been a faithful servant. He had just reached the stone when another shot rang out.

He flinched and tried to cover his head as he was showered with lumps of marble. He looked up, noticing the bullet had blown Our Lady's head off and he blessed himself automatically, immediately startled at the gesture and the fact he'd remembered it so readily after so many years. He crouched lower as another bullet crashed off the side of the headstone, taking a chunk off it. He glanced at the inscription which now revealed that Denis Donnelly was 'A Loving Husband & Fat – '

Tom lay low behind Denis' stone, though he realised that he'd have to move quickly now that they knew where he was. He didn't think the marble would be able to withstand too many bullets, and he felt Denis' grave had been subjected to enough desecration for one day.

Harrison heard the shots and immediately threw himself to the ground. He saw the flash of light from the gun – it was one of his men – and the head of a statue disintegrating. He was sure something moved beneath it and he shot at it, hitting the corner of the headstone.

He started crawling, watching for any sudden movement and ready to fire again. There were no further shots from the other direction, though he presumed his men would be closing in on the same position. After quickly moving forward about ten yards, Harrison stopped. He checked the target through his rifle sight, though he didn't see any further movement. He waited, finger poised on trigger, knowing it was now a waiting game and the man with the greater patience was the one likely to triumph.

Tom rolled across until he was behind another headstone, two down from Denis' damaged memorial. He wondered what the dead man's relatives would think the next time they visited the cemetery. Now that he knew there were men in front of him and behind him, he could figure out his next move. He needed to get to the far side of the cemetery so that they would all have to come towards him, and then it might make things a bit more straightforward for him.

The obvious move was simply to crawl towards the graves at the end of this row of dead souls, but he knew Harrison's guns were waiting for any sudden movement to unleash their deadly load. The problem was, if he stayed where he was, then they would eventually close in on him and he'd have nowhere to hide.

He slipped his jacket off after taking the knife out of his pocket, and delicately hung it on the corner of the headstone before perching his cap on top of it. Then he fired two shots in quick succession and bolted away as a volley of bullets slammed into the jacket, obliterating the headstone.

Harrison reached what remained of the memorial just ahead of two of his men. Pieces of marble were strewn across the grave but there was no sign of Costello. He picked up the jacket which was riddled with bullet holes, noticing that the cap on the ground had suffered the same fate. He glanced round, his eyes scanning the graveyard but he could see no movement other than his own men approaching. He crouched down slowly, trying to lessen the pain in his knee. It now felt like a knife was being thrust in and out of it every time he bent it.

A couple of the men had reached him and they both glanced at the clothing. One of them knelt down beside Harrison while the other leant against a nearby headstone which had managed to escape unscathed from the hail of bullets. He wiped his forehead with his sleeve and shook his head as Harrison handed him Costello's hat.

There was a snap like a firecracker and suddenly the man was writhing on the ground and howling like a hungry child. It was a sound loud enough to waken the dead and

Harrison scrambled across to him, swiftly followed by the other man, both of them eager to see the extent of the injury and also to try and quieten the man.

'My hand!' he screamed. 'He's shot my feckin' hand!'

He held up a bloodied fist and Harrison could see that several of the fingers were missing. Blood was pouring out of the wound and Harrison searched his pockets for anything that might help stem the flow which, in turn, would hopefully dull the screams.

Tom knew he had hit something – he could hear the screams – but they also told him that it hadn't been a clean kill and that his intended victim was still alive. He was on the move again, heading further into the cemetery.

He shivered slightly, suddenly aware of the early morning cold now that he was minus a jacket, but it didn't stop him moving. If anything, it helped speed him up. Suddenly he threw himself to the ground and rolled across the top of a grave until he was behind a black marble headstone. There was a man walking towards him – it was one of Harrison's gang – though he hadn't seen Tom. He kept turning his head to scan behind him as if he was anticipating an ambush, before focusing on the path in front of him.

Tom slid the knife out of his jacket and gripped the handle. He waited until the man was almost level with him before springing out from behind the headstone. He grabbed the man round his chest with his left arm and drew his right across the man's throat, slicing through his flesh. He pushed the body away and the man toppled to the ground. His hands thrashed blindly at the wound for a few seconds before the life drained out of him as quickly as the blood gushed out of his neck, and he rolled over. Face down, he stopped moving.

Glancing round, Tom stood up and prodded at the body, eventually using the toe of his boot to roll the body back over. He staggered back and almost fell over himself. His hand gripped the headstone for support and he stared at the body. Jimmy Dougall's lifeless face stared back up at him.

Harrison left the wounded man whimpering on his knees and advanced slowly with two of his men, though when the whimpering didn't fade but continued to follow him, he realised that the man was on his feet and following them. Not that he was going to prove useful in any way once they encountered Costello again since he didn't have the use of his hand and wouldn't be able to fire a weapon. Still, he hoped that strength in numbers would still provide some tiny advantage over an enemy who was winning the battle so far, though Harrison was determined that he wouldn't win the war.

Tom had marked the grave he'd always intended reaching and he knelt down quickly, taking out a box of matches. A momentary urge for a cigarette was quickly suppressed and instead he checked the short fuse on the stick of dynamite that lay in front of the headstone like a macabre memorial.

He reckoned he had no more that sixty seconds to get away safely before he'd feel the full force of the blast himself, and he scanned his escape route one final time just for reassurance that there had been no last-minute obstacles put in his path.

As soon as he saw movement in the distance, he fired in that direction, even though he wasn't sure whether it was a man or an animal, perhaps a stray fox or deer ambling through the sedate and deserted surroundings. Either way, he knew that the shot would attract Harrison and his men, though he fired another shot just to be sure.

Harrison and his men fell to the ground the instant they heard the shot, though this one didn't appear to be successful. He glanced round at the other men, noticing that Jimmy Dougall was missing. He thought of shouting out the man's name, but decided against it.

Slowly, they began crawling forward and a third shot rang out. This time one of Harrison's men returned fire, and he was quickly followed by a colleague. Harrison knew it was unlikely they'd hit anyone or anything, but it might help them feel better if they were at least able to discharge their weapons. Another of the men did the same thing, though after a couple of bursts of fire, he signalled for them to stop and an eerie silence descended on the graveyard.

Tom watched Harrison's men getting nearer and realised that, in those vital sixty seconds, they might spot him fleeing and shoot him before he got away. He glanced at the box of matches before taking one and striking it against the rough panel on the box. A flame instantly sparked up and he held it against the fuse until it caught fire.

He began sprinting away from the grave, even as a couple of bullets whistled past his ears and he had barely managed to drop himself into the freshly-dug grave nearby and pull the wooden planks back over the hole when there was an explosion and Tom could feel the ground shake beneath his feet. There was a delay of about ten seconds before earth began raining down on his covering, like a sudden winter hailstorm as he lay silently but alive in the freshly-made grave.

Moment of Truth

Bernie closed the door gently so that it barely clicked shut at all. It was a force of habit more than anything else since there wouldn't be anyone in the house. She'd wanted to get away from the hustle and bustle of the other flat, and this was a safe house that only she and Connor knew about. She felt sick and was tempted to go to the sink and put her fingers down her throat to expel the bile that was festering in her stomach. She didn't know if Tom was dead or alive. He was out there now, in the middle of a cemetery, facing a man who wanted to kill him. She prayed that he wouldn't be lying dead among the other bodies which had permanent residence there, but she was worried God would turn a deaf ear to her, given that she'd ignored him for long enough.

She knew she couldn't wait in the other house with all the comings and goings and pretend that there was nothing bothering her. No-one else knew where Tom was or what he was up to; no-one asked and she certainly wasn't going to volunteer any information.

Connor was gone when she'd woken up, no doubt out somewhere with Jimmy, and she was glad of that. He would have been the very one to ask about Tom and she knew she wouldn't be able to satisfy him with vague explanations. Of course, she could have said she didn't know, but she wasn't a good liar and when her face turned the same shade as her hair, Connor would realise something was up.

She thought of Tom, remembering those eyes which could visually caress her body so that she would feel herself tingle as he stared at her; she'd also seen another side to those eyes, when they were cold and dead and then she really did shiver like she feared for her life. It didn't stop her from being drawn ever closer to him, however, like a moth to a bright flame, not even after he'd brought the knife out. She knew it was stupid. It was more than that. It was insane. She sensed that, at some point down the line, Tom Costello would withdraw from any emotional engagement. It would be completely unannounced and it would leave her angry and confused. Not that he would care. He would be well away, moving on to his next victim, while she would have to learn to cope with the pain of his absence, while regretting the decision to choose him over Connor.

Her heart told her that this would be her choice when the time came, even though her head was counselling other-wise. Connor would be surprised. Furious. Probably even devastated, though that was an emotion he was unlikely to display in public.

Maybe it would be better if Tom didn't come back today? It would certainly make her life a lot easier, if less exciting. Yet, even as the thought entered her head, she dismissed it, knowing that she wanted to see him again. She needed to see him, to hold him and feel his crushing weight on top of her, to sense his breathless excitement and to look into those soulless eyes and try to detect even the tiniest trace of life or love.

She said another prayer in her head, this time to Our Lady. If God wasn't listening directly to Bernie, then maybe a word from his mother might help. The words kept repeating themselves in her head. Keep him safe. It was short and simple, but heartfelt. That was all she asked for and she hoped that someone somewhere was listening to her and taking heed. It wasn't that she now regretted having turned her back on her faith. Politics had long since been more important in her life than religion, but now, when she felt helpless and needed to ask for help, it wasn't a plea to the Irish republican movement that she offered up. She turned to God like it was a death-bed conversion, and with the same doomed conviction, hoped that redemption was not beyond her.

It was a selfless act in any case, she told herself. She was pleading for someone else, rather than for herself, though God knew that wasn't entirely true, since she wanted Tom alive so that she could be with him. She blessed herself automatically and muttered a Hail Mary as she walked down the hall and into the front room.

'Hello, Bernie.'

She stopped, frozen to the spot, her prayer shuddering to a halt and she felt she was having to battle to control her balance to stop herself falling over.

'What – are – you – doing – here?' she eventually managed to say, forcing each word out like it was the first time she'd ever spoken and her mouth was having trouble with the unfamiliar sounds.

'Waiting for you.'

Bernie nodded but still didn't move. She wasn't sure she could and was worried that, if she tried to put one foot in front of the other she'd stumble to the ground. Her heart was racing now, though she sensed that her face, rather than matching her hair, was the same shade as the four grey walls of the room.

'I thought –' she began, though she wasn't sure what word followed next. 'Jimmy,' she eventually said, knowing it didn't make any sense.

'Jimmy's dead,' Connor said with a casual shrug.

'He's dead? How?'

'He was stabbed.'

'Oh, God, that's terrible.'

Connor shrugged again.

'Did the Brits do it?'

'Sit down,' Connor said, gesturing towards the wooden chair facing his own in the centre of the room.

Slowly, Bernie shuffled forward like she was taking her first footsteps and she focused on the chair even though she sensed that Connor's eyes were tracking hers. Lowering herself gently on to the chair, she smiled weakly at him but he didn't return the gesture. Instead he glanced down towards his feet where Jackie sat, cross-legged, staring at Bernie.

The boy's face was dirty and snot hung lazily from his nose which Bernie hoped he would soon sense and wipe away, even if it was only with his sleeve. She noticed that the hole in the knee of his trousers had grown bigger and a patch of bloodied skin peeked out shyly. He'd obviously fallen at some point in the past day or so, and no-one had seen fit to at least try and clean or bathe the wound.

Connor rested his hand on Jackie's tangled web of hair, occasionally patting his head like an owner would do to a favourite dog; the touch didn't appear to bother the boy who continued to stare at Bernie. She couldn't hold his gaze and looked up at Connor, who now smiled.

'I was wondering whether there was anything you wanted to tell me?' he said.

'About what?' Bernie said with a frown, though her insides were churning and her heart was thumping so loudly she felt it was going to explode at any moment.

'I don't know,' said Connor with a shrug, taking his glasses off. 'Whatever's on your mind.'

'So what happened with Jimmy?'

'I told you, he's dead.'

'But how –'

'It doesn't matter.'

'Of course it matters. He was our ally. He was your friend. It matters.'

'It doesn't matter to you.'

'What's that supposed to mean? I knew him too. What's wrong with you, Connor?'

It was a nervous anger which had pushed the words out of her mouth and Bernie almost recoiled as Connor glared at her.

'You tell me,' he said.

'Tell you what?'

'What's going on, Bernie?'

'What are you talking about?'

Connor patted Jackie's head and the boy smiled. He was rocking back and forth now, his eyes remaining locked on Bernie, and she tried to out-stare him though it was an impossible task. He didn't appear to blink at all and his blue eyes were dangerously hypnotic. Bernie looked away again.

'Jackie told me about the broken table,' Connor said.

Bernie glanced between Connor and Jackie, feeling like her eyes were trapped and there was no other place she could look. She gulped loudly but could find no words to give Connor. What was the explanation for the broken table? She couldn't believe that the boy would have known what had caused the damage. He was just a child, after all, and his imagination could hardly conjure up pictures of Bernie lying on the table with Tom on top of her.

What had he heard from inside the bedroom, however? Would he have known what those groans and sighs and screams, and later, the satisfied laugher and the gentle murmurings of their conversation signified? How could he, she thought again. He was only a child. Yet, when she managed to hold his gaze, it was as if his eyes were telling her that he knew what she'd been up to. And if he knew, then it was certain that Connor did too, since the boy told him everything.

Bernie felt sick and this time she didn't think she'd need to contemplate sticking her fingers down her throat. She looked at Connor who continued watching her while patting the boy's head.

'I know,' he said through gritted teeth. 'I know . . . '

'Know what? Connor, what are you talking about?'

Connor shook his head and stood up.

'Don't treat me like a fool, Bernie. I know.'

'Know what?'

'Do you want the boy to tell you what he told me?'

Bernie looked at Jackie who grinned like he was relishing the prospect of repeating his tale. She closed her eyes for a moment and let out a low groan. Images of her sitting on top of Tom and savouring the feeling as his eyes drank in every inch of her body danced before her, but they no longer excited her or set her heart soaring as they had done before. Now, alongside those pictures was another one, of a small figure with his ear pressed against the wooden door, or perhaps with one blue eye looking through the keyhole and memorising every writhing movement of naked flesh, his ears detecting every frenzied noise and his brain already wondering how quickly he would be able to tell Connor about this; more importantly, he'd be calculating how much the information would be worth. She opened her eyes as Connor took a step forward.

'Why?' he said, shaking his head.

She opened her mouth as if to speak, though not knowing if she was going to continue pleading innocence or whether she'd try and explain how she'd stumbled into this situation.

'No, don't bother,' he said, holding up his hand and cutting her off before she could utter a sound. 'I don't want to know. I don't want to hear any of your excuses or lies.'

He shook his head, looking as though he was ready to start crying. He took his glasses off and rubbed his eyes furiously, perhaps to dispel any tears that were threatening to spill out.

'I'm sorry, Connor,' she whispered.

'So am I,' he said.

He put his glasses back on and walked towards her. She tensed up, bracing herself for the inevitable blow.

'What are you doing?' he asked.

'I don't know. I thought – '

'What? That I'd hit you. Jesus, Bernie, what sort of man do you think I am?'

'Sorry.'

Connor shook his head and moved slowly past her, gesturing with his hand towards Jackie, who stood up and scurried over till he stood beside Connor.

'Is that it?' Bernie asked as she heard the door open. She didn't turn round.

'What?'

'Are you just going to walk away without saying or doing anything?'

Connor sighed. 'You've obviously made your choice and there's nothing I can do about that.'

Bernie continued staring ahead at the empty chair in front of her, though she sensed Connor was still standing at the door.

'You will have to leave Glasgow,' he said and she looked round. 'You can't stay here now, not after what's happened.'

'I'll go home,' she said quietly.

'You're not going back to Ireland either.'

'What?'

'I know about Harrison,' he said. 'I know you told him where he could find . . . find Costello.'

'But Tom told me to tell,' she said.

'One telegram home and you know what'll happen. And it doesn't matter what your excuse is. The movement doesn't take kindly to informers.'

'But Tom. . .'

'The telegram will be in Dublin before your train's left Central Station.'

Bernie stood up, clutching the back of the chair for support. Jackie stared at her, wearing a sneer that deserved to feel the back of her hand, while Connor seemed to be looking beyond her.

'But where will I go?'

'I don't know, but you've got twenty-four hours to decide or I'll send the telegram.'

Bernie could feel her bottom lip beginning to quiver and she bit down on it, determined that Connor wouldn't see how upset she was.

'And don't think Tom can save you. I've already informed the Chief about everything that's happened here, with Eugene getting shot and him killing Duffy. I think he's the informer.'

'That's ridiculous.'

'You can defend him if you want, and I'm sure that you will, but he'll have to answer to Michael Collins when he goes home.'

'But where will I go?'

'I don't care, Bernie, but I want you out of my city,' he said, leaving the room with a final shake of the head, Jackie bounding out behind him.

Bernie remained standing in the middle of the room as tears began to move silently down her cheeks. She didn't know what she was going to do next, but she wanted desperately to speak with Tom. The only thing was, she didn't know if he was still alive.

She didn't hear the door opening again, her mind still in turmoil about Tom, and Connor, and the fact she might never see Ireland again. A floorboard creaked and she looked up, a tiny hope in her heart that it would be Tom standing before her. It wasn't. She'd seen the man with Connor before plenty of times but as he walked towards her, pistol in hand, she couldn't remember his name. Connor would know. She could shout out and ask him and he'd probably hear her from the hall where she presumed he waited. It didn't matter anyway, she realised, as she closed her eyes, conjuring up an image of Tom. It made her smile.

Back from the Dead

Tom sat at the kitchen table smoking a cigarette, the white stick grasped between dirty fingers. He found the nicotine a calming presence in his body and as soon as he'd finished it, he quickly lit another one and smoked it too. The flat was empty again. Connor and Bernie were gone, while the handful of communists had headed off after he'd told them about Jimmy. He presumed they were going to break the news to his family, though it may well have been blind panic at suddenly becoming leaderless.

He had waited in the grave for about five minutes, surprised at how quickly he'd become accustomed to his new surroundings. Tiny strips of sunlight broke through the gaps in the planks of wood which covered the hole, and it had helped steady his nerves. This was going to be someone's final resting place, and soon too, given that it was a freshly dug plot, but it was helping to save his life. Tom was ready to shoot anyone who might lift up the wood above him out of curiosity, which would have provided the grave with a dead body, even if it was minus a coffin and without the benefit of a proper ceremonial send-off.

He didn't know how many the explosion had killed, but the chaos had allowed him to escape to this temporary resting place, though he knew he'd have to move soon. The blast would have been heard from miles away and the area would be crawling with soldiers and policemen, and then he'd be trapped here for hours, maybe even days; the prospect of staying overnight in the cemetery, and in this hole in the ground, was enough to chill even the bravest soul.

Thankfully there had been no sign of life when he'd peeked out from the grave and scrambling to the surface he made his way out of the cemetery, heading in the opposite direction from the explosion. He'd walked back to the house as quickly as possible, ignoring the stares from passers-by who eyed him up and down. He glanced at himself after it had happened several times, noticing that he looked as if he'd been immersed, fully clothed, in a bath of mud.

He was smoking his cigarettes like a thirsty man in the desert who'd stumbled upon an oasis and he knew he'd soon run out. He didn't want to leave the house, however, so he tried to slow down the rate at which he was devouring them. He didn't have a change of clothing though he'd probably have been able to find something in the flat that would have made him more presentable, but he preferred to remain where he was.

His mission to Glasgow was slowly turning into a disaster and he'd still not had the opportunity to do what he came here for in the first place – kill Maxwell. What would Michael Collins make of it all? No doubt he was receiving reports on his progress – Connor would be gleefully informing on what had been happening – and Tom knew he'd have to explain to the Big Fella what had been going on when he eventually returned to Ireland. It would make his explanation a lot easier if he was able to accompany it with news of Maxwell's demise, but for the first time since he'd arrived in this city, a fragment of doubt was beginning to imbed itself in his mind.

The thought that he might not complete his mission was one that disturbed Tom. He wasn't used to failure, or even the prospect of it, and regardless of what else he did achieve during his time in this God-forsaken city – his mother had been right about that – if that list didn't include Maxwell's death, his superiors would judge the operation a failure, and him too.

Stubbing his cigarette out, which took its place with the butts already assembled in the saucer, Tom stood up and shuffled over to the sink for some water. The cool liquid rushed down his nicotine-coated throat, though it felt like he'd swallowed a ball of smoke which made him feel nauseous for a moment.

He had been stunned when he'd rolled the body over in the cemetery and saw that it was Jimmy, though he'd always had his suspicions about the young communist leader. All these idealistic fools who traipsed in and out of the house, blindly taking orders from him had been duped. He was a Brit all along and, like all traitors he got what he deserved. Whether the communists ever discovered what Jimmy had been up to was unlikely. Tom wasn't going to say anything while the Brits weren't going to announce that they'd lost a spy. More likely, they'd be trying to recruit someone else to do their dirty work for them, if they hadn't done so already.

He didn't trust any of them so he would remain wary, though he hoped it would only be for another couple of days. Once he'd seen Bernie, then he was heading out on his mission, and from there it would be back home. He knew he would have to ask Connor for help in this regard. He needed transport and money, but they'd all been instructed by Michael Collins to help him in any way that he wanted, so the other man had no choice.

It was Bernie he wanted to see. He wanted to hold her and kiss her and breathe in her scent so that he would still remember it when he was an old man propping up a Donegal pub and muttering about days gone by. He wasn't going to ask her to come home with him. It wasn't fair, for a start. He was going back to fight the Brits and that would remain his priority for as long as the war continued. There was no place for her in all of that, and he didn't think she'd accept the role of secret lover, waiting by the fire every time he went out on a mission and not knowing if he'd return. In any case she would want to be involved herself, and he knew he'd find it too difficult if he had to worry about her as well as concentrate on staying alive. Still, if she asked to come back to Donegal with him, he wouldn't say no.

There was a click at the door as the handle began turning and Tom was instantly on edge, his hand automatically reaching towards the pistol in his belt. The door opened and Connor strode in, followed by two men, both of whom were pointing guns at him. He knew he'd be dead before he managed to pull out his own weapon, so he kept his hands at his side. Connor sat down at the table while the two men remained standing. Tom knew better than to move without an invitation.

'You're leaving Glasgow,' Connor said after a few minutes of silence.

'What are you talking about?'

'Did you not hear me first time?'

'I heard you fine.'

'You're leaving this city.'

'Nobody's going anywhere until you tell me why,' said Tom. 'I've still got a job to do here.'

'Not any more. I've informed Dublin about what you've been doing here and they've ordered you back.'

'I don't believe you.'

'You don't need to,' Connor said. 'I've got the telegram.'

He slowly prised a sheet of yellowed paper from his pocket and held it out. Tom walked over and snatched it out of his hand.

'TC TO RETURN HOME. STOP. URGENT FAMILY MATTER. STOP. CANCEL GLASGOW PARTY. STOP.'

Tom glanced round at the two armed men and then at the telegram again.

'Your train leaves in two hours,' Connor said.

'My train?'

'To Liverpool. You'll be met there for the boat back to Dublin.'

'This doesn't make sense. I've still got a mission to complete.'

'Is the telegram not clear enough for you? It's over. Finished. The mission's been cancelled.'

'But I don't understand,' said Tom. 'It was the Big Fella's orders.'

'And now he's changed those orders. I told him of my suspicions about you and he wants you back.'

'Suspicions?'

'That you're the traitor in the ranks.'

'That's ridiculous, and you know it.'

'Is it? What about the army raid on the flat after you arrived? Or Eugene's death . . . and God knows what happened at the cemetery.'

'You know about that?' Tom said.

'The whole city knows about that. It was a blast fit to waken the dead, and now the Brits will be coming down on us even harder.'

'But Jimmy Dougall. . .'

'Jimmy's dead,' said Connor.

'I know –'

'How do you know?'

Tom hesitated. He looked at Connor and then at the two men, knowing that if he made a move towards any of them a bullet would stop him in his tracks. He needed time to think but Connor had said the train was leaving in two hours. There would be explaining to do back home, he knew that, but he still felt sure that the Big Fella would believe him when Tom had a chance to tell him everything. He'd be disappointed that Maxwell wasn't dead, but at this moment, that was not Tom's top priority, and he'd take the consequences of failure when that time came.

He nodded towards the empty chair opposite Connor, moving hesitantly towards it. Connor's gesture of approval was aimed more towards his men, who relaxed their guard, though only slightly as Tom sat down. Their guns, however, remained trained on him.

'Mind if I smoke,' Tom asked, gesturing towards his inside pocket where his cigarette tin was.

'Yes, I do,' Connor said, and Tom's hand hovered in the

air for a few moments before he took it away from his pocket. He wasn't going to pick a fight he couldn't win over a cigarette.

'I wouldn't get too comfortable,' Connor said. 'You'll be leaving soon enough. I wouldn't want you to miss your train.'

'This will all get sorted out when I'm back in Dublin.'

'We'll see.'

'You really think I'm a traitor?'

'I know what you are,' Connor said, and there was menace in his voice. Tom realised some of that came from the security the two armed men provided, but there was a hint of something else. Tom desperately wanted a cigarette and wondered whether they would actually shoot him if he lit up. He looked at Connor again, at his eyes which glared at him, and he decided against it.

More than a cigarette, however, he wanted to see Bernie, if only to let her know what was happening, so she didn't think he'd just disappeared. What else he would tell her would depend on the time and the moment, though he knew he was fooling himself if he thought that it would be a romantic scene when he declared his undying love to her. He grinned at the thought of it; he wasn't like that at all – what Irishman was – and so he could only hope that she would guess how he felt from what was left unsaid.

'What's so funny?' Connor asked.

'Nothing,' said Tom, shaking his head. 'Just imagining having a cigarette. I'm gasping.'

'Okay then,' Connor sighed with a shrug. 'Condemned man and all that. . .'

Tom nodded and took out his tin, gratefully lighting a

cigarette and inhaling deeply. As if on cue, Connor took off his glasses and began rubbing his eyes. Tom resisted the temptation to blow smoke directly at him, but he found the other man's discomfort only added to his enjoyment of the cigarette.

'What about Bernie?' Tom asked.

'What about her?'

'Can I see her before I go?'

'No.'

'What do you mean, "No"?'

'You can't see her,' said Connor.

'What's it got to do with you anyway?'

Connor stood up, his chair scraping across the floor as he did so.

'It's got everything to do with me,' he said. 'This is my city, and she was my girlfriend.'

Tom started to speak but thought better of it. Instead, he watched as the other man began pacing across the room, occasionally shaking his head as if he was having a private conversation with himself. Eventually he stopped and glared at Tom. He knows, thought Tom, again sensing the value of remaining silent.

'Bernie was an informer,' Connor said, slowly and deliberately.

'What?'

'She told the Brits about you. She set you up at the cemetery so that they could kill you.'

'But I told her to do that. It was me who made her tell them.'

'How very chivalrous of you to take the blame for her.'

'But it's true. She only did it because I told her to.'

'And why would she do that, do you think?

Tom was being challenged. He glanced at the two armed men, who remained silent but vigilant observers to the conversation. Their only contribution, he knew, would be to shoot him should that be required. He didn't want to give them an excuse, though he knew Connor was trying to push him in that direction. He remaining sitting, knowing that he needed to hold his own nerve and, more importantly, to control his temper.

'She's no more a traitor than you or me,' said Tom. 'Let her come back to Dublin with me and I'll explain to the Big Fella.'

'That's not possible.'

'What do you mean?'

'You know what happens to informers?'

Tom let his cigarette fall. It seemed to do so in slow motion and he watched it twist and turn as it dropped inexorably to the floor. Just as slowly, he stood up, staring at Connor as he puffed out his chest. His fingers flexed anxiously, desperate to grab hold of his gun, and they moved towards his waist. The click of a pistol safety catch stopped him.

'I wouldn't, if I were you,' said Connor.

Tom glanced at the two men as the other safety catch was released.

'It's time for you to say goodbye to Glasgow.'

'Bernie?' Tom said, almost in a whisper.

'She was a traitor,' said Connor, 'and so she suffered a traitor's fate.'

'You killed her?'

Connor shrugged but said nothing.

'And now you're going to kill me too?'

'Unfortunately, that exceeds my authority,' said Connor. 'The bullet for you is waiting in Ireland.'

'Bernie,' Tom muttered, his eyes suddenly focused on the smouldering cigarette end at his feet.

'It's time to go, Costello,' Connor said, now standing behind the two armed men. 'It's time for you to leave my city.'

Tom looked up. This isn't your city, he wanted to say, but when he opened his mouth, the only sound that escaped was 'Bernie.'

Revelations

Tom sat by the window, his hands gripping the rifle and his eye, open and unblinking, staring through the sight. He had maintained this position for at least half an hour and he was prepared to wait as long again, if not even longer, until Maxwell appeared. It didn't matter that his limbs were beginning to stiffen up, or that his lungs were almost crying out for a fresh infusion of nicotine. It didn't even matter that he saw images of Bernie dancing in front of him whenever his other eye – the one not trained on the house across the street – began to wander.

He knew she was dead. His mind kept telling him that, but he tried desperately to push the thought out of his mind, even as he remembered her flaming hair that he'd grasped passionately just days before. He didn't even get a chance to say goodbye. There had been no goodbyes the last time they'd spoken; only 'good luck'. Now he wished he had said something, anything, which had let her know how he felt, though he knew that, given the opportunity again, he would still stumble and stutter over words that felt awkward and uncomfortable in his mouth.

There wouldn't even be a chance to say goodbye at her graveside. There was no way of him finding out when the funeral would be, or whether it was in Glasgow or back home in Ireland; that wasn't quite true since he could ask questions and eventually stumble upon the right answer. He didn't want to draw any more unwelcome attention to himself, though, and he was sure there would be people at the funeral who would ignore the solemnity of the occasion if it meant they were able to capture an IRA man in their midst. She might already be in the ground for all he knew.

All Tom had left now was his mission. It had been easy enough to get off the train. Only one of the armed men was accompanying him to Liverpool. As soon as he realised that, he knew he was going back to Glasgow to get Maxwell. Ideally, he wanted to get Connor too, but he wouldn't know where to start looking for him, and he was sure the other members of the Brigade would have been warned what to do should they catch sight of Tom.

It seemed that Connor had underestimated him in only sending one guard with him on the train. Either that, or maybe he thought that with Bernie dead and an armed man sitting alongside him, Tom would accept his fate and meekly return to Dublin. His first trip to the toilet dispelled that notion.

The guard had waited outside the toilet and Tom reappeared after a few minutes, heading back towards their seat. As they passed one of the outside doors, Tom appeared to stumble, and as the guard automatically moved forward to help him, Tom straightened and grabbed the man in a head lock. Before he could offer any resistance, the door was open and the man was out the train. Tom didn't bother looking towards the shocked and stunned faces he was sure his actions had produced. Instead, he leant out the door, the wind buffeting his face. He waited a few seconds before stepping out, flying through the air before crashing heavily into a field, tumbling across the grass before he finally came to a halt with a long groan.

This was Tom's last chance. He knew that and he realised, too, that he'd be lucky to escape with his own life if he shot Maxwell, or even if he tried to. They would be after him in an instant, and alone in this city, he wasn't sure if he'd be able to evade capture, or even his own death. He was on his own now. At least if he was going to die, he wanted to make sure that Maxwell did too. That was the main mission Michael Collins had sent him to complete, and he was determined to succeed. Tom was beginning to accept in his mind that his own death was a likely outcome after he squeezed the trigger. It didn't scare him as much as it should have. What was there to live for, he asked himself, not able to provide a satisfactory answer.

If he made it home to Donegal all that waited for him was his mother's grave. If he stayed here then, eventually, he might locate Bernie's grave and spend tortuous hours in front of it. His own grave seemed to be beckoning, and if it did, then he would accept his fate, even if it did mean that other business remained unfinished. He was sure the Big Fella would understand.

It had been stupid of him to even contemplate a future with Bernie. It was out of character and he didn't know why he should have felt so differently about her. Every other woman he'd been with he had been able to discard without too much difficulty or feeling, but something was different this time. Maybe, if they had made it back to Ireland, things would have changed and he'd have ended up feeling the same way as before, but he had caught himself occasionally dreaming of life on a Donegal farm. He'd be tending the fields while Bernie was at home, feeding the children and making his dinner. The children always had her hair, burning with character and intensity, though they reminded him of lit matches when they stood up.

He smiled at that thought as he slowly returned to reality. It was dangerous to dream during these times, especially about the future. Many a man had those dreams ended by a bullet and he didn't want to be one of them. For one thing, these were only dreams he was having. He hadn't even said anything to Bernie and he couldn't fathom whether or not she felt the same way that he did. He suspected, or hoped that she did.

Now he would never be able to ask her and the realisation sent a sudden pain through his heart. He adjusted his position at the window and stared with even greater intensity through the sight, ignoring the occasional soldiers who marched in and out of the house, loading boxes into a truck parked outside. He was absolutely certain that Maxwell would appear, sooner or later, and he would wait here for as long as it took to get the British general.

Tom knew, even without looking over his shoulder, that the owner of the house was lying unconscious on the floor. The old man, his hair as white as freshly fallen snow, was alone when Tom broke in. He had planned to tie the man up and lock him in a cupboard while he took up his position, but he had proved to be particularly troublesome, and rather than struggle with him until he inevitably subdued him, Tom simply led him into the upstairs bedroom at the front of the house and cracked his skull with the butt of the pistol. The blow knocked the old man out instantly, and after checking to see that he hadn't killed him, Tom knelt down at the bedroom window, hoping that the old man wouldn't wake up before he was able to finish his own job.

The door of the house across the road opened and Connor walked out of the house. Tom almost fell over as the leader of the IRA's Glasgow Brigade stopped and turned round. Behind him, two soldiers appeared. One of them was carrying a small black case and he headed straight towards the car parked in front of the truck. The other soldier stopped beside Connor and the two men exchanged a few words. It was Maxwell.

This was his chance, the moment that he'd been sent here for. One squeeze of the trigger and General Sir John Maxwell, the man who had killed the leaders of the nineteen sixteen uprising, would be dead. Yet, Tom's eyes wouldn't leave Connor. Suddenly, it all started to make sense; the shoot-out in the house when he'd first arrived. The Brits had been too quick to know he'd arrived in Glasgow and now he realised why. He remembered Eugene and knew once again that the bullet which had claimed Connor's brother's life had been meant for him. Maybe Bernie had found out too and that's why he killed her? Bernie was no traitor but Connor was.

He gripped his rifle and aimed it out the window, balancing the barrel on the window sill. It moved from Connor to Maxwell and back again. He did this several times, not sure who deserved to get the first bullet. He should carry out his orders and shoot Maxwell. He knew that was the right thing to do, though even as he trained his sights on the General, he kept thinking of Bernie, and the gun seemed to move involuntarily towards Connor.

His hand reached inside his shirt and he touched the medals round his neck for a moment, glancing automatically to his right where he still imagined the smiling face of his cousin, Danny, would be, winking at him in a gesture of reassurance. His finger was now on the trigger and Maxwell's head was in his sight, but he was struggling with the emotions threatening to overwhelm him. It was Connor who was the traitor and had murdered Bernie, and he deserved to die. The sights on the rifle travelled to Connor.

Tom pulled the trigger but its normally smooth sliding action came to a sudden halt. It had jammed. He tried again but still the gun wouldn't fire. He checked the loading action of the rifle, noting that the bullets were lying there patiently to be fired, while still glancing out the window where the two men were still talking. He took up position again, aimed, and pressed the trigger. It still jammed.

He threw the rifle across the room and took out his revolver, quickly checking that it was loaded, though as he did so, he saw Maxwell step into the back of the car. It rumbled into life and slowly began its journey along the street. Tom couldn't see inside it to catch a glimpse of the General. That was his chance and it had gone.

He found he didn't care. All he could think of was revenge. He should have realised before now that Connor was a traitor. If he had, then Bernie would still be alive and then there would be something worth going home for.

A cocktail of rage and grief swirled around in Tom's head. He slumped to his knees and silently sobbed into his lap, his eyes tightly shut as he remembered what it felt to have her lips pressed against his, and knowing that the memory of it would eventually fade despite his best efforts to preserve it.

Connor stood at the front door watching the General's car reach the end of the street. Slowly, he turned, though just as he took one step forward a bullet slammed into the back of his skull, catapulting him into the house. A thin red spray seemed to hang in the air where before there had been a head and Tom stared at it for a second before slipping the revolver back into the waist of his trousers and scrambling away from the window.

Escape

It was a biting wind which seemed to gleefully attack his face, though Tom had long since become used to its relentless assault. He'd been on the boat for nearly two hours now, sitting up on the open deck despite the offer of a warmer position inside from one of the crew. He'd simply shaken his head, muttered a few syllables that he hoped sounded like 'I'm fine,' and remained sitting out in the freezing cold. The man had shrugged but didn't press his offer, which Tom was grateful for, and he continued staring out at the water, which seemed to have a restless anger about it, each choppy wave mischievously buffeting the boat which still managed to move forward with a gritty determination despite the water's best efforts to hinder it.

A fleeting temptation to plunge into the icy depths was quickly suppressed. Tom knew that was the coward's way out and he had never been one to run away from anything. No-one would have noticed if he had gone overboard, and even if they did, he knew it was unlikely any of the crew or other passengers would have attempted a rescue, knowing that the only outcome would be their own death. He could have disappeared, unknown and unmourned, into this watery grave, but instead he chose the penance of a physical assault from the elements.

He was soaking wet from the constant bursts of spray

which splashed up off the side of the boat and almost invisibly washed on to the deck. The first couple of times they had hit him, Tom shuddered, but now he more or less ignored it. In truth, it was almost strangely comforting, like he deserved to suffer and he was grateful that the water realised this.

The sky scowled, black and furious, down on him, threatening to make its own contribution, but so far the rain had abated and he was sure everyone else on board was grateful for that, even if he wasn't bothered. There had only been a handful of passengers who'd shuffled on to the small steamer, most of them carrying suitcases which indicated they were going home.

His only possessions were his revolver and his knife, both of which remained out of sight. A few disdainful glances were thrown in his direction, no doubt due to his appearance, but he didn't care what anyone else thought. It was better that he sat away from them, however, in case he should take exception to any sneering eyes which would no doubt lock on to him throughout the journey.

He hadn't looked back at the mainland when the boat had slowly pushed away from the dock, and he knew he'd never set eyes on Glasgow again. He wondered whether his mammy had felt the same thing when she'd returned home to Ireland all those years ago, and he was sure her pain was a similar one. He was annoyed, too, that he had failed in his mission to kill Maxwell, and he knew how disappointed Michael Collins would be with that, but mainly he thought of Bernie, now lying in a cemetery somewhere in the city.

He didn't know if anyone would have gone to the

funeral, or was she now lying in an unmarked grave? Did anyone send word home to her family? Most likely, they would still believe she was alive, though when letters remained unanswered for months, if not years, doubts and fears would begin to creep into their minds, though they'd probably never find out what had happened to the flame-haired girl who had left Ireland's shores.

It wasn't for him to visit and inform them. Perhaps someone in the movement would do so, supplying mean-ingless platitudes about how she had given her life for her country and that everyone should be very proud of her. The news would come like a bolt of lightning on a sunny day, and her father would slip away outside to mourn privately for his daughter, out of sight of other grieving relatives. Perhaps he'd think of his wife, too, and hope that mother and daughter were now reunited?

Seagulls were tracking their choppy journey across the water, flying high in the air before swooping low and scanning the boat for any sign of food. Disappointed, they would glide away again and wait for a few minutes before repeating the move. It was captivating to watch how they could effortlessly hover in the sky despite the best efforts of the wind to knock them down. It wasn't as though their wings were flapping frantically to do so, which would only have made them exhausted and eventually weak enough for the wind to succeed. It was graceful and natural and almost hypnotic. Tom was content to stare up at the birds and follow them as they accompanied him on his journey.

He didn't hear the footsteps approaching across the deck, and a nudge on his shoulder startled him. The same man who had invited him inside stood there again, a white mug in one hand and a thick clump of bread in the other. He held them out to Tom who took them gratefully.

'I thought you might be hungry,' he said in a voice that was almost melodic.

The mug was filled with soup – broth of some kind – and the aroma which wafted up towards him made his stomach rumble. He didn't remember the last time he'd eaten and he held the cup up like it was a pint before taking a gulp. The liquid poured down his throat and he coughed and spluttered, spitting some on his trousers.

'It's a bit hot,' the man said with a smile.

Tom smiled back and nodded. He dipped the bread into the mug and bit off a corner, munching hungrily on it while the man stared at him with a smile that seemed to grow wider with every movement of Tom's jaw.

'Good,' Tom mumbled through the mouthful of bread.

'My Eileen's soup is the finest in Benbecula,' the man said proudly. 'Maybe in all of the islands. She's famous for it.'

Tom nodded as he dipped the bread into the soup again.

'You'll come and have a bowl at our house,' the man said. 'Eileen always likes to feed visitors.'

'I'll not be staying long,' Tom said.

'Long enough,' the man replied with a grin. 'Eileen will be pleased to see you.'

He turned and walked unsteadily back along the deck as the boat rose and fell and rocked from side to side, though he managed to navigate a safe passage to the door and disappeared inside, slamming it shut behind him. The man had been right about one thing. Eileen's soup was delicious, almost as good as his aunt Theresa's, though the fact he was hungry may have had something to do with his appreciation. Still, he was grateful for the gesture even if he had no intention of visiting for more soup when they reached the island. He was only there for one reason and it wasn't to get fed.

Tom stood outside the church and studied the small stone building. There was a small wooden sign which read 'ST. MARY'S CHURCH' fastened into the ground at the front and he stared at the words for a few minutes. He felt like he was still on the boat even though he'd been on solid ground for a while now, and as he stood with his feet rooted to the soil, he could feel himself swaying back and forth as if he was about to faint. He was still damp, though the Atlantic wind had dried some of the water which had drenched him on the journey over. The wind was a constant presence since they'd set sail from Oban and, if anything, it seemed to be crueller and more vicious now that he was on dry land.

He had resisted all efforts of the crewman – his name was Roddy – to head straight for his cottage to meet Eileen and enjoy another bowl of her famous soup.

'Maybe later,' Tom had muttered, hoping that Roddy could sense in his tone that 'later' was Tom's way of saying 'never'. The man had been kind enough to organise a lift for him, and he'd clambered gratefully on to the back of a cart which trundled slowly along bumpy, rock-strewn paths until the horse was brought to a halt.

'St Mary's is that way,' the driver said, pointing directly at a hill that only seemed to contain a few grazing sheep. 'Keep walking for about two miles and then you'll see it. You can't miss it. It's the one with the cross on top of the roof. I'd take you there myself but I'm not going that way today.'

Tom thanked the man as he jumped down from the cart and he stood and watched it move away before setting out on his trek across muddy fields and hills until he did, indeed, catch sight of the church in the distance just as the driver had told him.

Now he stepped up to the door of the church and turned the handle. He opened the door slowly, hesitating as it creaked, before pushing it open and looking inside the small building. It was empty. He walked inside, closing the door behind him and crept quietly towards the altar, though every footstep seemed noisy and amplified in this silent space.

Reaching the front, he sat down on a wooden bench, suddenly grateful to rest weary legs which he stretched out, noticing that his boots were caked in mud. He glanced back up the aisle and saw the trail of soil which he'd left in his wake, and realised that whoever was responsible for cleaning the church would be annoyed. The wind continued to whistle outside but in here it was warm and relaxing and Tom yawned several times.

Strips of sunlight pushed through the glass, warming the inside of the church and without thinking, Tom stretched out on the bench, yawning again and feeling like a heavy hand was pulling on his eyelids, even though he battled to keep them open. When he'd stretched to his full length, his head was basked in a shaft of sunlight, which was warm and comforting, and he quickly lost all desire to keep his eyes open.

It had been a deep sleep, a peaceful one too, and one not haunted by the horrors he had seen or done. Tom lay on his back, his eyes still closed, and his head still framed by the sun, and sighed deeply. It had been the best sleep he had enjoyed for as long as he could remember, though he had no idea how long he had lain here. He heard a cough and wondered how that fitted in to any dreams he might have had. He heard it again and slowly opened his eyes.

A figure stood a couple of feet away from him, at the front of the altar, and coughed a third time. The figure was blurry at first, though as Tom wiped his watery eyes on his sleeve, the man came into focus. It was a priest. Slowly, Tom swung his legs off the bench until his feet hit solid ground and he sat up, stretching himself with a tired groan.

The priest stood, arms folded, staring at him. Tom searched in his pockets until he found a packet of cigarettes, taking one out and putting it in his mouth. He held out the packet to the priest who shook his head.

'This is a church,' he said.

Tom stood up and walked over to the tray of white candles which burned devotedly under a statue of Our Lady and held his cigarette close to one of the flames until he got a light, taking a deep draw and filling his lungs up with nicotine. He sat back down and continued smoking as the priest's face began to smoulder with fury.

'How dare you,' he said, though Tom held up his hand to stop him. Taking three heavy draws, he dropped the cigarette on the ground and stood on it, extinguishing it on the wooden floor and leaving a black mark.

'Sorry, but I'm no good after a sleep without a smoke.'

'Get out of my church,' the priest said, almost hissing between gritted teeth as he pointed towards the door at the back of the building.

'All in good time, Father Costello.'

'How do you know my name?' the priest said with a frown. 'Who are you?'

'I'm really disappointed you don't recognise your own nephew.'

'What'

'I'm Kate's son,' Tom said, standing up and noticing he was almost the same height as the priest. 'My father was Michael Costello... your brother.'

The priest stared at Tom as though he'd just been punched in the stomach, and he almost stumbled back. Unsteadily, he sat down on one of the altar steps and began shaking his head.

'That's not possible. You're lying.'

'Do you think I'd come all this way just to pretend I'm someone I'm not?'

'But Mick died . . . Kate went home . . . I got the letter . . .'

'My mammy was pregnant when he was killed. She had me after she went back home to Donegal.'

'No, no, this can't be true,' the priest said, shaking his head furiously. 'Mick would have told me. You're lying.'

'I don't know if he knew, to be honest with you, but it's the truth.'

The priest shook his head again.

'I'll not have you lying in a place like this,' he said angrily, standing up.

Tom shrugged and tugged at the medal round his neck,

snapping the chain and throwing it at the priest who caught it.

'My mammy gave me it just before she died. She said it belonged to him.'

The priest studied the medal in his hand, glancing up and every now and then at Tom.

'I gave this medal to Mick,' he said slowly, staring at his palm. 'But it can't be possible.'

'It's not just possible, Father. It's true.'

'So you're . . . you're Mick's son?'

'I'm Tom Costello.'

'Tom?'

The priest almost fell over but managed to regain his balance. He stared at Tom, his head shaking almost involuntarily and his eyes narrowing as if they were peering through a sheet of rain and trying to focus on a shadowy figure.

'Your name is Tom?' he eventually asked again.

'Yes.'

'But I'm . . .'

'You're Father Thomas Costello.'

'You've got my name. I thought Kate would have named you after Mick.'

'I'm Thomas Michael Costello, to give you my full name. But Tom will do.'

Tom took out another cigarette and Father Costello gestured for one as well. He lit both of them and handed one to the priest – his uncle – who drew on it hungrily while clutching it between trembling fingers.

'Your mother. . .' he said after a few minutes of smoky silence.

'She's dead.'

'Kate's dead?'

'Two months past now,' said Tom. 'She gave me the medal the last time I saw her.'

Father Costello looked at the medal again and Tom wondered whether he was remembering when he'd given it to his brother. It was a strange feeling to be sitting here in front of a man who knew his father so well. This would be the time to ask questions and get some answers as to who Mick Costello really was. Yet, he could see that the priest was still in shock. He would look up every now and then at Tom and then back at the medal, his mind no doubt filling up with a million thoughts and images and memories he'd believed had been buried for good.

'Kate's dead,' he muttered to himself in an accent that was still recognisably Irish, but there was a melodic lilt to it similar to Roddy from the boat. It was understandable, given that the priest had been here for about twenty-seven years, since Tom's father had been murdered and his mother had gone home to Ireland. Father Costello knew her. Tom could tell from the way he kept muttering her name over and over again while staring at his father's medal, as the news of her death slowly took hold of his thoughts.

Tom didn't think there had been any contact in the intervening years. He didn't remember any letters arriving from Scotland, while his mother couldn't write, so there was no way she had corresponded with him.

'So why are you here?' Father Costello suddenly asked, looking up.

'I'm here for you.'

'For me?'

'You have to answer for Dan Foley.'

A look of puzzlement slowly changed to alarm as the priest recognised a name he'd not heard for a very long time.

'What do you mean?' he asked in a shaky voice.

'You have to answer for Dan Foley,' Tom repeated.

'I don't know what you're talking about.'

Tom sighed as he finished his cigarette and extinguished it on the floor again, making another black mark on the wood.

'You betrayed Dan Foley to the Brits and now you have to pay.'

'But I don't know what you're talking about. As God is my witness, I had nothing to do with any of it.'

'Walsh is dead. Father McNeill is dead. Archbishop Eyre is dead.'

'You killed the Archbishop?'

'No,' Tom said with a laugh. 'Unfortunately God got to him before me. . . They're all dead, Duffy too.'

'You killed Duffy.'

'Everyone has to answer for their sins, Father. Surely you should know that. And everyone has. . . except you. Until now.'

The priest held the tiny remnants of the cigarette between his fingers, not flinching as it began to burn his flesh. He let it fall and it tumbled on to the floor where it continued to smoulder. His eyes opened wider as Tom brought out the revolver which he'd kept inside his jacket. He flicked open the barrel and twirled it noisily around in its carriage before clicking it back into place, having checked that it held six bullets.

'You have to answer for Dan Foley.'

'You're going to shoot me?'

Tom shrugged.

'But this is a house of God. You can't kill me. Not here.'

Tom clicked the safety catch off.

'You can run but you can't hide, Father Costello,' he said as the priest made the sign of the cross and closed his eyes.

He looked at the old man and paused . . . hadn't enough blood been spilled already?

The Last Post

They buried the priest on a morning when the sun appeared to cast its warmth over the whole island. In truth, it felt like everyone on the island was gathered in or around the small church. They were there to say goodbye to someone who had arrived as a stranger but who, over the many years of bleak winters and warm summers, had become one of them. He had baptised many of them, married a good few of them, counselled lots of them and heard enough sins to have lasted a lifetime; he had buried many of their friends and relatives too, and it was said for many a long mile that no-one conducted a better funeral than Father Costello of St Mary's.

Now it was his turn and Father Macdonald from Barra had made the journey up to lead the final farewell for his brother priest. He spoke warmly of the Irishman who had made his home on this island. Why he had first arrived on Benbecula no-one knew, and it was so long in the past that it hardly seemed to matter. What was important to them all was that he had wanted to become part of their lives and community, with him eventually being central to that, as the Church was in these places and on this island.

He was still an Irishman through and through. They could hear it in his voice every time he said Mass, but his accent had been softened round the edges through speaking their Gaelic tongue rather than his own and it remained a reassuringly distinctive sound to them all every Sunday.

The simple wooden coffin sat in front of the altar as Father Macdonald progressed round it, first with holy water which he sprinkled, some drops falling on the Bible which sat on top of the coffin. Then came the incense, again to bless the coffin, but the smoke rose up and filled the whole church, which was packed full of mourners, and a few coughs broke out as the incense tickled sensitive throats.

At a signal from the priest, six men moved out from the first couple of rows and took up position either side of the coffin. Then, as Father Macdonald turned and walked down the aisle towards the door of the church, following a small boy who was struggling to hold up a large crucifix, the men gripped the coffin and hoisted it on to their shoulders before beginning the slow procession out of the church and across the short patch of grass to the graveyard where a freshly dug hole lay waiting for Father Costello.

Everyone was grateful that God had, indeed, shone on his servant, particularly those who were forced to stand outside during the service. They were able to relax among neighbours and friends in the comforting heat of the sun and there would be a few heads burnt red before the day was out.

As the men stepped from the shade of the church into the glare of the sunlight, a lone piper struck up a lament, his pipes groaning like a hungry dog until he'd engaged them and *The Flowers of the Forest* floated in the air above them. People blessed themselves as the coffin passed them, and then they too shuffled towards the graveside where Father Macdonald was now approaching.

Seagulls hovering above the church, intrigued by the large gathering of people and hopeful that something would be left when the crowd had evaporated, contributed their own sounds, which mingled in with the music of the pipes.

Many people were thinking of their old priest, though some had already begun to wonder who would replace him. Would it be another incomer, an Irishman or perhaps a Scot from the mainland? Or would it be one of their own? That's what they would all prefer, if truth be known. It didn't matter that they had grown to love and respect Father Costello. Centuries of tradition had built in them a fear of the outsider and, even if they didn't always articulate it, they were all more comfortable with one of their own.

The coffin was laid on top of the planks of wood which covered the hole in the ground, and rope cords were looped under it – eight in total – which were taken up by the six coffin bearers and two other men who stepped forward from the crowd. Then the wood was taken away and the men slowly lowered the coffin into the ground as Father Macdonald prayed at the foot of the grave.

'Out of the depths I cry to you, O Lord. Lord, hear my voice. Let thine ears be attentive to the voice of thy supplication. If Thou, O Lord, should mark iniquity, Lord, who shall endure it. For with Thee there is merciful forgiveness, and by reason and by law I have waited for thee, O Lord. My soul hath relied on his word. My soul hath hoped in the Lord. For with the Lord there is mercy, and with Him plentiful redemption, and He shall redeem Israel from all its iniquities. Eternal rest grant unto him, O Lord, and let perpetual light shine upon him. May he rest in peace. Amen. May his soul and the souls of all the faithful departed, through the mercy of God, rest in peace, Amen. *In nomine Patris et Filii et Spiritus Sancti.* Amen,' he said, making the sign of the cross, at which everyone else followed suit, and then closed his prayer book.

Slowly, the crowd started to break up and fade away like clouds on a windy day, but a few gravitated towards the graveside, waiting their turn to throw a handful of earth on top of the coffin and make their own prayer for their priest. Several studied the headstone already placed at the end of the grave, though it would have to go back to the engraver to add another name.

It had been a strange business and no-one ever really uncovered the heart of it. Certainly, Father Costello had been reluctant to offer too much of an explanation except to inform them solemnly at Mass one Sunday that his nephew had disappeared at sea.

'He was a troubled young man,' Father Costello had said. 'He had hoped to find peace here, on this island, but that has been cruelly snatched away from him. We pray he has now found that peace and, by God's grace, he may enjoy eternal salvation.'

There would now be two names on the headstone. The first read simply, 'Tom Costello, 1892–1919.' The other would record that Father Thomas Costello was a much-loved priest who had died in 1920 at the age of fifty-nine. Future generations could speculate as to the relationship between the two men with the same name, no doubt some of them wondering whether the priest was a 'father' in title alone. Only the two men, and God, knew the absolute truth. Everything else was just another chapter in the never-ending story of the island.